OFF TH

MW00990470

#1 NEW YORK TIMES BESTSELLING AUTHOR
BARBARA FREETHY

"PERILOUS TRUST is a non-stop thriller that seamlessly melds jaw-dropping suspense with sizzling romance, and I was riveted from the first page to the last...Readers will be breathless in anticipation as this fast-paced and enthralling love story evolves and goes in unforeseeable directions."

— USA Today HEA Blog

"Barbara Freethy's first book in her OFF THE GRID series is an emotional, action packed, crime drama that keeps you on the edge of your seat...I'm exhausted after reading this but in a good way. 5 Stars!"

— Booklovers Anonymous

"What I love best about Freethy's books are the characters and the depth she puts in them, the story can be as good as ever, but if you don't care about the characters you can't help but be unbothered by the events unfolding. RECKLESS WHISPER has so many twists and turns that I read it in one sitting.....a must read for everyone, I don't want to ruin anything so I will just say.....WOW"

— Booklovers Anonymous Blog

"You will love RECKLESS WHISPER. From the first sentence of the book until you end, you are on a suspense filled ride. I loved it and couldn't put it down."

Janel – Goodreads

"LOOK OUT! There's danger up ahead. Off the Grid is a labyrinth. Each tale pulls readers deeper into the abyss. DESPERATE PLAY amplifies the chill factor. Freethy intensifies the fear as the danger level rises. Unpredictability is a seductive aphrodisiac. Barbara Freethy uses it in a way that will chill, thrill and appeal."

Isha Coleman — Goodreads & I Love Romance Blog

"DESPERATE PLAY is definitely a page turner! Once you think you have something figured out, something else happens and your trying to figure out what's going to happen next. The question is can you love and trust someone after they lie to you so many times?"

Brandi – Goodreads

"It's been a while since I have had the fun of reading a brilliant romantic suspense book – Perilous Trust gets me back into this genre with a bang!"

— For the Love of Fictional Worlds

"A uniquely seductive, gripping and exhilarating romantic suspense that is fast paced and action packed...Barbara Freethy is the ultimate seducer. She hooked me and slowly and keenly reeled me in. I was left in a trance. I just cannot wait for the next book."

— MammieBabbie.com

"This was my first time reading Barbara Freethy and I loved this story from start to finish. Right from the start the tension sets in, goodness, my heart was starting to beat a little fast by the end of the prologue! I found myself staying up late finishing this book, and that is something I don't normally do."

— My Book Filled Life Blog

"The suspense and action continued throughout the whole novel really keeping the pacing going strong and the reader engaged. I flew through this story as Sophie and Damon went from escaping one danger into having to fend off another. I'd definitely recommend this novel to anyone who like suspense romance or even contemporary romance. Its fast paced, entertaining and filled with sexually tense moments that would appeal to any romance lover!"

— PopCrunchBoomBooks.com

"This was just a well-written story with lots of twists and turns. Who's bad? Who's good? Who killed Sophie's father? There's also lots of hot and steamy romance! I'm looking forward to the next installment! 5 Sexy Stars!

— Knottygirlreview.com

Also By Barbara Freethy

ELUSIVE PROMISE

Off The Grid: FBI Series #4

BARBARA FREETHY

HYDE STREET PRESS
Published by Hyde Street Press
1325 Howard Avenue, #321, Burlingame, California 94010

© Copyright 2018 by Hyde Street Press

Printed in the United States of America

Cover design by Damonza.com

ISBN: 978-1-944417-47-5

One

The last time Parisa Maxwell had been at a consulate party she'd been sixteen, and she'd spent the evening peeking around a heavy, thick curtain, looking at all the beautiful, powerful people sipping champagne and speaking in a half-dozen different languages. That party had been on the other side of the world, at the US embassy in Bezikstan, a small country tucked between Nepal and Bangladesh on India's northeastern border.

Her stepfather, Harry Drummond, had served as the ambassador to Bezikstan for almost three years, and she'd loved living in the mountainous and mostly peaceful country. While she'd been a teenager, listening to the music and imagining a time where she'd be one of the guests at the party, she'd had no idea of the chaos and terror that would soon follow.

Her body tightened at the memory. It had been fifteen years, but that night was forever imprinted on her brain.

However, there was no reason to be nervous now. This evening was not about world political events, but rather personal ones. The consul general of Bezikstan, Raj Kumar, was hosting an engagement party for his daughter Jasmine at the consulate in New York City, which was located in a three-story building just a block away from Central Park.

She'd been a little surprised to get an invitation to the party. Her relationship with the Kumars had ended years ago. She assumed she'd been invited now because of her stepfather's relationship with Raj Kumar, which had continued after they'd left Bezikstan, and the fact that a very long time ago Jasmine and her sister Anika had been her classmates and her best friends.

She wished her mother and stepfather could have attended the party with her, but they were at a yoga retreat. It was up to her to represent the family, and it wasn't a terrible chore; she was actually looking forward to seeing the Kumars again. Since her assignment in San Francisco had recently ended, she had time for a short vacation, and one that was very much needed.

She'd been moving at breakneck speed for years, and she didn't know how to shift into a lower gear, but she might need to find that gear soon, because with each engagement party she attended, she was reminded that her whole life was work, and that might not be the healthiest way to live.

She accepted a glass of champagne from a nearby waiter and looked around the crowded foyer. She didn't immediately recognize anyone, but she was only in the outer reception area. The family was probably in the living room.

Despite the happy occasion, she still couldn't quite shake the feeling that she needed to be on her toes. She'd spent the last four years working as an FBI agent, and she never went anywhere without subconsciously noting every detail: the security at the entrances and exits, anyone who looked out of place, a subtle movement, someone watching instead of participating. Being acutely aware of her surroundings was a hard habit to break, but she needed to take a breath and just relax, enjoy the party.

She'd only taken a few steps forward when she heard her name called.

Whirling around, she saw the beautiful and exotically pretty Anika Kumar, who at thirty-one, was the same age as herself, but much more sophisticated. While they both wore black dresses, Anika's cocktail dress was much shorter and glittered under the lights. Her dark-brown hair was cut short and angled, framing her oval face, which was expertly made up, highlighting her red lips and dark eyes.

"Parisa, it is so good to see you," Anika said.

"You, too. You look amazing, Anika." The thin girl with the long, gangly legs and arms had grown up to be a spectacularly pretty woman.

Anika smiled in a way that told Parisa she was very much aware of her beauty. And then they exchanged a brief, airy hug.

"How long has it been?" Anika asked.

"Fifteen years."

"I can't believe it. How are you? What are you doing now? I think I heard you were working for the state department."

That was the cover she'd been using since she'd left Quantico. It fit her background and was vague enough not to generate many questions. It also afforded her an easy opportunity to move in international circles with little scrutiny.

"Yes," she said. "I work as a translator."

"You were always good at languages."

"What about you?"

"I'm working at WNN as an associate producer for the show: *Around the World with Bill Haskins.*"

"Really? That sounds amazing." The renowned and intrepid foreign correspondent Bill Haskins hosted an hour-long segment on cable news, featuring important world events, and he often went to remote and sometimes dangerous locations to get the story. "Do you travel with him?"

"I wish. Hopefully, some day. But it's actually fine that I'm stuck here in the city for now, since there will be a lot of planning required for Jasmine's wedding. With her marrying Westley Larimer, heir to the Larimer fortune, the wedding will be an event."

"How long have they been together?"

"Only three months, but Jasmine is head over heels in love, and Westley feels the same way."

"I'm happy for her, but that is fast."

"Jasmine says when you know, you know," Anika said, with a touch of sarcasm in her voice.

"Well, I wouldn't know," she said with a laugh.

"Neither would I," Anika agreed. "And I'm enjoying my single life. I'm sure you are as well."

"Yes."

"Have you seen my parents yet? They were really happy that you reached out to them."

"Reached out?" she echoed in surprise.

Before Anika could reply, she was distracted by a young woman wearing a conservative gray skirt and blazer, probably a staffer of some sort.

"Excuse me," Anika said, giving Parisa an apologetic smile. "I have to attend to something. Please enjoy yourself. Who knows? You might find yourself a handsome billionaire here. Westley invited many of his friends."

"That would be something," she murmured.

After Anika left, she made her way into the living room. The Kumars were standing in front of a massive stone fireplace, with a fire blazing behind them. It was early January, and the temperature outside was in the forties, with slushy, dirty snow lingering from a midweek snowstorm, but this room was warm and cozy.

Raj Kumar was a tall, lean man, whose once black hair was now pepper gray. His wife Kenisha was almost a foot shorter than her husband with brown hair, dark eyes and generous curves that were quite visible in her coral-colored silk dress. Both of them looked extremely happy as they chatted with their friends.

Since the Kumars were surrounded by people, she decided to wait a bit before approaching them. As she glanced around the room in search of the bride-to-be, her gaze caught on a man who was watching her in a way that set off an internal alarm.

He was quite attractive in a black suit with a white dress shirt and dark-maroon tie. His hair was dark brown and wavy, a little longer than a businessman might wear. His face was square, his features rugged, but clean shaven. She couldn't tell the color of his eyes, but they were light—maybe blue or green. His mouth had a cocky set to it that matched his confident stance, and while she could find nothing at all wrong with his appearance—in fact, there was quite a lot she liked about it—his gaze bothered her.

Then he smiled, and a shiver ran down her spine. She felt suddenly nervous, excited, with a knot in her throat. *Why? Because a handsome man had smiled at her?* She really needed to think about working on her social life.

She was just so often not herself when she was at a party like this. She'd forgotten what it was like just to flirt, without working some hidden agenda.

The man lifted his champagne glass in her direction, and she found herself doing the same. But despite their connection, he made no move in her direction.

She wondered who he was. He could be a friend of the groom-to-be, Westley Larimer. He appeared to be in the same age range—early thirties—and he had a look of wealth and sophistication about him.

"Parisa?"

She turned quickly at the sound of a familiar male voice and saw a tall, gray-haired man in his early sixties. It was Vincent Rowland, former FBI agent and father of Jamie Rowland, a fellow trainee at Quantico, who had tragically died during a training exercise. "Mr. Rowland, what are you doing here?" she asked in surprise.

She'd met Vincent on several occasions and had attended a memorial for Jamie the previous year. Vincent had always been friendly and charming, but there was also something about the man that bothered her. She just couldn't put her finger on it.

"Westley Larimer is my godson," he explained.

"Really? I had no idea."

"I was in his parents' wedding. Phillip and I have been friends for a very long time, and I've known Westley since he was born. What about you? What brings you to this engagement party? I didn't realize you were working out of New York."

"I'm not. I just came for the party."

"Do you know Westley?"

"No, I know his fiancée, Jasmine. I was actually just looking for her. Have you seen her?" She looked around the room, hoping to catch sight of Jasmine, but her gaze fell once again on the mysterious stranger. He didn't smile at her this time. Instead, he turned and walked toward the line for the bar.

"There is the happy couple now," Vincent said.

Following his gaze, she saw Jasmine and her fiancé walk into the room, holding hands. Jasmine wore a light-blue silk dress and had long brown hair that almost reached her waist, a petite frame, big brown eyes, and a rather fair complexion compared to the rest of her family.

Westley Larimer was a big guy, at least a few inches over six feet, with a long, lean build. He had dark-blond, short hair and rather plain features that were made more attractive by the smile on his face and the beaming pride in the woman at his side.

As Parisa's gaze dropped to their locked hands, she was almost blinded by the enormous diamond on Jasmine's finger. It had to be fifteen carats—at least. It was then she noticed the two men in dark suits flanking the couple, looking very much like well-dressed security guards.

"That ring is spectacular," she murmured, glancing at Vincent.

"A very rare and perfect blue diamond, 16.6 carats, worth around fifty million dollars. It has been hidden away for many years, however, because of the curse."

"The curse?" she asked doubtfully.

A gleam entered his eyes. "You're not a believer in curses?"

"No, I'm not."

"Well, apparently neither is Westley. He has been quite eager to give the diamond to his bride-to-be."

"What is the alleged curse?"

"I don't know the details, but the diamond is passed to the bride of the first son of each generation, and some of those brides did not live happy lives."

"Westley's mother seems to be fine."

"Ah, but she never wore the diamond. She was too afraid of the curse."

Vincent paused as Jasmine and Westley stopped in the center of the room. The crowd grew quiet. Westley accepted a hand-held microphone from one of the consulate staff members.

"I want to thank everyone for coming," he said, with a welcoming smile. "Jasmine and I are eager to celebrate the official beginning of our lives together at this lovely engagement party thrown by her generous and wonderful parents, Raj and Kenisha Kumar, and her sister Anika."

The Kumars nodded as the guests gave them an appreciative round of applause.

"I'd also like to thank my parents—Phillip and Grace Larimer—and my siblings: Jonathan and Holly," Westley added, tipping his head toward his family, who were standing quite close to the Kumars. Then he turned his gaze on Jasmine. "I am the luckiest man in the world. The day Jasmine agreed to be my wife will always be the best day of my life. We come from very different worlds, across several continents, but miraculously we found our way to each other. I'd like to make a toast. To my future wife—Jasmine." He raised his glass.

"To Jasmine," the crowd echoed.

Parisa clinked her glass against Vincent's and then with a few other people in the immediate vicinity.

"Now, please," Westley continued, drawing the attention of the crowd back to him. "Enjoy yourselves. Eat, drink, talk. We hope to speak with each and every one of you before the night is over."

Westley finished his statement by giving Jasmine a loving kiss, and then the couple walked over to her parents.

Parisa was a little disappointed that Jasmine hadn't said a word, but Westley clearly had a strong personality, and Jasmine had grown up in a culture that kept women in the background.

"I'm going to speak to the Larimers," Vincent said. "If you'll excuse me."

"Of course." As Vincent left, she smiled in delight at another face from her past. "Mr. Langdon?" The blond-haired British man with the sharply intelligent brown eyes had taught at the school she'd gone to in Bezikstan.

"Parisa Maxwell? I thought that was you," he replied.

"I can't believe you remember me."

"One of my best language students, as I recall, and one who liked to speak her mind."

"Too much sometimes. How are you? Are you still teaching?"

"Yes. I moved to the university in Bezikstan about six years ago. But this year I'm actually a guest professor at Everly College, where my son Ben is a student."

"Ben is old enough to be in college?"

"Yes, he's twenty-one now. He goes to school at Everly, where Jasmine teaches economics. They've become very close. She's like his big sister." Neil tipped his head toward a line by the bar. "That's Ben in the blue suit."

Seeing the skinny male with the dark hair and short beard, she didn't even recognize the child she'd babysat a very long time ago. "He's all grown up."

"Time flies." He gave his son a wave, catching Ben's attention.

Ben got out of line and came over to join them.

"Ben, this is Parisa Maxwell. She used to watch you a long time ago when she lived at the embassy with her parents."

Ben gave her a guarded smile, but it was clear he didn't remember her. "Nice to see you again."

"Don't worry if you can't remember me. You were barely five when I saw you last," she said with a laugh.

He tipped his head. "Then I won't feel bad. Would either of you like a drink? I was just going to get one."

"I'm fine," she said.

"Nothing for me," Neil replied.

As Ben left, she said, "Your son is very handsome. He looks like Elizabeth. Is your wife here?"

"Somewhere, and, yes, Ben does look like her, which is fine with me. She's the pretty one."

She smiled at his affectionate words. She'd always thought the Langdons had a great marriage. "I hope to have a chance to speak to her tonight."

"I'm sure you will. Are your parents here as well?"

"Unfortunately, no. I am the sole representative of the family tonight."

"Well, I'm glad you could make it."

"As am I," a woman cut in.

She smiled as the bride-to-be joined them. "Jasmine. You look beautiful."

Jasmine opened her arms, and they exchanged a hug that was much warmer than the one she'd shared with Anika.

"I can't believe it's you, Parisa." Jasmine shook her head in amazement. "You're stunning."

"So are you. I'm very happy for you. You must be incredibly excited."

"It's hard to put into words."

"I'll let you girls chat," Neil said. "I know you and Parisa haven't seen each other in a very long time."

"Maybe we'll speak again later," Parisa told him.

"I'd like that. I'd love to hear about your life now."

"Of course."

"I would like to know about your life, too," Jasmine added, as Neil walked away.

"Believe me, your life is far more interesting than mine. When is the wedding?"

"June. It's a wonderful thing that has happened—love finally found me."

Jasmine's words took Parisa back in time, to a question they'd asked each other as teenage girls—*when will love ever find us*? "Yes, it did. You're lucky."

"We used to wonder all the time when it would happen, how it would happen. Remember?" Jasmine asked. "All the times we talked about boys and our futures?"

"I do." But she'd never really expected love to find her. She wasn't a passive person by nature. She didn't like to wait for things to come to her; she preferred to go out and get them. Unfortunately, so far, love—real, everlasting love—had eluded her.

Jasmine glanced toward the two very obtrusive security guards, who were standing nearby. "I feel like everyone is watching us. I heard you wanted to speak to me, and I really want to hear what you have to say. It's been so long since we've spoken. Shall we go upstairs?"

"I'd love a few minutes, but are you sure you can leave the party?"

"It will be going on for hours. And you are my dear friend from so long ago." Jasmine glanced over her shoulder and spoke to the older of the two men. "My friend and I will be going upstairs for a few minutes."

The man nodded, and they were escorted through the crowded room, into the hallway, and past a guard posted at the bottom of the grand staircase.

They made their way up to the third floor and into a luxurious bedroom. At first impression, everything seemed white or pink, from the king-sized bed with a dozen soft pink and lavender pillows, to a white love seat by the window with more pillows, an ornate dresser with matching silver mirror, and thick plush carpeting.

As the door closed behind them, with the guards on the other side, Jasmine blew out a breath of relief and sat down on the couch, then moved an overnight duffel bag from the sofa to the coffee table so Parisa could sit next to her.

"This is actually a nice break," Jasmine said.

She suddenly realized that there was more stress in Jasmine's eyes than joy. "Are you all right, Jasmine?"

"All of this is—it's a lot. When I saw how many people were here, I almost couldn't breathe. And this ring..." Jasmine held up her hand. "Ever since Westley put this on my finger, I've felt like my world is spinning."

She leaned in to take a closer look. The blue diamond was sheer perfection: the rectangular cut, the clarity, the sparkle. "I've never seen a diamond this big or this blue."

"It's one of a kind. It has been in the Larimer family for two hundred years."

"That's a long time."

Jasmine licked her lips. "Westley's mother Grace told me I should refuse to take it. She said it's cursed, and that Westley's grandmother, who wore the ring at her wedding, died in childbirth a year later. Apparently, there were other tragedies before that. Grace told Phillip she'd never wear it, so it's been sitting in a vault for a very long time."

"I'm sure that sad event didn't have anything to do with the ring."

"That's what Westley told me. He said it's silly for this magnificent diamond to be hidden away, and that he wants it to be a symbol of how big our love is. How could I say no to such a romantic gesture?"

She smiled. "You couldn't."

"I know. I'm acting crazy. I'll only be wearing it a few times a year. Westley is having a much smaller, but still beautiful, diamond ring made for me to wear every day. Anyway, enough about rings. How are you, Parisa?"

"I'm great."

"I had no idea you were here in New York."

"I'm not actually here. I came for the party."

"Oh…I guess I didn't understand. You work for the state department, though, right? You followed in your stepfather's footsteps."

"Yes. I'm putting my language skills to good use. What about you?" She was more eager to learn about Jasmine than to talk about herself.

"I'm a professor of economics at Everly College, or at least, I was—I quit at the end of the fall semester. Once Westley asked me to marry him, I realized how many events he has to go to, and how much traveling he does for work. Westley is a vice president at Larimer Enterprises. He needs a wife who can travel with him and help him entertain and truly be his partner. I wouldn't be able to do that with a full-time job."

"That makes sense."

A shadow passed through Jasmine's eyes. "Does it? Sometimes I wonder if I'm giving up who I am to be a part of who Westley is. Am I surrendering my life for his? I guess that's what marriage is. My mother certainly became my father's most ardent supporter. He has changed jobs many times, and she has always been there to do whatever he needed her to do. And they're happy, at least, most of the time."

She didn't really know what to say. She was surprised to hear the doubts in Jasmine's voice. "I'm not an expert on relationships or marriage, so I'm not in a position to hand out advice, but I think you should talk to Westley about your concerns. I'm sure he wants to make you happy as much as you want to make him happy."

"He is very devoted. I never really thought anyone could love me as much as he does, but he tells me all the time how wonderful I am. He truly swept me off my feet." She paused. "Is there a man in your life, Parisa?"

"Not at the moment."

Jasmine gave her a disbelieving look. "I can't believe that. Look at you. Are you too picky?"

"Quite possibly," she said with a laugh. "I also work a lot. I travel. I'm busy. And I'm happy."

"That's good. I've thought of you often over the years. We never really got to say a formal good-bye—at least not in person. The letters were great, but they weren't the same. Anika and I both missed you terribly after you had to leave. We were so excited when we heard you wanted to reconnect tonight."

She blinked in confusion as Jasmine's words echoed those her sister had said earlier. "What do you mean?"

Before Jasmine could reply, a heavy scent blew into the room.

She coughed as she looked toward the vent and saw thick, swirling air coming through the slats. Instinctively, she put a hand over her mouth.

"What is that smell?" Jasmine asked, getting to her feet. Then she suddenly swayed and sank to the floor.

She got up to help Jasmine but found herself tumbling to the ground, feeling light-headed and dizzy. She covered her mouth and nose with her fingers and tried not to breathe. Something was terribly wrong.

The bedroom door opened, and she was relieved, thinking the guards were coming to rescue them.

But as two pairs of men's shoes rushed by her, they seemed—wrong. One man was wearing black Nike's; the other had on brown boots.

She tried to lift her head, to say something, but she couldn't move. She felt paralyzed. Someone kicked her leg. She didn't know why. She tried to see but realized her eyes were closed. She was sinking into oblivion, and she willed herself to keep fighting, because if she fell asleep, she didn't think she would ever wake up.

Two

Jared MacIntyre had his target in sight. He took out his phone and pretended to be reading a text when he was in fact taking photographs of guests, who were engaging in conversation with the person he'd been following for the past week.

As he finished snapping the latest group he couldn't help glancing back at the camera roll, at the beautiful brunette with the deep-brown eyes, sexy smile and killer curves, who had crossed paths with his target a half hour earlier. He'd definitely had a visceral reaction to her, but what had really bothered him was the fact that he didn't know who she was.

He'd studied the party guest list at great length, matching names to faces, long before he'd come to the consulate. But he didn't remember *her* face, which was extremely odd, because she had the kind of heart-stopping beauty he would not have forgotten.

Her long, thick, dark-brown hair fell over her shoulders in flowing, silky waves, and her facial features and olive skin, implied that she was a mix of cultures. He'd seen her greet several people, including the bride-to-be, with a warmth that seemed very familiar. So, who was she and why hadn't she been on the guest list?

He opened up a text and sent her photo with one questioning word—*name?*

He'd no sooner done that when a waiter passing by with a full tray of glasses suddenly stumbled, sending sparkling wine in every direction, including the front of his shirt.

"Sorry, so sorry," the young man said.

He gasped at the sudden, cold wetness. His shirt was drenched.

A woman who'd been standing quite close to him began squealing about her dress, and there was a general commotion as waitstaff came to clean up the mess and offer towels and apologies to those who had been soaked in champagne.

He pushed the conciliatory waiter away, muttering that he was fine, and stepped out of the fray, searching once more for the person he was supposed to be watching.

It took him only a minute to realize his target was no longer in the living room.

He walked through the crowd with a growing sense of uneasiness. He couldn't help but wonder if the dropped tray hadn't provided the perfect distraction to slip out of sight. He could have been made and the sudden champagne spill might not have been an accident at all.

He quickened his pace, walking out of the living room and down the hall.

He'd studied blueprints for the consulate in great detail. He knew there were nine rooms on the first floor: the main living room where most of the partygoers were gathered, a smaller sitting room, the library, the dining room, which was filled with several long buffet tables, two restrooms, a small office, and a small bedroom with attached bath. There were additional offices, bedrooms and bathrooms on the second floor, while five bedrooms and five bathrooms took up the third floor, and where the more private and personal rooms for the family in residence were located.

He also knew there was a back stairway off the kitchen and if one needed to make a discreet exit or entrance, there was a short tunnel out of the basement that led to an alley a block away. He'd used that tunnel to get into the party without an invitation.

As he moved through the rooms, he couldn't help noticing that the bride-to-be didn't seem to be present, either. Nor did the beautiful brunette he'd seen talking to Jasmine and to his target.

He made his way down the hall. He needed to get upstairs, but he wouldn't be able to get past the guard without bringing attention to himself. The back stairway was a better bet.

He moved into the banquet prep area next to the kitchen, walking confidently among the servers. No one paid him any attention, which was exactly as he wanted it. He stopped by a pantry closet, shrugged out of his suit coat, and grabbed a chef's coat, putting it on over his clothes. Then he entered the kitchen.

It was controlled chaos: smoky, steamy heat coming from the ovens, lots of people rushing around, and beyond all that noise was a back hallway, a stairway. He expected to find a guard there but there was no one stationed at the bottom of the stairs. That seemed odd, too. The Kumars had brought in additional security because of the Larimer diamond.

He went up the stairs, bypassing the second floor in favor of the third. There was a door at the top landing. He opened it and peered down the hall, shocked to see the two security guards who had been following Jasmine sprawled on the floor, unconscious. There was no sign of blood, but there was a terrible smell in the air.

He pressed the material of his chef's coat across his nose and mouth and made his way toward the guards. A nearby door was ajar. He pushed it open and saw a woman lying on the ground. She was struggling to move, her eyes flickering open, then closing.

His heart jumped. It was the beautiful brunette in the clingy black dress. He rushed over to her.

"Jasmine," she stuttered. "Took Jasmine."

Her words sent a rush of alarm through him, but first he had to get her away from the terrible and obviously toxic smell.

He pulled her to her feet.

She swayed against him. "You? Who?" she murmured, her gaze meeting his.

He didn't bother to answer as he half-dragged her, half-walked her out of the bedroom and down the hall to the back stairwell. He closed the door to keep the fumes out, then opened a small window at the top of the stairs.

He pushed the woman as close to the window as he could. She took several breaths and seemed to gain strength with each one.

"What happened?" he asked.

She stared back at him in bemusement, her eyes cloudy and unfocused. "Someone…took Jasmine. Didn't see. Air…bad."

He heard a shout from the hallway. The guards had been discovered. It would be only seconds before security would be all over this area, and he couldn't allow himself to be caught up in whatever was about to happen. "Stay here. Someone will find you. They'll help you."

"Wait. Who are you?"

He didn't answer her question as he dashed down the stairs. As he hit the bottom step, he ran into several guards coming through the kitchen. "Heard a woman scream," he said, pointing toward the stairs. "Up there."

The men ran past him, probably thinking he was just one of the cooks. He made his way into the kitchen, where the servers were still moving about, although there was some chatter about an emergency. He slipped through the door leading into the basement without anyone noticing. He jogged down the steps, into the wine cellar, and out another door, past old furniture and boxes, reaching the far end of the room where a large bookcase had previously blocked the door to the tunnel.

He quickly realized that the bookcase had been moved, and the once hidden door was clearly visible. He went through the door with wary steps, pulling out the gun he'd tucked under his coat, keeping it at the ready as he maneuvered his way through the tunnel. The final door led to four stone steps and an alley behind a restaurant near Central Park. There were no lights, no security cameras—nothing but dumpsters and dark shadows.

He walked down the alley, ending up at the park, as sirens blazed through the air. He wandered down another path, disappearing into a thick thatch of trees, and staying in the shadows as he worked his way back to the front of the consulate.

There were four police cars out front. They'd set up barriers around the front of the consulate. A steady stream of people flowed out of the building in their cocktail dresses and expensive suits.

Was his target among them? Or had his target been involved in whatever had happened to Jasmine Kumar?

Unfortunately, he was too far away to identify anyone, and he'd just lost the best chance he'd had in weeks.

As ambulances pulled up in front of the building, he took out his phone, his hot breath swirling in the cold night air. He punched in a number, then said, "We have a problem."

Parisa was only dimly aware of being carried downstairs and put in an ambulance. Upon arrival at the hospital, she was treated with oxygen in the ER, and had blood drawn to see what toxins she'd been exposed to. With an IV in her arm, providing some much-needed fluids, her head finally began to clear.

Through the glass window of the examining room, she could see numerous people milling about in the hallway, including uniformed police officers and men wearing suits and badges. She also saw Jasmine's father, Raj Kumar, as well as Westley Larimer and his father Phillip.

Everyone looked impatient and terrified as they listened to a female doctor report on her condition. She knew that the doctor would tell them what she'd already told her—that while they didn't have the bloodwork back yet, her vitals were strong, her oxygen levels were returning to normal, and barring any other unforeseen problems, she should make a full recovery.

But the people in the hallway probably weren't that interested in her prognosis. They wanted to know if she was ready to talk about what happened.

First, she had to remember…

She'd been chatting with Jasmine in her room when something had been pumped into the ventilation system. Two men had come in and grabbed Jasmine. But she hadn't seen anything, had she?

Closing her eyes, she willed her memories to come back. She saw shoes, black and brown. Men's shoes. *What else?*

She was frustrated that her mind couldn't come up with more details. She felt like she was trapped in a thick fog, a terrible nightmare.

The door clicked, and her eyes flew open as Raj, Westley and two men in suits entered her room. As the door was about to close, a third man stepped inside, and she caught her breath at the familiar blue eyes of Special Agent Damon Wolfe, one of her best friends at the bureau.

His gaze widened when he saw her, and he gave her a short nod, but made no mention of their relationship, or her real job, as he introduced himself as a special agent with the FBI.

The dark-haired man in the gray suit was Kabir Bhat,

director of security for the consulate, and the balding man in black slacks and a wool coat told her he was Martin Vance, an NYPD police detective.

"Parisa, how are you feeling?" Raj asked, his innate sense of politeness probably prohibiting him from asking what he really wanted to know.

Westley had no such problem. "What happened to Jasmine?" he demanded. "Did you see who took her?"

"Give her a chance to answer," Damon cut in. "Ms. Maxwell, can you tell us exactly what happened?"

"Jasmine and I were in her bedroom when we smelled something very strong. I looked at the vent, and I could see thick particles of air blowing into the room. Jasmine jumped up and then she immediately fell to the floor. I tried to get to her, but as I hit the ground, I could barely breathe. I felt paralyzed. The door opened, and I saw men's shoes: black Nike basketball shoes and dark-brown boots."

"What about their clothes?" Detective Vance asked.

"All I saw was black. I'm not sure if they were wearing jeans or slacks."

"Did they say anything?" Kabir Bhatt asked.

She thought about his question. She felt like she had heard something, but what? Had it only been her own thundering heartbeat, her own breath? "I don't think so."

"If you couldn't move, how did you get out of the bedroom?" Westley demanded. "The guards found you in the stairwell."

"I—I don't know," she stuttered, not sure if the handsome man with the penetrating green eyes had been real, or if she'd somehow made her way there in search of clean air. Everything seemed very dreamlike. "I remember trying to crawl out of the room. I kept blacking out. And then I woke up by the stairs."

"Why did you and Jasmine go upstairs?" Westley continued, his gaze suspicious. "Why did she leave the party?"

"She said she wanted to catch her breath. She felt overwhelmed." She paused. "The guards—they were outside the door. What happened to them?" She looked at Damon as the other men exchanged a long look.

"They didn't make it," Damon said. "One died at the scene, the other in the ambulance on the way to the hospital."

Her heart twisted at that piece of news. *How had they died, and she'd managed to survive? And what was happening to poor Jasmine?* She had to be terrified. She had such a gentle, sweet soul.

"What did you and Jasmine talk about?" Mr. Bhatt asked.

"Her engagement, how she met Westley, wedding plans, that kind of thing. We were catching up."

"And you hadn't seen her before tonight in how many years?" he continued.

"Fifteen." She glanced at Raj. "I'm so sorry."

He nodded, his expression grim. "This isn't your fault. We're just trying to piece together what happened and why."

"Isn't the *why* fairly obvious—the ring?" she asked.

"Yes, but we don't understand why they didn't take the diamond and leave Jasmine behind," Raj answered.

"That would have made more sense," she murmured. Unless there was going to be a ransom demand for Jasmine.

"I never should have given Jasmine that ring," Westley said, shifting his weight back and forth, his face tight with tension. "I just wanted her to feel like a princess for one night. But she didn't want to wear it. She felt awkward and nervous. That's why she left the party, isn't it?"

"She did say the ring felt heavy, and she was glad she wouldn't be wearing it that often." As the blood drained from Westley's face, she felt guilty at her words. "But she also said how much she loved you, and that she appreciated the magnificent gesture."

"She did?" Westley asked, eager to hang on to that thought.

"Yes. How did the kidnappers get Jasmine out of the

building?" she asked. "There were so many people around. Was everyone rendered unconscious?"

"No, only the people on the third floor were affected," Raj said. "It appears that they left through a tunnel in the basement that we were not aware of. It was a brazen kidnapping."

"And well-orchestrated," Detective Vance put in. "They had to have had inside help."

Mr. Bhatt bristled at that comment. "We were extremely diligent in providing security for the event."

"It wasn't good enough," Vance said, angering the Bezikstani official.

"The FBI is happy to offer our resources moving forward," Damon interrupted.

"The consulate is under Bezikstani jurisdiction," Mr. Bhatt reminded Damon.

"And we'll cooperate with the American authorities," Raj said, sending his security guy a stern look. "Getting my daughter back is all that matters."

"Is there anything else you can tell us, Ms. Maxwell?" Detective Vance asked.

"I really wish there was," she said.

"Why do you think the kidnappers left you behind?" Westley asked, giving her a hard look, as if he thought she was somehow involved in the kidnapping.

"They probably thought I was going to die as the guards did, or that I offered no value to them."

"Are you sure it was Jasmine who wanted to go upstairs and not you?" Westley persisted.

"It was Jasmine." She wasn't going to take offense at the innuendo. The man was beside himself. She could cut him a break. "I want to help find her. I just don't remember anything else."

"Perhaps more details will come back to you as you recover," Damon said.

"I hope so."

"The doctor told us that she wants you to have additional breathing treatments before you're discharged," Damon continued. "While you're doing that, I'm going to have someone collect your things from your hotel, and we'll make sure you have a safe place to stay until we know what's going on. While you can't identify the kidnappers, they may not know that."

She was relieved to have Damon take charge. When the others left, she could speak more freely with him, and he might have information that the others didn't want to share with her.

While she didn't believe the kidnappers would come back for her now, the fact that she hadn't died along with the guards might trouble them down the road.

"Please take care of yourself, Parisa," Raj said, genuine concern in his eyes.

"I will. I am praying for Jasmine's safe return."

"We all are," he said, as he and Westley left the room, followed by Detective Vance and Mr. Bhatt.

She looked at Damon with a sigh of relief. "Thanks for putting an end to that."

"It didn't seem like you had anything else to add. Unless you were holding back?"

"I wasn't. And I didn't want to break my cover if I didn't have to."

"But you weren't working a case tonight, were you?"

"No. The Kumars are old family friends. I lived in Bezikstan from the age of thirteen to sixteen when my father was the US ambassador to Bezikstan. Raj Kumar was the minister of commerce at the time. They became close friends as they worked together, and our families did the same."

"Were your parents at the party?"

"They're traveling; they couldn't make it. I just finished up an assignment in San Francisco, so I thought I'd take a few days off and come to New York. I was planning on getting in touch with you and Sophie as well."

"We're always happy to see you. Preferably not in a hospital room. How are you really feeling?"

"My chest is tight, and my throat is sore, but considering the alternative, I can't complain." She paused as the nurse came into the room.

"It's time for your treatment," the nurse said.

"I'll leave you to it," Damon told her. "What hotel are you at?"

"The Parker, room 307." She looked around for her bag, so she could give him her key, but it was nowhere in sight. "I guess my purse is still at the consulate."

"I suspect so. The building has been evacuated while they test the air levels for toxins, but when the authorities can get back in there, we'll get it to you. I'll have someone retrieve your things from the hotel. I'll come back when you're done."

"Thanks." She was happy to have a few minutes to regroup. She needed to collect her thoughts and see if there was any detail she'd forgotten that might help them find Jasmine.

Three

Jared MacIntyre slid onto a stool at O'Malley's Pub near Times Square just after ten. The pub was crowded, as expected on a Friday night, with the usual mix of singles and couples, many of whom were tourists staying at the nearby hotels. He'd picked the pub for that reason. There weren't a lot of locals. The crowd turned over every weekend, and no one would remember him being there. He ordered a beer from the bartender. When it came, he drank half of it before setting it down on the bar.

"Looks like you needed that," a man said, as he took the stool next to him.

"It's been a night." He turned to look at the thirty-nine-year-old man with the short, neatly trimmed brown hair and intelligent brown eyes. Although, they'd been in contact almost daily the last month, he hadn't actually seen him in person in over six weeks. "You look better than the last time I saw you."

"Considering I was in the hospital then, that's not saying much."

"I'm glad you've fully recovered. How has it been—being back in New York?" Gary Heffernan had been living overseas for almost three years, and until a few months ago had been sporting a full beard and long hair.

"Different," Gary said, then shrugged. "And yet the same. I'm happy I still have a job. Although, I don't know how long I'll have it if I keep helping you."

"Speaking of which, do you have something for me?"

"I do. But first I need a drink. I'll have what he's having," Gary told the bartender, then gazed back to him. "You're a little overdressed for this place."

"I didn't want to take the time to go home and change. I'll do that later. Do you have a name for me?"

Gary waited until the bartender set down his beer, then said, "Parisa Maxwell."

"She wasn't on the guest list."

"She was a last-minute entry. Her stepfather is Harry Drummond, longtime US diplomat. He was assigned to the embassy in Bezikstan eighteen years ago. He and his wife Riya, and his stepdaughter Parisa, spent three years there. They were close friends with the Kumars. Raj Kumar was the minister of commerce at the time that Mr. Drummond was stationed there, and the two men facilitated trade agreements with the US. Parisa went to school with the Kumars' daughters."

"Which was why she was at the party."

"I would think so. It might interest you to know that Drummond and his family left Bezikstan after an attack on the embassy fifteen years ago. Several staffers were injured, and a Marine guard was killed. They barely got away with their lives."

"I don't remember seeing her parents' names on the guest list."

"They weren't. Parisa's mother and stepfather arrived in Bali a week ago with an expected stay of at least a month. They're participating in a yoga meditation retreat, which involves complete isolation and technological disconnect—no phones, no computers."

"So, they probably haven't heard anything about their daughter."

"Doubtful."

"What about her biological father?"

"I only have the basics, but Doug Maxwell divorced his wife when Parisa was about three. He runs a residential moving company in Florida."

"What else do you know about Parisa? What does she do for work?"

"Like her stepfather, she also works for the state department, but she serves as a translator. She's been working in San Francisco for the last several months. She flew in last night and checked into the Parker Hotel, which is located about six blocks from the consulate."

"Where is she now? Do you know her condition?"

"She was taken to St. Paul's Hospital, where she has been receiving treatment and undergoing interviews with the local police, the FBI, and Bezikstani security."

"Any mention of me?"

"Not that I've heard."

"Good. Do you know her prognosis?"

"They're expecting a full recovery. She's lucky. The two security guards didn't make it."

His gut churned at that piece of information. He'd gotten to her just in time. "And my target?"

Gary shook his head. "I don't know. All of the party guests will be interviewed, but there were over a hundred people at the consulate and evacuation took priority over getting statements. It will take some time to get to everyone. What's your next play?"

"I'm not sure. This kidnapping has changed everything. I don't know if it's related to Paris, but I need to find out. I need more access to the investigation."

"You can't have it. You've been ordered to stand down."

"I'm aware of my orders," he said, anger running through him at the reminder. "But I'm on leave, so no one needs to know what I'm doing."

"That will be permanent leave if you don't behave. And there's only so much I can do without drawing attention. Look, I know April was important to you—"

"She was important to all of us," he said quickly. "Or she should have been. I just need to find another way in."

"How?"

He had one idea, and it was probably a bad one...

———————

It was almost one o'clock in the morning on Saturday when Parisa was finally released from the hospital. Damon escorted her to a black SUV parked just outside the hospital door, and she was relieved to have him by her side. She also wasn't going to complain about staying the night in a safe house. While she normally had every confidence in her ability to take care of herself, after the night she'd had, she was still feeling a little wobbly and off her game.

"I guess your vacation isn't going the way you thought it would," Damon said, as he started the car.

"Definitely not. This was actually the first party I've been to in a long time where I was just going as myself and not working an angle. And then I end up in the middle of a kidnapping. Thanks again for not blowing my cover."

"No problem. I just followed your lead."

"I was very happy to see you at the hospital. It made things a lot easier." She looked out the window at the city lights, wondering where Jasmine could possibly be right now. Turning back to Damon, she said, "I'm surprised there hasn't been some word from the kidnappers yet. Unless you heard something while I was getting my treatment?"

"There has been no word from anyone," he said tersely.

"Was anyone else taken ill by the toxins?"

"No. The third floor was on its own ventilation system."

"But how did the kidnappers know Jasmine would go to the third floor during the middle of her party?"

"Perhaps their plan was meant to occur later in the evening when she went to bed, but when she showed up earlier, they took the opportunity to act."

"Seems a little risky, considering the house was full of people. I don't understand how Jasmine could have been taken out of the building without anyone seeing her. I know they went down the back stairs and through the basement, but why wasn't there a guard there? And how did they make it into the basement without anyone in the kitchen seeing them?"

"The guard who was posted to the back stairwell has disappeared."

"So, it was an inside job."

"Looks like it."

"I wish the kidnappers hadn't left me behind. If I was with Jasmine now, I might be able to help her escape."

"If she's still alive," he said darkly, then immediately added, "Sorry, I forgot she's a friend of yours."

"Believe me, I'm aware of the odds."

"Did you happen to speak to Vincent Rowland at the party? He called me a half hour ago and said he was there, that he's Westley's godfather, and he wants to do whatever he can to help our investigation."

"I did speak to Vincent. I have to admit I was startled to see him there, especially in light of the warnings Bree and Wyatt sent us a few weeks ago." Two fellow FBI agents and close friends of hers had suggested that Vincent could be tied to some of the dangerous situations they'd recently been finding themselves in, and she should watch her back. "But when Vincent explained his relationship to Westley, it made sense." She paused. "What do you think of Bree's theory about Vincent wanting to get revenge on us?"

"I'm keeping an open mind. Each case, taken on its own,

doesn't mean anything. But when you look at what happened to me, to Bree and Wyatt, it looks like there could be a pattern. Someone could be targeting our Quantico team. And the fact that our mentor and teacher, Alan Parker, is also dead, and Alan could have been held responsible for Jamie's death, it makes me wonder if someone—possibly Vincent—could be seeking revenge against the people who let his son die."

"But it has been four years. Why would Vincent keep inviting us to Jamie's memorials if he blames us for his son's death? And why would he wait so long to get revenge?"

"I don't know. It seemed ridiculous when I first heard it, but I trust Bree's instincts, and Wyatt also seems to be on board. Also, when I think about my own situation last year with Sophie, I wonder if we plugged all the FBI leaks. Vincent was an agent for twenty plus years. He knows how to work the system. He has friends all over the world."

"Or we could just be running into problems on our own. It's not like we don't do dangerous work and make enemies along the way. I can't imagine Vincent being as devious as everyone is suggesting. And why would he have an innocent girl kidnapped to get to me? He could have just kidnapped me. Or killed me."

"You might have been supposed to die tonight—just like the guards."

"Maybe." She frowned. "Jasmine did say something odd to me—she was happy that I'd reached out to the family for an invitation to the party and that I'd asked to speak to her. I didn't do, either. The invitation was forwarded to me from my stepfather's assistant."

Damon's profile tightened, as he thought about her comments. "It sounds like someone wanted you at the party."

"It might not be about Vincent; it could have to do with my ties to Bezikstan or even to my stepfather."

"Well, I'll call Vincent back in the morning and see what else he has to say. Any other interesting guests at the party?"

"I spoke to Neil Langdon, an old teacher of mine, and his son Ben. I also talked to Jasmine's sister Anika." She paused, debating her next words. Maybe she needed to say them out loud to see if they made sense. "There was a man at the party. He was watching me. I don't know if he was just flirting or if there was more behind his smile, but I felt myself not wanting to look away."

He glanced over at her. "Did you speak to him?"

"Not then." She cleared her throat. "I honestly don't know if I dreamed this, but it's possible he might have pulled me out of the bedroom and into the stairwell."

"Seriously? Why didn't you say that before?"

"Because my brain is foggy. Everything feels very dreamlike in my head. I don't know his name, but I'm also pretty positive he didn't have anything to do with the kidnapping."

"How can you be sure of that if you don't even know if you dreamed him up?"

"I guess I'm not sure, but if my dream was real, then I can say he was shocked to learn Jasmine had been taken. He didn't know what was going on."

Damon sent her a concerned look. "What did he say to you?"

"He asked me what had happened, but I couldn't really speak. He dragged me into the stairwell and opened the window. Then he told me to wait until help came, and he left."

"Why wouldn't he have waited with you? He clearly didn't want to talk to security."

"No, but why would he rescue me if he was one of the kidnappers?"

"I can't answer that. Would you recognize him if you saw him again?"

His handsome face and compelling green eyes flashed through her head. "Yes. I think so."

In fact, she didn't think she would ever forget him, and

that bothered her more than a little bit.

"It's possible one of the security cameras caught a glimpse of him as he moved through the party. Maybe you can come down to the office tomorrow and take a look."

"I will do that. I just wish I could do more. I'm really scared for Jasmine. The kidnappers murdered the two guards. They won't be afraid to kill Jasmine."

"They could have left her in the room to die and just taken the ring. So, I'm going to go with the assumption that they want to use her for ransom."

"Then why haven't they made contact yet?"

"I don't know," he said grimly.

She didn't, either, and her gut told her no news was probably not good news in this case.

A few minutes later, Damon pulled up in front of a two-story brownstone in Greenwich Village. "There are two flats in this building. The bottom apartment is empty. You'll be on the second floor. We'll have an FBI police officer posted downstairs for extra protection."

"Okay." She'd spent time in FBI safe houses before. She knew the drill. She just wasn't used to being the person who was in danger.

Damon walked her up the stairs and into the building. A uniformed male with sandy-brown hair and brown eyes, who appeared to be in his early thirties, was waiting in the lobby.

"Officer Briggs," Damon said with a nod. "This is Special Agent Parisa Maxwell."

"Pleased to meet you," the officer said. "I'll be here all night."

"I appreciate that," she said with a tired smile, then followed Damon up the stairs.

Damon unlocked the apartment with a code and waved her inside.

The living room had a card table and four folding chairs. The bedroom had a queen-sized bed, a dresser, and an armchair. Her suitcase was on the floor by the bed.

"It's not much," Damon said. "Sorry."

"It will be fine."

"Maybe I should stay with you."

"You don't need to do that."

"I would have taken you home, but Sophie has a friend staying with us."

She let out a breath and sank down on the edge of the bed, kicking off her high heels. "It's fine. I'm fine. I have a gun in my suitcase, and I'm well trained. Plus, the officer is downstairs. You don't have to worry about me."

"I know you're capable of taking care of yourself. But you almost died tonight, Parisa."

"I'll be okay. I'm more concerned about Jasmine. I want to talk to the Kumars again tomorrow."

"That's a good idea. They may speak more freely to you as an old family friend. When were you last in Bezikstan?"

"When I was sixteen years old. I'm sure the country has changed a lot since I was there."

"Yes. The Bezikstan government is currently under attack from a couple of rebel groups, who are growing in strength and radical thought. That diamond could buy a lot of weapons."

"I know. I also know that Raj Kumar is very close to the government leaders. Perhaps Jasmine's kidnapping is part of a bigger play."

As she yawned, he said, "I'll let you get some rest. We can talk tomorrow."

"Thanks." She walked him back out to the living room, turning the dead bolt after he left the apartment. Then she returned to the bedroom, opened her suitcase and pulled out her gun.

Just as a precaution, she took it into the bathroom with her. She would take a hot shower and then go to bed. When she woke up, maybe she'd remember something important, something that would help Jasmine.

Four

⸻➤➤❮❮⸻

Parisa didn't know what woke her up—it might have been the click of the door, or the sudden stream of light—but instinct brought her out of bed and to her feet as a dark figure came toward her. She saw the glint of a badge and for a moment, she was confused.

Was it the police officer who was supposed to be downstairs by the front door?

"What's going on?" she demanded.

Then she saw the gun in the man's hand, and her training kicked into gear.

Her first goal was to disarm him, which she managed to do with a swift waist-high kick that sent his weapon flying. She battled on, using her fists and her feet to fight. The man was bigger, but she was quicker.

She dodged several blows, but a stumble by the dresser gave her attacker an advantage, and he landed a punch against the side of her face that sent her reeling, and for the second time in twenty-four hours, she had to fight to stay conscious.

As he came at her again, she jerked to the right, knocking

him off-balance.

She sprang back up to her feet, but he was too fast, and suddenly his hands were on her throat, and he was bending her over the dresser with a deadly force. As she looked into his dark, evil eyes, she knew this was not the man who had been assigned to watch her door.

Where the hell was he?

She grabbed at her attacker's arms, kicking her feet, trying to find leverage, but she was losing air. Her brain was spinning. Lights were flashing before her eyes.

And then a man charged into the room.

He grabbed her assailant by the arms, pulling him off her.

She sank to the floor, gasping for breath as her rescuer went after her attacker with deft, trained moves. While they were fighting, she crawled across the floor and grabbed the gun her attacker had discarded. As she stood up and took aim, her attacker bolted out of the room.

Her rescuer turned his face into the light that was coming from the living room, and she gasped.

"You?" It was the mysterious stranger with the compelling green eyes. "What the hell are you doing here?"

"Saving your life—again."

She glanced at the clock on the nightstand. "It's five o'clock in the morning."

"I was going to wait until the sun came up to speak to you, but when I saw that guy go into the building, I had a bad feeling. My instincts were correct."

She didn't know about his instincts, but hers were screaming caution. "How did you find me? How did you get in here? Where's the guard that was downstairs?"

"He's by the front door—unconscious. I'll answer all your questions, but right now, we need to go." He didn't look at all concerned by the gun in her hand. "Someone just tried to kill you."

"I'm aware of that. Is the guard dead?" Her stomach

turned over at the thought of that man being killed because of her.

"He's still breathing."

"Good. We need to get him help."

"You can call from somewhere else. Put on some shoes, grab what you need—"

"I'm not taking orders from you," she interrupted.

"I saved your life twice. Doesn't that offer some sort of trust?"

"No. And I was perfectly capable of saving my own life."

He gave her a speculative look. "You sound pretty confident—for a translator who works for the state department."

He knew who she was, and she had no idea who he was. That put her at a disadvantage, and she didn't like it. "I've taken a lot of self-defense classes. How do you know what I do?"

"I know a lot of things. And I want to talk to you, Parisa. But we need to get out of here before your assailant comes back with some friends."

She wanted to argue, but he made a good point, although how he'd found her at an FBI safe house raised a lot of red flags. Maybe he was undercover for some other agency. Judging by his combat skills, he'd been trained somewhere.

"What's your name?" she asked, as she put on her sneakers and threw her long, wool coat over her leggings and T-shirt.

"Jared."

It might be a bad decision but going with him seemed less risky than staying put. She threw the attacker's gun into her suitcase and then tucked her own gun into the waistband of her leggings. Jared grabbed her bag, and she followed him down the stairs.

She stopped by the door to check on the guard. He was lying face down, with a big bump on the back of his head, but he had a pulse and was breathing, with no evidence of massive blood loss. She'd call Damon as soon as they got out of the building.

Jared went out the front door first, motioning her to hang back for a moment. Then he said, "It's clear. My car is nearby. Let's go."

She didn't want to hop into his car, but there were no taxis around and she couldn't wait to get a ride. Hoping she wasn't making a huge mistake, she got into the silver Ford Focus, while he put her bag in the trunk and then slid behind the wheel.

"Don't worry, you're going to be fine," he said as he started the engine. "And you do have a gun, so…"

"So, don't mess with me," she finished, pulling it out from under her coat.

"You seem pretty comfortable with a weapon. Was that also part of your self-defense training?"

"It was," she said, ignoring the sarcasm in his voice. "Where did you learn how to fight?"

"I took some martial arts classes."

"More than a few, I'm guessing. Where are we going?"

"There's an all-night diner not far from here. Why don't we get breakfast?"

"You want to eat now?" she asked in surprise.

"I'm hungry. And I'm sure you're going to argue if I try to take you anywhere but a public place."

"Fine. Give me your phone. I need to get someone to take care of the officer."

He handed it over. She couldn't help noticing it was a cheap throwaway phone that didn't even have a lock on it. She punched in Damon's number, which she had memorized.

He answered with a wary, "Yes?"

"It's Parisa."

"What's wrong?"

"I was just attacked at the apartment. I'm all right, but the guy got away."

Damon swore. "What about Briggs?"

"He was knocked out, but he's alive. Can you get someone over there to check on him?"

"Yes. Where are you now?"

"I'm going somewhere else."

"On foot?"

"No, I'm in a car."

"Come to my house."

"That's not a good idea."

"Then go to the FBI office or to the police station."

"I can't. The person who attacked me was wearing a uniform. I don't know if he was an FBI police officer or NYPD, but someone discovered my location. I can't trust anyone. I need to stay out of sight for a while."

"What else can you tell me about your attacker?"

"Not much. It was dark. I saw a uniform and the gleam of a badge. He had dark eyes. I'm assuming his hair was also dark. Beyond that..." She was frustrated with the lack of detail she could provide. "I know it's not much to go on."

"Maybe we can get more from Officer Briggs."

"I doubt it. He was hit on the back of the head. I have to go. Don't call me back on this phone. It's not mine. I'll be in touch with you when I get a chance." She set the phone down on the center console.

Jared gave her a speculative look. "Was that the police or the FBI?"

"Does it matter?"

"They want you to come in. But you can't trust them."

"I can't trust you, either." He knew her name. He knew about her job. He'd found her at the safe house.

What else did he know, and who the hell was he?

"Then why didn't you tell them about me?" he challenged.

As their gazes met, a shiver ran down her spine. It was a good question. Why hadn't she told Damon about him?

"Well?" he pressed.

"I honestly don't know. But you're right, we need to talk."

Parisa's right eye was swollen and her dark hair was a tangled mess, but her brown eyes were sharp and alert, and even in leggings, a T-shirt, and a black wool coat, she was a very attractive woman. She was also an enigma, an equation that didn't quite add up. She'd fought her attacker like a pro. And she'd handled her weapon as if it were a natural part of her. Was she really a translator for the state department?

Jared suspected she was not.

She had secrets. So did he.

He wondered who would break first.

Parisa sipped her coffee as they waited for their breakfast. She sat facing the door to the diner. The sun was starting to rise as the clock moved toward six thirty, but it was still dark outside. There were only a few other people in the restaurant: a woman in a nurse's uniform and an older man who was reading the newspaper. One waitress worked the counter while a male cook appeared to run the kitchen.

He would have preferred to be in Parisa's seat, but she'd slid in to that side of the booth before he could stop her.

"Well?" she prodded. "You said you wanted to talk, so talk."

"You said you wanted to talk, too. Why don't you begin?" he countered.

"All right. What's your last name? Were you invited to the party at the consulate or did you crash?"

"My last name is MacIntyre, and I was not technically invited to the party."

"You might want to think of a better answer. The police and FBI are going through the surveillance video from the party. I'm sure you're on it. They'll be contacting you."

"Good to know. Did you see who took Jasmine Kumar?"

She stared back at him, her gaze assessing. "Someone obviously thinks I did, based on what happened at the apartment."

"That's not an answer."

"What were you doing upstairs at the consulate?"

"I was looking for an available bathroom. The ones downstairs had long lines."

"You were wearing a black chef's coat—as if you were in disguise. I think you came up the back stairs by the kitchen."

He tipped his head. "So, you do remember something."

She frowned. "I just remembered that."

"What else?"

"I know you didn't want security to find you in the stairwell, that's why you rushed away. How did you get out of the building? Did you use the tunnel exit from the basement?"

"There's a tunnel from the basement?" he asked, preferring to get more information than he wanted to give.

"The police said the kidnappers probably took Jasmine out that way." She paused, tilting her head to the right as she gave him a speculative look. "What's your deal? Who are you? What do you want from me? How did you find me at the safe house?"

"That's too many questions."

"Take them one at a time."

"I can tell you this—I didn't have anything to do with the kidnapping."

"That's not enough. Tell me more," she said, a determined glint in her eyes. "Are you working for someone? Homeland Security? FBI, DEA, ATF?"

"That's a lot of initials. What you need to know is that I want to help you find Jasmine."

"All those agencies have a better chance of finding Jasmine than you or I do."

"Maybe not. We might have the inside track."

"I can't imagine why. And I'm not going to work with you, until you tell me who you are."

"You think working with the FBI is a better option after one of their officers just tried to kill you?" he asked.

"I'm sure he wasn't really an officer."

"But he knew where you were, and that apartment was clearly a safe house."

"Most people wouldn't know what a safe house looks like."

"An empty apartment with a guard—it wasn't a tough guess."

"How did you find me there? You better tell me something, or I'm going to walk out the door."

He smiled at her challenging words, feeling remarkably charged up by the conversation. He liked a woman who could keep up, and this woman was not only keeping pace with him, she was charging ahead. He had no doubt she would make good on her threat to leave if he didn't give her something. "I followed you from the hospital to the apartment."

"Why didn't you come looking for me when I first got there?"

"I decided to wait until morning, until you were awake, but then I saw a guy approaching the building. He had on a uniform, but the way he was moving gave me pause. When he went inside the building, the front door stayed open. That seemed odd. I went to investigate and saw the guard on the ground. That's when I knew you were in trouble."

She shook her head in bemusement. "I can't believe you followed us from the hospital, and we didn't see you."

He shrugged. "Maybe the person who took you to the safe house isn't that good at spotting a tail."

"He's very good, which means you must be good at avoiding detection."

He ignored that as he leaned forward and rested his arms on the table. "Now, it's your turn. Who are you, Parisa Maxwell?"

"You already know. I work for the state department."

"What I know is that you fought your attacker like someone with training. You picked up the gun like you knew exactly what to do with it. You didn't scream for help. You didn't call the cops or the FBI until we were away from the building, and when we came into this diner, you picked this table and your seat, so you could watch the door."

"I was being cautious."

"Are you a cop? Private security? FBI? Military? A spy?"

"I asked you the same exact questions, and you didn't answer. Why don't we cut to the chase? What's your job? And why were you at the party?"

He decided to tell her something, so they could move the conversation along. "I'm a reporter. I came to the event looking for a person who might have information for a story I'm writing."

"Who? And what's the story?" she asked suspiciously.

"Ben Langdon. You were talking to him at the party. It looked like you were friends."

Her eyes widened. "Ben Langdon is a college student. Why do you want to talk to him?"

"I've recently discovered that Mr. Langdon was in Paris at the time of an explosion at a Left Bank café. Two people died."

"Are you talking about the bombing at Café Douceur before Christmas?"

"Yes." His gaze narrowed. "I'm surprised you know about it. It didn't get much public attention here in the States."

"Why on earth would you think Ben was involved in a terrorist attack?"

"I'm not sure of the level of his involvement. But I do know Ben dated a woman in Paris named Sara Pillai. Sara is a Bezikstan citizen. Her stepbrother Isaac Naru belongs to the radical group taking credit for the Paris explosion— Brothers of the Earth. Both Sara and Isaac disappeared after the bomb went off. Ben stayed in Paris for four days and then returned to NYC two weeks ago. When I learned he was going to a party at the Bezikstan consulate, I went there to see if he might use the opportunity to meet up with Sara or Isaac again."

She stared back at him, clearly weighing his story for the truth. "Okay," she said slowly. "Did that happen?"

"I don't know. I was watching Ben, and then a waiter crashed into me. When I untangled myself from the crush of champagne glasses, Ben had disappeared. That's when I went looking for him."

"Upstairs."

"Yes. When I got to the third floor and saw the guards on the floor, and you struggling to get up, I pulled you out of the room. I wanted to find Ben before I got caught upstairs and questioned by security."

"Did that happen?"

"No. Which is why I decided to look for you at the hospital. I wanted to talk to you about Ben. When you left with the FBI agent, I followed you. I'm hoping you might be willing to help me out. You have a connection to the Langdons, and you owe me for saving your life."

She frowned. "That's an interesting story, but I don't feel like it's the complete truth."

He didn't answer as the waitress set down their plates. When she left, he said, "Tell me about your relationship with the Langdons—that's not top secret, is it?"

She dug into her eggs and took several bites. He did the same, hoping he could get her to open up.

Finally, she said, "I lived in Bezikstan for three years when I was a teenager, while my stepfather served as the US ambassador. Ben's father, Neil, was my teacher. He was more than a teacher, actually. He was a mentor and a friend. He and his wife, Elizabeth, often came to dinner at the embassy. I babysat Ben several times during those dinners. He was about five at the time. He was a sweet, loving kid. He loved playing cards. I taught him how to play spades."

"Sweet kids sometimes grow up to be terrorists. Did you know Sara Pillai or Isaac Naru?"

"I don't believe so. How old are they?"

"Isaac is twenty-nine. Sara is twenty-two. Sara and Ben attended the same schools in Bezikstan, but she was one year older. Isaac actually grew up in Mumbai but moved to Bezikstan when his father married Sara's mother when he was seventeen and Sara was ten. Any of that ring a bell?"

"No. Isaac is two years younger than me and didn't arrive in Bezikstan until after I was gone, and Sara would have been seven when I left." She paused. "Do you think that Jasmine's abduction is tied to this terrorist group?"

"I was shocked by the kidnapping, so I honestly don't know. But it's something to consider."

"Jasmine is like a big sister to Ben. Ben's father told me that Jasmine took Ben under her wing when he started college here in New York. I don't think he would be a party to anyone hurting her."

"Maybe he's not. But Ben did visit the consulate several times this week. And someone had to know the layout very well in order to pull off this kidnapping in the middle of a huge party."

"Have you shared these thoughts with the police, the FBI or the Kumars?"

"I haven't had a chance yet."

"You had a chance to track me down," she pointed out.

"I thought you might be more willing to share information with me than those agencies."

"Why would I be?"

"Remember that part about how I saved your life..."

She finished off her eggs and hash browns while she thought about that, and he downed the rest of his omelet. He hadn't told her everything, but hopefully it was enough to get her interested in working with him. She hadn't told him who she was yet, but he was damned sure she was working for one of the agencies she'd just mentioned. He didn't think she was a cop so that left FBI or possibly Homeland Security. With her international connections, she'd make a valuable asset. But had she been working tonight? Or was she just a guest at the party?

She wiped her mouth with a napkin and sat back in her seat. "You said you haven't talked to law enforcement about the kidnapping, but have you spoken to anyone about Ben's possible connection to the Paris blast—to Sara Pillai and Isaac Naru?"

"Yes, I've spoken to the authorities, and there are multiple agencies looking for Sara and Isaac. I'm not sure who's aware of Ben's relationship with Sara, but I assume I'm not the only one who knows Sara was dating Ben in Paris. They were not in hiding. They went on picnics by the Eiffel Tower, went dancing at night, like two young lovers."

"Who do you work for, Jared?"

"I work for myself. I'm a freelance journalist."

She sighed. "I can believe you're freelance, because you seem very comfortable operating off the radar, but I don't believe you're a journalist. Or, you're not *just* a journalist."

"Well, I don't believe you're a translator, or *just* a translator. But we can still work together, Parisa."

"How would we do that?" she asked.

"I'd like you to talk to Ben, use your family connection to get in the door, maybe get me in the door. Ben won't know you have any idea that he could be involved in the Paris bombing."

"I'm not against helping to determine whether Ben was involved in a terrorist attack in Paris, but my priority right now is finding Jasmine."

"The events could be connected. Brothers of the Earth originated in Bezikstan. Have you heard of them?"

"I've heard the name, but I haven't been following politics in Bezikstan." She paused, her lips tightening. "Here's the problem—I just don't trust you, Jared MacIntyre—if that's even your real name."

"Jared is my name. And you don't have to trust me. You just have to trust your instincts."

"My instincts are telling me that probably every other word out of your mouth has been a lie."

"At least some of my words are true," he said lightly. "Don't forget I've saved your life twice."

"How could I forget when you keep reminding me?"

"That was the last time."

"Sure." She pushed her plate away. "Okay. Here's the deal. I need to drop out of sight for a while."

He liked that she was moving on to more practical matters. "I have the perfect place."

"I also need to pick up a prepaid phone, but I don't have any money. My purse is still at the consulate."

"I can help you out. Should I call you Officer or Special Agent or what?"

"Parisa works." She paused, giving him a hard look. "I want to make something else perfectly clear, Jared. If you are playing me, you will not be happy with my response."

Purposeful fire burned in her dark eyes, and his gut clenched with inexplicable desire. Since the first moment he'd seen her, he'd felt like he'd been sucker-punched. Even now, bruised and exhausted, she was stunning, and he was swimming into dangerous waters. This beautiful woman had a ruthless—possibly deadly—side. On the other hand, so did he.

"That goes both ways," he told her, then extended his hand across the table. "Shall we shake on it?"

She slid her hand into his, and he held on to her fingers for seconds too long, feeling again that odd sense of intense connection. He didn't know her. She didn't know him. They were both probably lying about a lot of things. But there was some innate truth between them.

One of these days, he'd figure out what that truth was.

Five

After leaving the diner, they picked up a prepaid phone at a drugstore, and then Jared drove her to an apartment building in Midtown Manhattan, parking in the underground garage. They took the elevator to the sixteenth floor and stepped into a one-bedroom unit that looked like it had been professionally decorated. The hardwood floors were slick and smooth. Recessed lights cast a beautiful glow over the gray sectional couch, black coffee table, and entertainment center. The adjacent kitchen gleamed with new appliances that were top of the line.

Peeking into the bedroom, she saw a king-sized bed with a black bedframe, matching tables, and some books on the nightstand. The way the books were situated felt more like décor than books that were actually being read. Also, notably, there were no personal items in the apartment: no photographs on the walls, no shoes kicked off by the coffee table, no used coffee mugs, or even an old magazine.

As she moved back into the middle of the living room, she glanced out the windows, taking in a rather amazing view of Chelsea and the Hudson River. Turning back to Jared, she said, "This is much nicer than the last safe house I was in."

"It's not a safe house. This is my apartment."

"It doesn't feel like you actually live here."

"Well, I've been traveling recently, so I haven't completely made myself at home. You should be happy about that. The place is spotless."

"Does that mean you're normally a slob?"

"I wouldn't say that, but I don't spend a lot of time thinking about cleaning. There are more important things to worry about."

"Yes, there are," she said with a sigh, thinking about Jasmine and how every minute that passed made the odds of getting her back safe and unharmed that much longer.

"Can I get you anything?" he asked.

"Some water would be nice."

"Sure." He moved into the kitchen and opened the cupboard by the sink and then moved to the one by the stove and pulled out a glass.

So, he didn't know where his own glasses were kept—interesting. That just confirmed her suspicions that this place was a safe house or he'd moved in yesterday. He filled her glass with tap water and brought it back to her.

"I should have asked how you're feeling," he said. "Do you want some ice for your eye?"

"It's fine. It's not that bad."

"Most women would get more upset about a black eye."

"Well, I'm not most women."

He gave her a thoughtful look. "I'm beginning to realize that."

She wandered over to the window as she sipped her water. It was eight in the morning, and the city was waking up. In the distance, she could see the new Freedom Tower that had replaced the World Trade Center, destroyed in the attacks of 9/11. It rose up in the sky like a proud phoenix, and it made her feel happy to see it.

Closer in, the High Line Walkway built over old train tracks and now a popular walking and running path wound its way above the city streets. There were the shops and restaurants in Chelsea, a farmers' market a few blocks away and a parade getting ready to begin. Tourists were coming out of their hotels and venturing into cafés, ready to eat and walk and explore one of the biggest and most interesting cities in the world.

She'd thought about living in New York more than once, but the kind of work she did for the bureau kept her out in the field and renting an apartment that would be empty more often than not in one of the most expensive cities in the world did not seem like a good idea.

"Something interesting out there?" Jared asked, coming up next to her.

"There's already so much going on." She waved her hand toward the view. "Manhattan is chaotic, energized, vibrant, alive..."

"It is all that and more. The best part is the food. You can travel around the world in cuisine without walking more than a few blocks." He folded his arms in front of his broad chest. "From the way you're speaking about the city, I don't get the feeling you live here."

"I think you already know that I don't. I've been in San Francisco the last six months. It's a beautiful city, but a much different vibe."

"Where were you before that?"

She waved a careless hand. "Here, there, and everywhere. I move around a lot."

"With the state department?"

"Yes. And you still haven't told me how you know that about me."

"It's easy to find anything on the internet."

She let that go, because, clearly, he wasn't going to give her a direct answer. "What about you? Are you a native New Yorker?"

"I was born here, yes." A shadow moved through his eyes. "I've both loved and hated this city."

There was a ton of emotion packed behind his simple statement, and, for the first time, she felt like Jared had said something truthful. But he didn't seem inclined to continue talking.

He was definitely an enigma—a very interesting, handsome, sexy puzzle. Her fingers tingled in memory of the handshake they'd shared at the diner, reminding her that she needed to keep her wits about her. This man had an almost irresistible attractiveness. Last night, in his expensive suit, acting debonair and sophisticated, he'd given off a James Bond vibe. Today, in dark jeans and a gray pullover, a shadow of beard on his face, his eyes a bit tired from his sleepless night, he looked even more appealing.

As their gazes clung together, something shifted in his eyes. Unfortunately, she had a feeling he'd just pulled a curtain down, instead of up. Maybe he regretted his candid comment.

"I'm going to run out for a few minutes," he said, surprising her with his words.

"Where are you going?"

"I have to make a call."

"And you can't make it here?"

"I can, but I thought you might want some privacy to make your own calls. I'm being thoughtful and considerate," he added with a smile.

"Or using this opportunity to pursue your own secret agenda." But since she did want some privacy, she let it go at that.

"I won't be long," he said, as he headed to the door.

After he left, she punched in Damon's number. "It's me, Parisa," she said, when he answered. "I picked up a new phone."

"Good. Are you safe?"

"I think so. What's happening? How is Officer Briggs?"

"He has a concussion and is fuming about getting jumped. Otherwise, he's fine. Unfortunately, he did not see his assailant."

"I figured. Any word from the kidnappers?"

"Not yet. We're going through security cameras in the area near the consulate, hoping we get lucky and can pick up the kidnappers somewhere near the exit to the tunnel, but so far nothing. We're also interviewing guests, staffers, servers, anyone who was at the party last night, who might have seen something."

"What about the missing guard, the one who should have been on the back staircase?"

"In the wind. I do have one interesting piece of information. The security company that the Larimers hired to protect Jasmine and the diamond has only been in business for two months. The owner lives in South Africa and the number listed on the website is disconnected. The men who died were paid a lump sum of five thousand dollars the day before the party. They were both American, both veterans, and both dishonorably discharged—one for theft, the other for assault on a fellow officer. One is survived by a sister, who said she hadn't seen her brother in fifteen years. The other had no relatives."

"Who hired the company?"

"Phillip Larimer said Tim Hutchinson, the director of his security team at Larimer Enterprises, hired the company. Mr. Hutchinson had worked for the company for nine years. Phillip had no reason to distrust him."

"You said *had* worked…"

"You probably won't be surprised to learn that Mr. Hutchinson quit the company last week and left the country after draining his bank account. Phillip Larimer said the departure hadn't made him suspicious, because Hutchinson had been talking about wanting to retire for a long time, and that the security for the party had been put into place days earlier."

"So, Hutchinson hired a shady security company to guard a fifty-million-dollar diamond, and no one questioned him about the firm's credentials?"

"They trusted Hutchinson to do his job."

"What does Westley have to say about all this?"

"He's distraught, angry, and feels guilty that he should have done his due diligence on the security. He also said that because the consulate had its own security, they thought their guys were just extra muscle. Their sole mission was to protect the diamond."

"Is there any chance Westley is involved?" she asked.

"There's always that chance, but he has been very cooperative. He willingly turned over his phone and computer and spent most of the night talking to detectives and agents. He's not acting like anyone who has something to hide."

"How are the Kumars holding up?"

"Mr. Kumar went back to the consulate this morning."

"Is it safe?"

"It appears to be. However, the rest of the family, as well as the consulate staff, are staying at the Clairmont Hotel until the building can be thoroughly cleaned. Mr. Kumar wanted to be there in case the kidnappers call that number with their demands. We have an agent with him. The police are also there, as well as the consulate security team."

"The kidnappers would be fools to believe that law enforcement wouldn't be listening in on any calls. I wonder if they'd reach out to someone else, someone not as visible, but who could pass the demands along to Mr. Kumar. The kidnappers might try to contact Westley. In fact, that makes more sense to me. The real money belongs to the Larimers."

"We have an agent at Westley's apartment and have strongly suggested that he not act on his own if he wants to save Jasmine's life."

"I hope he takes that advice, but we both know what desperation can make people do." She paused, as she looked out the window at the Freedom Tower. "We talked about political motivation last night. Anything new on that angle? Could Jasmine's kidnapping be tied to a rebel group in Bezikstan? Raj is a government official."

"I spoke to Mr. Kumar about that. He hasn't been in touch with anyone tied to a rebel faction. Nor has he received threats. He's been in the US for over a year, and while he does have connections with people in the government back home, he has no direct power to influence anything, so he can't imagine what anyone would want him to do. Or what he even could do. He's, of course, willing to cooperate in any way that will bring his daughter home."

"He must be terrified about Jasmine. The Kumars are a close family. My heart breaks for them."

"It's a tough situation," Damon agreed. "I also have one of our diamond experts tapping into his network of dealers. If someone tries to sell or cut the diamond, hopefully he'll know."

"Good."

"I'm still concerned about your safety, Parisa. Obviously, you weren't expected to survive last night's attack, and when you did, someone tried to shut you up. Have you remembered anything else that might be helpful?"

"No. I'm making a lousy witness."

"You're not just a witness, you're also a victim. And you were still coming down off the toxic fumes in your bloodstream. If anyone should be feeling guilty, it's me. I put you in that safe house. I'm wondering if someone at the bureau leaked the information—maybe Rowland. I saw Vincent this morning in Deputy Director Hunt's office."

"What did he say?"

"He expressed all the right sentiments, including concern for your health. Both Rowland and Hunt want you to come into the office, so we can get you additional protection."

"That's not going to happen, especially not with Vincent hanging around. I need to stay off the bureau's radar. We probably shouldn't use your phone anymore."

"This is a new number since Christmas and is only known by the five people in our group. I don't use the phone for anything else. We're okay."

"All right. Before you go, Damon, I need to talk to you about something else. I don't know if it's connected, but it might be."

"What's that?"

"About three weeks ago, there was a bombing at Café Douceur in Paris. A radical group called Brothers of the Earth, that has ties to Bezikstan, took credit for the attack. Two names have come to my attention: Sara Pillai and Isaac Naru. Sara grew up in Bezikstan and was living in Paris at the time of the attack. Her stepbrother, Isaac, has ties to Brothers of the Earth, and he was also believed to be in Paris when the bomb exploded. Can you find out what the bureau knows about the attack and whether Isaac or Sara have surfaced anywhere since the blast? I'd love to know if they're in New York City."

"I can do that," he said slowly. "But do you want to tell me where you're getting this information?"

"Yes." She took a breath, her grip tightening on the phone. "I didn't escape the safe house attack on my own. The man from the party—the one who pulled me out of Jasmine's bedroom—also found me at the safe house. He followed us there from the hospital. He was going to wait outside until dawn to speak to me, but when he saw the man in uniform go into the building and leave the front door opened, he followed."

"What the hell?" Damon exclaimed. "We were followed from the hospital? I checked for a tail several times."

"I'm pretty sure the guy is in law enforcement; I just don't know which branch. But he definitely has skills to avoid detection. He claims his name is Jared MacIntyre and that he's a freelance journalist chasing down a story on the Paris bombing. He was at the consulate party because the woman I just mentioned, Sara Pillai, is believed to have been dating

Benjamin Langdon, while Ben was studying abroad in Paris. The Langdons are very close to the Kumars. I knew the family from my time in Bezikstan and spoke to Ben and his father last night."

"You got all this information from the journalist?"

"Yes. He alleges that he was following me because he saw me talking to the Langdons and figured I might help him get more information on Ben since he saved my life at the consulate."

"And you believe him?"

"I believe some of what he's telling me. Like I said, I think he's working for someone—I just don't know who."

"I'll run him through our databases. Where is he now?"

"I'm not sure," she hedged. "But he'll be back."

"You're playing with fire, Parisa."

"Maybe. But my gut tells me Jared is not a danger to me. He did save me twice."

"Because he wants something from you."

"Yes. But I don't mind helping him get to Ben if it means finding who might have been behind the terrorist attack. And if that event is tied to Jasmine's kidnapping, then he might have given us the best lead we have."

"He could have given that lead to the police or to the bureau—why didn't he?"

"I don't know. And I probably have no right to ask this of you, Damon, but could you keep his name off this lead until we know who Jared is? If he does work with another agency, we could suddenly find ourselves tied up in red tape and territorial fighting. That will only slow down the search for Jasmine."

"I can do that for now. I'll start digging into everything you gave me."

"Great. I'm going to talk to Anika and Kenisha today. Call me if you find out anything."

"You do the same, and watch your back, Parisa. You're still a very loose end."

"I know." As she ended the call, the apartment door opened. She was relieved to see Jared, although that seemed like a foolish thought. He could be as dangerous as anyone.

"Any news?" he asked, a curious gleam in his green eyes.

She slid her phone into the pocket of her coat. "Not really. What about you?"

"Same."

"Well, we're not getting too far too fast," she said dryly, quite sure he'd gotten an update from someone.

He gave her a smile that sent an unwelcome wave of heat through her body. She couldn't remember the last time a man's smile had had such an effect on her. She reminded herself it was a smile she couldn't trust and to think otherwise would be foolish.

"Something wrong?" he asked with a quirk of his brow, as his gaze swept her face. "You seem a little on edge."

"I'm debating my next move."

"I didn't realize translators had moves," he quipped.

"I'm feeling more like a detective at the moment. I want to do everything I can to help find my friend. The Kumars are staying at the Clairmont Hotel. I'd like to check in on them."

"Good idea. I'll drive you."

"Fine, but you're not coming inside. I can't bring a stranger into their midst. Not now. Not after everything that has happened."

"I understand, but perhaps you can find out if they've been in touch with Ben or the Langdons."

"I can probably work that into the conversation."

"How did you find out they're staying in a hotel?"

She shrugged. "A friend told me that while Mr. Kumar is at the consulate with several law enforcement officials, the vents in the building are still being cleaned, so family and staff are staying in the hotel." She paused. "Where did you go?"

"I had to check in with one of my friends," he said, deliberately using her word.

"Did your *friend* have anything to say?"

"Unfortunately, no."

She wondered if that were true, or if Jared was holding out on her, but she was going to concentrate on what she needed to do next.

"Are you ready to go now?" Jared asked.

"Actually, I'd like to take a shower and change clothes first, if that's all right."

"The bedroom and bath are yours," he said, with a wave of his hand. "And the bedroom door locks, in case you were wondering."

"Good. But I'm not afraid of you."

"Why not?" he challenged.

"Because I still have my gun." She took it out of the waistband of her leggings as a pointed reminder that she could take care of herself.

He smiled and then pulled up his long-sleeve shirt and took out his own gun.

She couldn't stop her jaw from dropping. "Why didn't you show your gun before—like in the safe house when I was being attacked?"

"I didn't need to."

Her gaze narrowed. "Since when do reporters carry guns?"

"It's a dangerous world, Parisa."

"Don't I know it," she muttered, grabbing the handle of her suitcase and dragging it into the bedroom. She didn't bother to lock the door, because he could easily break through the flimsy lock. And while she didn't know who he really was or what his long-term game was, her instinct told her she could trust him—*for now*.

Six

J ared put his gun down on the table, waiting to hear the click of the lock on the bedroom door, but it didn't come. He was surprised. Parisa definitely didn't trust him, but, apparently, she trusted him enough. He wished he could say the same.

She'd clearly been speaking to someone in law enforcement, probably the man she'd called earlier. And she had some kind of credentials. If she'd just been a witness to the kidnapping, she would not have been given any facts about what was happening at the consulate or where the Kumars were now staying.

If he had to guess, he'd say she was FBI. Her driver to the safe house had been Special Agent Damon Wolfe. And when she'd made her call from the car earlier, even though she'd been careful in her word choices, it had been clear that she knew the person she was speaking to.

Pulling his laptop computer from the top drawer of his desk, he opened it, and logged into an encrypted site. There, he found a copy of the police report that Gary had sent him— the interview between the police and Parisa. He skimmed through the report, noting that Parisa had stated that she'd gone upstairs with Jasmine, because the bride-to-be wanted a break from all the attention. Had that really been it?

The kidnappers had only put the toxins in the third-floor ventilation system, which was a newer system and separate from the one servicing the first two floors. Someone had to know that Jasmine would go upstairs. Had Parisa actually been the one to set Jasmine up? To get her to go to her bedroom?

His gaze narrowed on that thought. But that would make Parisa a conspirator, and he didn't believe that. If he hadn't found her and gotten her out of the bedroom, she could have easily died along with the guards.

But who else would have known that Jasmine would even go upstairs during the party?

Or had the kidnappers planned to do it later that evening?

He frowned, hating when a piece of the puzzle didn't fit. Jasmine could have easily gone home with Westley that night. In fact, she probably would have.

There was something he was missing. *But what?*

Leaving that question hanging, he spent the next fifteen minutes reading through witness statements, none of which were of value to the investigation as far as he could see. He noted that Gordon Roberts, the security guard who had been posted at the back stairway, had disappeared. Two waiters had also vanished after the kidnapping—Victor Salgetti and Ray Bateen. Gary was already researching the three men, and he was sure the other agencies involved were doing the same. Hopefully, someone had left a clue behind.

Clicking out of the police report, he pulled up photos of Sara Pillai and Isaac Naru. He wanted to show them to Parisa. She claimed she'd never heard of them, but there might be a chance she'd seen them somewhere, possibly at the party.

Sara was a slim girl of twenty-two, with brown hair that she almost always wore in a ponytail. She had striking features, and he could certainly see why twenty-one-year-old

Ben had fallen for her. The photograph of her had been taken in Paris a week before the explosion. She and Ben had had a picnic in front of the Eiffel Tower and Ben appeared to be completely infatuated with the woman sitting on the blanket across from him.

The moment, the relationship, seemed innocent and not at all noteworthy, if not for what had happened a week later.

His gaze moved to the second photo. Isaac Naru was a short and stocky man of twenty-nine years, with a square face and a brooding, shifty expression. His photo had been caught by a security camera at London's Heathrow Airport as he'd waited to board a plane to Paris three days before the explosion. Had he been contemplating what he was about to do?

Neither step-siblings had been seen since the blast at the café. There had been no record of them leaving Paris or arriving anywhere else. Ben had departed Paris four days after the blast. He'd taken a direct flight to JFK Airport. For the past two weeks, he'd been staying with his parents at the apartment they'd rented a year earlier. Ben didn't appear to be taking classes, although he had not yet graduated from Everly.

He opened another computer window and pulled up a photograph of Ben that he'd taken at the party. He really wished now that he'd made a move on Ben while he'd had the chance. He'd been waiting to see if he'd connect with Sara or Isaac, but he'd waited too long.

He heard a click and as the bedroom door opened, his attention moved to Parisa. She'd changed out of her leggings into dark-blue jeans and a cream-colored ribbed V-neck sweater that clung to some very nice, full breasts.

A knot entered his throat as his gaze moved to her face. Her eye was not as swollen as it had been, but there was purple-and-black bruising around the lid and the bridge of her nose.

Despite the bruises, she had beautiful features with her

wide-set dark eyes, long, sweeping lashes, and a sexy mouth. Her skin had a warm, honey-glow, and was creamy, no freckles or skin spots—nothing to mar the perfection.

His pulse sped up as she looked back at him, as he felt the strong pull of attraction that had hit him the first moment he'd seen her. For a split second, at the party, he'd almost forgotten why he was there, what he was supposed to be doing. And he couldn't make that mistake now.

It wasn't going to be easy to concentrate with her around, but he would have to find a way. Later…maybe later…they could explore some other distractions.

Not that she'd probably stick around for later.

Not that he probably would, either.

But there was something exciting about that, too.

Parisa cleared her throat, as if her thoughts had been going down the same dangerous road. "What are you doing?" she asked.

He tried to remember what he was doing, but the blood in his brain was rushing to other parts of his body.

"On the computer," she added.

"Right. I want to show you some photos."

She moved next to him and peered over his shoulder as she took a look at the three pictures. "I recognize Ben, of course. I'm guessing the woman is Sara Pillai?"

"Yes. And the other guy is her stepbrother, Isaac Naru. Have you seen them before? Did you notice if either Sara or Isaac were at the party?"

She immediately shook her head. "I'm sure I've never seen them. When were the photos of Ben and Sara taken?"

"Several days before the blast."

"Ben looks happy, carefree, not like someone about to do something terrible."

"Maybe he didn't know what his girlfriend was involved in."

"Are you sure she was his girlfriend?"

"Look at the photo."

"I see two people having a picnic."

"They were inseparable for a week, spending every day and every night together." He paused, deciding to tell her a bit more. "Sara had been working in Paris for about two months before Ben showed up there during his study abroad program. She was a waitress at the Café Douceur."

"That's interesting." She pulled out a chair and sat down across from him. "What about Isaac?"

"He had been working in London but quit his job about six weeks before the explosion. He made a trip to Bezikstan during that time and another trip to Mumbai. When he got to Paris, he stayed at a hostel."

"Not with his sister?"

"Sara had three roommates in a very small flat. But once Ben arrived, she was staying in his hotel room."

Parisa gave him a thoughtful look. "You know a lot about them, Jared."

"I do my research."

"Was Sara working at the café the day of the blast?"

"She called in sick. Good timing, huh?" he asked, unable to hide the bitter note in his voice.

Parisa immediately picked up on it, her gaze narrowing. "This feels personal, Jared."

"I tend to get personally involved in my stories. It's a bad habit, but sometimes it makes the end result better. Because I care, I go the extra mile."

"Right. That might be true, but I don't really believe you. At any rate, you said the authorities are looking for Sara and Isaac, and I would assume for other members of this radical group. Why don't you just let them do it? Or work with them?"

"If the authorities find them before I do, that's great, but the more days that pass, the greater the odds that anyone will be held responsible for that explosion."

"All right," she said, getting to her feet. "I appreciate you sharing the pictures with me, and I think your goal is a good one. I would love to take down these terrorists, but right now, I need to focus on Jasmine."

"I understand."

"Are you ready to go to the hotel?"

"Sure." He closed the computer. "Before we leave—why do you think the kidnappers set up the toxin for the third floor when Jasmine had been staying at Westley's house almost every night last week? How could they guarantee she'd ever go up there with the ring on her finger?"

She stared back at him. "That came up in my discussion with the police. I don't have an answer. Although, I do believe that we were in Jasmine's bedroom. Her purse was there. She moved it from the couch to the table. I'm sure she would have gone upstairs to get it at some point, even if she was planning on leaving the building."

He nodded. "Good point. Have any other details from last night come back into your head?"

"I just remember seeing men's shoes go by. There are garbled sounds in my head, but I can't identify the word—if any were spoken. I might be imagining it. The sound could have come from my heart pounding loudly against my chest." She took a breath. "I knew—I just knew that if I gave into unconsciousness, I'd never wake up."

"Maybe that's why you survived. You were fighting." He gave her a thoughtful look. "Just like you were fighting last night when that guy was choking you."

At his words, she put her hand to her throat, and he could still see the faint traces of redness on her skin.

"I would have taken him down," she said. "I just needed one more second to get leverage."

"If you had one more second. You're not lacking in confidence, I'll say that."

"Neither are you."

He tipped his head. "That's true. I'm also a fighter. I don't quit."

"I don't quit, either. Let's go to the Clairmont. We'll have a better chance finding answers there than here."

The Saturday traffic was crazy busy. Jared maneuvered through crowded side streets in an attempt to make his way around several parades. It took them almost an hour to go about four miles, and the clock had just passed ten thirty. Every minute that passed seemed like one more minute wasted. Parisa grew increasingly frustrated. They needed information, a lead, something...

It would have been faster to take the subway, but she wasn't ready to throw herself into a big crowd just yet. There would be too many faces to scan, too few escape routes.

"We don't have a tail," Jared said, as she not only glanced in her sideview mirror but also looked over her shoulder. "I've been watching."

"Damon was watching last night, and he didn't see you."

"Damon?" he queried. "Would that be Special Agent Damon Wolfe?"

"Yes," she said, realizing she'd sounded a bit too familiar, but it was too late to take it back.

"Sounds like you got really friendly on your ride home from the hospital."

"He's a friendly guy."

"But not that good at spotting a tail."

She decided to leave that alone. Thankfully, they were nearing the Clairmont Hotel, which was tucked on a side street near the park and not far from the consulate. There was a valet in front, and Jared pulled into the line.

"You're not going in with me," she reminded him.

"I'll wait in the lobby. There's nowhere to park around here. I need to valet the car."

She didn't like it, but she couldn't argue. "Fine, but I'm getting out now. No one needs to see us enter the hotel together."

"Go for it. And, Parisa, while I know your goal is to save Jasmine, if you get a chance to ask about Ben—"

"I will," she said, cutting him off. Then she got out of the car and walked into the lobby.

The Clairmont was a five-star luxury hotel with a lobby that glittered with gorgeous glass chandeliers and sleek marble floors. There was a piano bar by the windows, where a gifted pianist was entertaining guests, some of whom were seated at cozy tables, others at the bar.

Her gaze moved to the front desk and the adjacent bank of elevators. There was a hotel clerk checking keys before guests went up in the elevators. In addition, there were several men in dark suits, who appeared to be watching the area as well. She was guessing those men were there to protect the Kumars.

Knowing that she wouldn't be able to sneak up to the top floor, she boldly approached the female front desk clerk. She gave her name and asked the woman to contact the Kumars and let them know she wanted to see them. The clerk told her to wait and then went into the back room.

She tapped her fingers impatiently on the counter, then turned her head, her gaze sweeping the lobby. Jared had taken a seat at the bar that faced the lobby area where she was standing and had ordered a drink. He gave her a subtle nod and a smile, reminding her of when she'd first seen him at the party. He definitely had the ability to slide into any scene and look like he belonged there.

A moment later, an attractive blonde dressed in boots and a short sweater dress took the seat next to him, giving him a warm smile.

She frowned at the weird feeling that ran through her. She had no reason to care that he was now talking to the woman, except that it felt a little *wrong*. He was supposed to be on guard, watching the lobby, keeping an eye out for problems, not flirting.

What if that woman was a plant, someone meant to

distract him?

But no one was after Jared. No one was aware of his activities at the consulate the night before—at least she didn't think so. She didn't really know for sure.

And she was being ridiculous. Maybe even a little jealous. *What on earth was wrong with her? Why was she even thinking about Jared when her focus should be solely on Jasmine?*

Glancing toward the elevator bank, she saw a man walking toward her. He'd been with Kabir Bhatt, the director of Bezikstan security, at the hospital, but she hadn't been given this man's name.

"Miss Maxwell," he said in a voice laced in a faint British accent. "I'm Sanji Gupta. I'll take you upstairs."

"Thank you," she said, accompanying him to the elevator. She was relieved that the Kumars had agreed to see her.

He put in a security card to access the penthouse suites, and within seconds, they reached the top floor. They walked down a thickly-carpeted corridor to the end of the hall where large double doors were being guarded by two uniformed men with guns clearly visible. The men nodded to Sanji and opened the door.

A female dressed in a black sheath dress greeted her and then escorted her into the living room. Kenisha and Anika were seated across from each other—Kenisha on a plush white sofa and Anika in a chair by a gas fireplace that offered a warming fire. They looked exhausted and terrified.

Both women came to their feet as she entered the room.

Kenisha gave her a teary smile as she opened her arms.

She embraced Mrs. Kumar, feeling her trembling shoulders, knowing that Jasmine's disappearance was ripping her apart. Then she turned to Anika, whose hug was much lighter, but whose gaze was just as troubled.

"Would you like some tea?" Kenisha asked, motioning toward the silver tray on the coffee table. "The water is still hot."

"That would be nice," she said, as she sat down on the sofa next to Kenisha. "My throat is still a bit sore."

"But you're feeling better now?" Anika asked. "We've been so worried about you."

"Yes. I'm better." She almost felt guilty admitting that she felt close to normal when Jasmine…who knew what condition she was in? But she couldn't let those fearful thoughts overwhelm her. "Is there any news?"

Anika shook her head. "No. It's as if my sister disappeared into thin air. I don't understand how no one saw her being carried out of the building, although there's apparently some tunnel through the basement that none of us knew about. But still, how did she get to the basement unseen? There were hundreds of people around."

"It's very disturbing," she agreed.

"You were lucky that you managed to get yourself out of the room and into the stairwell," Anika continued. "The guards were not so fortunate."

She couldn't help but see the question in Anika's eyes, the suspicion of something… "I guess the fumes were worse in the hall than in the bedroom."

"But you said Jasmine collapsed almost immediately," Kenisha put in.

"Yes. Jasmine jumped up, and I think maybe she was closer to the vent than I was. She fell to the floor. I tried to get to her, but I couldn't. I'm so sorry." Her voice broke as guilt swamped her.

"No one is blaming you," Kenisha said gently. "There was nothing you could do, Parisa."

"Why did you go upstairs?" Anika asked. "Mr. Bhatt told us that Jasmine wanted to speak to you alone, but it didn't sound as if your conversation was about anything too important, unless he didn't relay that information to us."

"Jasmine felt overwhelmed by the attention, all the eyes on her. She wanted a minute to catch her breath, so we went upstairs. She said the ring was weighing her down."

"Jasmine has always had a shy quality about her," Kenisha said, tears welling up in her eyes. "I wish she'd told Westley that she didn't want to wear that enormous ring. And I wish I'd encouraged her to speak up. She expressed some doubts to me about accepting such an expensive gift, but I told her that she would hurt his feelings if she didn't wear it at the party. This is my fault."

"It's not your fault," she said quickly. "It was Jasmine's choice, and she did tell me that she wanted to show Westley how much she appreciated his magnificent gesture."

"Westley loves a magnificent gesture," Anika said with an edge in her voice. "But the diamond was cursed, and he never should have given it to Jasmine."

"I don't believe in curses," Kenisha told her oldest daughter.

"Well, look what happened," Anika snapped back. Then her expression immediately shifted. "I'm sorry, Mother. I didn't mean that."

"I know you're upset," Kenisha said.

"Upset doesn't begin to cover it."

"What did you mean when you said Westley loves magnificent gestures?" Parisa asked.

"He likes a show. Wasn't that obvious last night? Most of the people at that party were his friends or his father's colleagues or were from his mother's country club. There were only a few people from Jasmine's world, from the university. It bothers me how she's willing to surrender her life to him."

"That's not what she's doing," Kenisha interrupted, frowning at Anika. "She's compromising. Love is about compromise. It's about being a good partner to the person you love."

"It seems to me that women do all the compromising. Look at you and Father. You were going to be a doctor once, but you didn't pursue your studies because of him."

"My dreams changed when I fell in love, as did Jasmine's. You will one day understand that, Anika."

"I seriously doubt it. I'm not going to give up my life for a man."

The woman in the sheath dress returned to the room, interrupting their conversation. "Mrs. Kumar? Mrs. Langdon is on the phone again. Would you like to speak with her? Or shall I take a message?"

"Yes, of course," Kenisha said, getting to her feet. "Excuse me. Elizabeth has already called several times. I need to talk to her."

Parisa nodded, taking a sip of tea as Kenisha left the room. Then she turned to Anika. "It's nice that your family and the Langdons have remained close over the years."

"It all started when your stepfather was the ambassador, and we all got together. After you left, we stayed in touch with the Langdons. Once Ben decided to go to Everly, and my father got the consulate assignment here, the Langdons rented an apartment so they could spend more time in Manhattan. In fact, Neil is a guest professor at Everly now."

"Jasmine must see a lot of Ben and Neil since they're both on campus."

"I don't know how much she sees Neil, but Jasmine took Ben under her wing as soon as he arrived in New York. They're really tight. He spends a lot of time at the consulate. Although, since Jasmine started dating Westley, I think she's seen Ben a lot less."

"Does Ben have a girlfriend?" She might as well get some information for Jared since Ben had come up so easily into the conversation. "When I saw him last night, I could hardly believe how grown up he is."

"He told Jasmine he got together with someone he used to know in Paris last month, but it was a mistake. He gave her another chance to hurt him, and she did."

"Ouch."

"Love doesn't last very long when you're twenty-one, at

least, not in my experience."

"Mine, either," she admitted.

"My mother thinks I'm jealous of Jasmine and Westley's love, but I'm not," Anika said, surprising Parisa with her words.

"Why would she think that?"

"Because I challenge Jasmine to stand up to Westley. I'm not trying to sabotage their relationship. I just want to make sure that she asserts herself as his equal, as someone he should respect."

"You don't think he respects her?"

"Honestly? I'm not sure. I think he loves her. But respect is something else. Is she just a pretty wife to introduce to his friends, his exotic flower, as he likes to call her? Or will she really be his partner? I just don't want him to break her heart, and I think he's the kind of man who could do that."

"Well, he looked pretty heartbroken last night."

"Yes, he was very upset, and I'm sorry for speaking negatively about him. I guess it's easier to be angry with Westley for giving Jasmine that damn ring and making her a target for thieves than thinking about where she is right now and what she's going through. I'm really worried, Parisa."

"I know. Me, too." She took another sip of her tea, then said, "Have you spoken to Westley today?"

"He called earlier, and we exchanged a few tense words, but that was about it. He's waiting for a ransom demand. So is my father. I just don't know what we're going to do if nothing comes. I also don't know what we'll do if we get a demand. How can we be sure they'll let Jasmine go, even if whatever they want is paid? They already killed those two guards. Will they be afraid to kill Jasmine? It doesn't seem like it."

Anika was painting a dark but accurate picture. "I would try to concentrate on the positive," she said gently. "We still have hope."

Anika blew out a breath as she twisted her hands together. "I just keep asking myself what if I'd done something differently...what if I'd never introduced Jasmine to Westley, what if I'd convinced Westley not to give her the ring, what if I'd stayed closer to her last night..."

"*What-ifs* will drive you crazy, Anika."

"I know, but my brain won't stop going around in that vicious circle. Westley was doing the same thing when I spoke to him earlier. He's also worried that he's going to be a person of interest."

"Why would he be worried about that?"

"Isn't the boyfriend always a suspect in cases like these?"

"I guess. But the diamond belongs to his family, so I don't think he'd steal it."

"Probably not."

"What do you mean?" she asked curiously. "Do you have some doubt?"

"No, it's stupid."

"Just say it, Anika."

"Jasmine told me that Westley and his father had a big fight one day, that Westley wants to start a new branch of Larimer Enterprises, but his father has a tight hold on the purse strings, that he doesn't pay Westley close to what he deserves, so he can keep him subservient to him. Phillip is apparently that way with Westley's brother and sister, too. The only reason Phillip agreed to give Westley the ring is that it's a Larimer tradition to pass that diamond on to the first son at his engagement."

She thought about what Anika had just said. "You're suggesting that that diamond might be worth more to Westley if he could sell it? But as long as it's on Jasmine's finger, he can't do that."

"I told you it was a stupid idea."

"Actually, it would be an incredibly clever way to get the diamond for himself."

"But it doesn't make sense that Jasmine would be kidnapped."

"Not if he really loves her, no."

"It could have been a mistake. Perhaps they were only supposed to take the ring. I do think Westley loves her," Anika said, but there was still some doubt in her voice. Her phone buzzed on the table next to her, and she reached for it, reading what appeared to be an incoming text. An odd expression flashed across her face, and then she set the phone down. "I need to go into my office. Bill wants me to talk about what he can do to help Jasmine. He has a lot of investigative connections through the WNN network."

"Of course." She didn't know why Anika was lying, but she was. *Had it been her boss sending the text? Or had one of the kidnappers reached out to someone who wasn't sitting next to a police officer or an FBI agent?*

"I should go, too," she said quickly, as Anika got to her feet. Maybe she and Jared could tail Anika and see if she did, in fact, go to meet Bill. "Should I wait and say good-bye to your mother?"

"When she and Elizabeth get on the phone, it usually goes on for some time."

"Then I'll walk down with you."

"Let me get my coat."

As Anika left the room, she texted Jared to get the car and told him Anika would soon be on the move. She didn't know if Anika was going straight to her office, but there had been something concerning in her gaze, and if there was a chance the kidnappers had contacted Anika, Parisa wanted to find out where she was going.

She put her phone into her bag as Anika returned to the room, having thrown a beautiful wool black-and-white coat over her black dress. Her legs were bare despite the winter weather, her feet encased in three-inch-high black pumps. She couldn't help thinking that while Anika's eyes showed signs of stress, her outward appearance was quite put together.

"I wish we could have had this reunion under better circumstances," Anika said. "There's so much I want to talk to you about. I'd love to hear about your life."

"I'd love to hear about yours as well."

"When this is all over," Anika said, determined hope in her voice.

"Yes. We'll do it then." She followed Anika out of the suite and past the guards, one of whom accompanied them to the elevator. "Do you normally live at the consulate, or—"

"No, I have an apartment in Midtown that I share with Jasmine. I would have gone there last night, but my mother was so distraught, and I didn't want her to be alone."

"So, the room at the consulate, where Jasmine and I were talking—that isn't her bedroom?"

"It is when she stays there. My parents have a room set aside for each of us, and we occasionally stay the night after a family dinner. Why do you ask?" Anika gave her a questioning look as they stepped onto the elevator, the guard staying close to Anika's side.

"I was just wondering how the kidnappers would have known that Jasmine would take me upstairs to that bedroom. Why would they have had reason to think she'd ever go up to the third floor?"

"I've wondered that, too," Anika admitted. "That's why I was asking you earlier why she suggested you go upstairs."

She saw something suspicious in Anika's gaze that she had to address. "If you're thinking I had anything to do with this, you'd be wrong."

"But you did survive an attack in which two men were killed and my sister was kidnapped."

She was surprised at the bluntness of Anika's statement. "I barely survived. I understand that you're looking for answers, Anika, but I like Jasmine very much and I would never hurt her."

"I want to believe that. It's just strange that she had to have a private conversation with you in the middle of her engagement party."

"I honestly think she just wanted to take a breath." Parisa paused, as they moved off the elevator, the guard walking a few steps ahead of them. "Did you tell Jasmine that I wanted to speak to her?"

"No, I didn't speak to Jasmine about you," Anika replied, pausing in the middle of the lobby. "Why do you ask?"

"She said something about how happy she'd been to learn I wanted to talk to her. And both you and Jasmine suggested that I reached out to the family for an invite, but I didn't do that, Anika. I didn't know about the engagement until I got the invitation to the party, which came through my stepfather's assistant."

Anika frowned. "My mother told me you reached out to her, saying how happy you were about Jasmine's engagement. Why would she make that up?"

"I don't know. Maybe my mother said something to her and just didn't mention it to me."

"That's probably it. My car is outside. Do you need a ride somewhere?"

"No, I'm going to walk. But can I get your number? I'd like to keep in touch."

"Of course."

She put Anika's number into her phone, noting that Anika did not ask for hers. Then she followed her out of the hotel.

Jared's vehicle was idling two cars behind a black SUV, where a man in a suit waited for Anika.

Once Anika was in the SUV, she walked over to Jared's car and slid into the passenger seat.

"Where are we going?" he asked.

"We'll soon find out. Follow that car."

Seven

As the SUV left the hotel, Jared followed, staying a few cars behind. There was still a lot of traffic, so they weren't going anywhere too fast.

"Why are we following Anika?" he enquired.

"She acted oddly after getting a text. She said she's meeting with her boss, Bill Haskins, at WNN, but it felt like she was lying. I just want to make sure that's where she's really going and that the kidnappers didn't reach out to her."

He gave her a sharp, approving look. "Good call. Did you learn anything else? Was Jasmine's mother there?"

"For a bit, until she went to take a call from Elizabeth Langdon."

"Dare I ask if Ben's name came up?"

"It did. But you already know everything Anika told me. Ben said that he reunited with an old girlfriend while he was abroad, but that it had ended badly, and he never should have let her hurt him again. It didn't sound like he and Sara were still together. Maybe he found out who Sara really was and got scared."

"Possibly. Anything else?"

"Anika doesn't seem to be as big a fan of Westley as her sister is. She believes Westley is taking over Jasmine's life. She even suggested that Westley might have set up the diamond theft to get money for a new company he wants to start that his father isn't inclined to bankroll."

"That's a new angle. And he had his fiancée kidnapped to get the ring?"

"It's a theory. Anika thinks the kidnapping could have been a mistake, that they were only supposed to take the ring. I'm not sure I buy any of it. But it is interesting that the ring had to be given to the oldest Larimer upon their engagement, so that was the only way Westley would have ever gotten his hands on it."

Jared stopped at a light, two vehicles back from the SUV. "Let's say that's true—where's Jasmine now? If the kidnappers took her by mistake, why hasn't she been left somewhere? It seems doubtful Westley would have the taste for murder."

"I'd agree, but two men have already died. Maybe he hired the wrong people for the job, and now he's caught." She paused, realizing she hadn't told him about the security company. "I did find out earlier today that the company hired to protect the diamond has only been in business for two months. The guards were both former soldiers, who had been dishonorably discharged. I'm not sure what difference that makes. The man in charge of hiring the company was Tim Hutchinson, director of security at Larimer Enterprises until a week or so ago when he retired and left the country after draining his bank accounts."

Jared gave her a sharp look. "That's a great deal of information to be holding on to. Why didn't you say any of that earlier?"

"I'm telling you now. Anyway, this shady company might play into the theory that Westley had something to do with the kidnapping. Westley could have been working with

Tim Hutchinson."

"Someone certainly was. And I suspect Hutchinson was paid well for hiring that particular firm."

"Yes. Well enough to be able to disappear without a trace. But we don't know if that someone was Westley or Phillip or a person outside the family. I just hope that the second part of this kidnapping plan is to ask for ransom, because if a demand doesn't come, then..." She couldn't bear to finish the thought. As an FBI agent, she knew bad things happened to good people all the time, but she couldn't stand the idea that Jasmine would not come out of this situation alive.

"You have to stay positive, Parisa. There are a lot of law enforcement personnel looking for Jasmine. They may be able to locate her even without contact from the kidnappers." He hit the gas as the light changed and the traffic surged forward. When the vehicle carrying Anika turned right three blocks later, he frowned. "I thought the WNN building was in the other direction."

"Maybe she's meeting Bill at his home. I just assumed she was going to the office, but that might not be true."

"It doesn't look like she's going to anyone's home," he said, as the SUV stopped in a loading zone in front of a department store. He pulled over at the corner. "I think she's going shopping."

"There's no way she would do that today, not with her sister missing." But even as she said the words, Anika got out of the car, accompanied by the man in the suit. As they walked toward the front door of the department store, Parisa made a quick decision. "I'm going to follow them, Jared."

"Keep your phone on. Let me know what's happening. I'll try to stay here as long as I can. Or I'll go around the block."

"Got it." She jogged down the street and into the store, hoping whoever was still in the SUV wouldn't make note of the fact that she was following Anika into the building.

For a few frantic seconds, Parisa thought she'd already lost Anika. Then she saw her old friend pausing by a perfume counter to spray cologne on her wrist.

What on earth was Anika doing?

At the moment, it didn't look like she had a care in the world, much less a sister who had been kidnapped twelve hours earlier.

The man following Anika turned in her direction, and Parisa quickly moved behind a rather large man and his elderly female companion. When she peeked back in Anika's direction, she saw Anika and her bodyguard walking toward the café on the first floor. They stopped at the hostess station. Then Anika was escorted to a table while her security detail took a seat at the counter.

Parisa wandered around the activewear department that was just adjacent to the restaurant, wondering who Anika was waiting for—maybe Bill Haskins? It was the only idea that made sense.

She pulled out her phone and called Jared. "Anika is in the café. She's sitting at a table, looking at a menu, and her bodyguard is at the counter. She could be meeting her boss here."

"Okay. I had to park the car in the garage. The traffic cops were after me. I'm walking into the store now."

"I'm in the activewear department on the first floor near the restaurant. Try not to stand out."

"I think you're more recognizable than I am, but you don't have to worry."

She ended the call but kept the phone in her hand as she pretended to look at a running jacket while keeping an eye on Anika.

A moment later, a waitress set a glass of ice water in front of Anika, and then took her order. The bodyguard also appeared to be ordering something. It didn't look like either of them was in a hurry to leave. When the waitress left, Anika pulled out her phone and swiped the screen several times, her gaze focused on whatever she was looking at.

Jared came around the other side of the display wall and pretended to be looking at the same rack of clothes that had captured her attention.

"Anika ordered something," she said. "She must be having a lunch meeting. Although, it seems really off to me. Her sister is missing. Her family is shattered. How can she just sit in a restaurant and order lunch?"

"Doesn't make sense," Jared agreed. "But her SUV left, so they must think she's staying awhile. She still has a guard with her, though. It can't be that private of a meeting."

"I'm sure Anika's father doesn't want her to be left alone for even a minute." A moment of silence passed between them. Seeing the furrowed look on Jared's brow, she said, "What are you thinking?"

"That this feels like a setup," he replied.

"For what?"

"I don't know yet."

Her instincts were screaming the same warning. She caught her breath when Anika got up and headed toward the ladies' room. "Do you think there's a back door?"

"Betting there is," he murmured. "I'll go into the restaurant. No one will recognize me. You check the street for another exit from the café."

She nodded, moving out of the department store as Jared entered the restaurant. When she reached the street, she saw another door down the side of the building, about twenty-five yards away. She huddled behind a parked van, watching the door. A moment later, Anika walked outside. She put on her sunglasses, then strolled briskly in the opposite direction.

A second later, Jared came out the same door. She stepped out of her hiding place and tipped her head in his direction. He turned, saw Anika, and followed her down the street.

She stayed a good distance behind Jared, keeping at least a few pedestrians between them, and noticed he was doing the same between himself and Anika, although he didn't have to be nearly as careful. Anika would not recognize Jared, although she still might get suspicious if she thought anyone was following her. She'd gone to great lengths to pretend to be dining at the department store café, then ditching her bodyguard. Why?

Was Anika meeting the kidnappers? Would she dare to do that on her own? And if she were meeting someone, where was the cash? What would she trade for her sister?

Anika suddenly stopped in front of a small hotel, standing under an awning, by the doorman, as she pulled out her phone once more.

Jared popped into a nearby recessed doorway leading into an apartment building so that he wouldn't be in Anika's view. She decided to join him there. When she reached him, she moved in behind him, so that Anika wouldn't see her if she happened to look in their direction.

"She's waiting for someone," he murmured. "And I don't think it's her boss, unless she's having an affair with Haskins and this hotel is where they meet."

"I would think that right now the last thing on her mind would be sex." As she finished speaking, a car pulled up at the curb. A man got out, handing his key to the valet, then walked toward Anika. "Oh, my God," she murmured, moving around Jared so she could get a better look. "It's Westley."

She watched in amazement as Westley and Anika embraced in a way that felt far more intimate than one might expect. Westley pulled back and brushed a strand of hair away from Anika's cheek.

"Looks like sex isn't the last thing on her mind," Jared said.

"Maybe they're just comforting each other in this terrible time."

"That's the first thing you've said that makes me think

you're not in law enforcement," he said dryly.

He was right. The truth was in front of her. She just had to see it.

Westley turned his head, and she jumped behind Jared. "Do you think they saw me? What are they doing?"

"They're coming in our direction."

"Dammit. They'll see us. Maybe we shouldn't care. Maybe we should confront them."

Jared turned to face her, pushing her back toward the door of the building. Unfortunately, it was locked, so they couldn't go inside.

"We should care, Parisa. They don't think anyone is on to them. We need that advantage."

And that advantage would be lost in about two seconds if she didn't do something. "You're right. There's only one thing to do." She wrapped her arms around Jared's neck and pulled him toward her.

He gave her a startled look, then settled his mouth over hers, as he backed her into the building, hiding her body behind his.

Jared's lips were hot in the cold afternoon air, and what should have been just a quick kiss turned into a longer, deeper exploration. It wasn't just the need to hide that kept her in Jared's arms; it was the fact that she hadn't had a kiss like this in a very long time, one that made her heart ache, and her toes curl, and her palms sweat—a kiss that made her think about more than just tasting his mouth. She wanted to touch him all over. She wanted to get through his layers and unravel his secrets, but he was letting her go, lifting his head, gazing down at her with a questioning, somewhat surprised, look.

It had been her idea to kiss him. *Maybe one of her best ideas. Or maybe one of her worst.*

She licked her lips, and his gaze flew to her mouth once more. Then he shook his head as if fighting his instincts and took a step back. He turned, keeping her behind him as he looked down the street in both directions.

She drew in a breath and ordered her brain to get back to business. She wasn't supposed to be fooling around with Jared; she was supposed to be looking for Jasmine and finding out what Anika was up to.

"Are they gone?" she asked.

"I don't see them anywhere."

She moved around him and saw no sign of Anika or Westley. Disappointment and frustration ran through her. "We've lost them. Did we make the wrong move?"

"I don't think so. They won't be that hard to find. We know where they live. We can get to them at any time. What will be more important is using what we just saw to dig in a different direction."

"You think they're having an affair?"

"There was something intimate about how they looked at each other."

"I thought so, too. But I don't get it. Anika said she introduced Westley to Jasmine. If Anika and Westley were in to each other, why didn't they just get together? It's not like there was a reason Westley had to marry Jasmine."

"Maybe they're in this together. Perhaps they cooked up the whole plot—the big engagement party, the diamond heist, the missing sister. When the smoke clears and after a period of bereavement, they end up together, with the diamond funding whatever they want to do."

"You're suggesting that Anika would kill her sister, but I can't go that far. I know both her and Jasmine. I've seen how much they care about each other."

"You knew them a long time ago."

"I might be able to buy into the diamond heist, but the rest...I don't think so."

"Let's go back to the car and regroup."

As they walked down the street, she wondered if Anika had returned to the café. But that seemed pointless. She'd obviously wanted to lose the bodyguard and meet with Westley in private. But they hadn't entered the hotel. So where had they gone?

When they reached the department store, they went inside, taking a look into the café, but the bodyguard was gone, and there was no sign of Anika. They took a store elevator to the underground parking garage and then got into the car.

As Jared started the engine, she fastened her seat belt and said, "Why meet in front of that hotel and then not go inside?"

"I have no idea. I'm surprised no one was following Westley. Where's your FBI friend?"

"When I spoke to Damon—Agent Wolfe—earlier, he told me that Westley had an agent with him, and that he had warned Westley about the danger of attempting to do anything on his own. Westley must have found a way to ditch his detail, too."

"Looks that way. Shall we go back to my apartment and talk about it?"

"We might as well. I don't know where else to go."

On their trip across town, her thoughts ran in dozens of different directions, but nothing seemed to make sense. She had a feeling Jared was taking the same mental journey, as he was unusually silent and contemplative.

Or maybe he was thinking about the crazy long kiss they'd shared, which she was trying really hard not to remember, but her lips were still tingling.

They really couldn't do that again.

Eight

When they finally got back to the apartment, it was almost three o'clock. They'd spent a lot of time following Anika around, and to what purpose? They'd only ended up with more questions instead of more answers.

Jared walked over to the refrigerator. "Do you want something to drink?"

"Do you have any juice?"

"Orange," he said, pulling out a carton.

"That will do."

He poured two tall glasses of juice and then came back to the couch. He handed one to her and then sat down next to her. "What are you thinking?"

"That I'm stumped."

He nodded in agreement. "I wasn't expecting Anika to meet up with Westley. That's a twist."

"I'll say. I don't know what to think about it. I suppose they could be having an affair, but why? If Westley wanted to be with Anika, why wouldn't he be? He's not married to Jasmine yet."

"Would Jasmine be more important to his business interests than Anika? Does she bring anything to marriage that her sister wouldn't?"

"Not that I know of. She's a professor. And whatever money is in the family is probably equally shared." She sipped her juice as she pondered the questions in her head.

"Maybe Anika wants to break Jasmine and Westley up, get the diamond and the fortune for herself."

She frowned at his suggestion. "I can't imagine Anika would set her sister up to be kidnapped."

"What's Anika like? What's her personality?"

She hesitated, wondering if she really knew what Anika was like. "As you said, I haven't known her since she was a teenager, but back then she was ambitious, driven, and a go-getter. She talked a lot about having a career, being known for something. Jasmine was more introverted. She loved books and music and her friends. But despite their opposite personalities, the two of them always seemed to have a strong bond. I was actually a bit jealous. As an only child, I had always wished for a sister, and during the three years that I was in Bezikstan, the Kumar girls were like sisters to me. We talked about everything—school, boys, dreams. I can't believe we've ended up here. Anyway..." She finished her juice, then set her glass on the coffee table. "We need to figure out what to do next."

He smiled, and her heart skipped a beat. She was suddenly very aware of how close he was, and her lips tingled in memory of their kiss.

"I have a couple of ideas," he drawled.

"From the look in your eyes, I'm guessing those are bad ideas."

"Sometimes bad is good."

"Or just bad," she countered, giving him a pointed look. "We need to stay focused, Jared."

"Who says I'm not focused?"

She licked her lips, feeling the heat of his gaze.

"Jared...if we need to talk about that kiss."

"I wasn't thinking we need to talk."

"Well, we don't need to kiss again. We have work to do. We need to find Jasmine."

His jaw tightened, and he blew out a breath. "You're right." He downed the rest of his juice. "All right, I have another idea. Why don't you call the Langdons? See if you can find out where Ben is. We may not have an immediate next move when it comes to Jasmine, but we can push forward with Ben. And there's a possibility the kidnapping is connected to Paris."

"I could do that, but I don't have their number."

"I do," Jared said, pulling out his phone. "Do you want Neil or Elizabeth?"

"Why don't I just call Ben directly? I'm sure you have his number, too."

"His phone is off or dead. I tried it last night and again this morning. It doesn't ring, nor does it go to voicemail."

"Okay. I'm a little closer to Neil, so I'll start with him then."

As Jared read off a number, she punched it into her phone. Unfortunately, the call went to voicemail. She decided she might as well leave a message. "Hi, Neil, it's Parisa. I was hoping to speak to you about Jasmine, about everything that happened. If you get a chance, please call me back. It's important." She left her number and then disconnected.

"Want to try Elizabeth?" Jared asked.

"Sure." Unfortunately, her second call also ended with voicemail. Since she'd already left a message for Neil, she hung up. "Sorry," she said, giving Jared an apologetic shrug.

"We could just go over there," he suggested.

She knew he was eager to make something happen, but she wasn't sure that was the right choice. "It's a thought. But if Ben isn't there, and the Langdons get suspicious about our intentions—"

"We could blow our hand," he finished, his lips

tightening with frustration. "I know it's a risk."

"Let's see if they call me back. I can't see why Neil wouldn't do that. He wouldn't have any idea that I'm trying to connect Ben to a bombing in Paris. And he'd surely be interested in hearing what I want to say about Jasmine."

"True. I guess we'll wait."

She gave him a compassionate smile. "Not my strongest trait, either, but sometimes patience is necessary to get the bigger payoff."

"I agree."

He'd no sooner finished speaking when her phone rang. She glanced at the number. "It's my FBI contact. I need to take this. Do you mind if I use the bedroom?"

"Why don't you speak to him here?"

"Because I don't want to," she said candidly, taking the phone into the bedroom. She closed the door behind her, knowing that she still needed to choose her words carefully in case Jared might be listening, which he probably would be. "Any news?" she asked, sitting on the edge of the bed.

"Yes," Damon replied. "The Larimers received a ransom demand."

Her gut clenched. "How much?"

"Ten million dollars."

She blew out a breath. "That's a lot of cash. How did the Larimers react?"

"Westley wants to pay it. His father is concerned that paying the ransom won't ensure Jasmine's safe return, but he's moving forward in trying to raise the money. The kidnappers gave him until ten Monday morning."

"What about proof of life?"

"There's a video of Jasmine. She's alive."

"Thank God!" Relief ran through her. "At least we have a little time. Can I ask when the call came in?"

"Around noon."

And Anika had abruptly left the hotel a little before one. She and Westley had gotten together after the ransom demand. *What did that mean? Had Westley been the one who'd texted Anika to meet him? But why all the subterfuge? Why hadn't they simply met at the café? Why ditch the bodyguard? Why act like they had something to hide?*

"Parisa?" Damon asked sharply. "You still there?"

"Yes. I was talking to Anika Kumar at the Clairmont Hotel, probably about the time the ransom call came in. She got a text and left quickly, saying it was from her boss, but I had a feeling she was lying. I followed her to a department store, where she ditched her bodyguard and then met up with Westley Larimer in front of a hotel. They said something to each other, and it felt very intimate, but they didn't go into the hotel, they took off down the street. Unfortunately, I had to move out of sight, and I lost them."

"Are you suggesting there's something between Anika and Westley?" Damon asked in surprise.

"I don't know—maybe. Anika also told me that Westley wanted cash to start a new company but couldn't get it from his father, who apparently has a tight hold on the purse strings. She wondered if Westley might have used the diamond to get the money he needed."

"She thinks Westley set all this up? That's a new angle."

"It might be worth looking into Westley's financials."

"That's already happening. And Anika's theory doesn't seem to gibe with her meeting Westley in secret."

"I agree. She seems to be playing a lot of different sides."

"Which makes her more suspicious in my mind. It's time to do some digging into her life."

"I agree."

"Anything else I should know about?" Damon asked. "Are you still hanging with your mysterious friend?"

"At the moment," she admitted.

"I ran a check on him, Parisa. He comes up as a freelance journalist. I located some news reports online with his byline."

"Really? I have to admit I'm a little surprised."

"Don't be that surprised. His life looks carefully orchestrated, very few details, and those details are difficult to trace. I found nothing on his family, nothing on his personal life, and he appears to live his life on cash. I think your first instinct was correct, that he's working for someone, but he's not working for us. What does he want from you?"

"Access to Ben Langdon. Jared believes that Ben may have information on the Paris bombing because of his relationship with Sara Pillai."

"I looked into the bombing as you requested. Isaac Naru and his stepsister Sara Pillai are persons of interest and are a high priority for questioning, but they have disappeared. There was no mention of Ben Langdon in the reports I read, but I have to admit I didn't get too deep into it."

"If Ben is tied to the terrorist group, then Jasmine's kidnapping could be as well. The group originated in Bezikstan. We can't overlook that tie. My next step is to talk to Ben, but I haven't been able to reach him. Did he give a statement to the bureau?"

"I'm sure he did, but I haven't personally read it."

"Since the Langdons are very close to the Kumars, Ben's statement might not have been scrutinized as carefully as it should be. I need to find Ben."

"If you do, let me know. And, be careful, Parisa. You're still a loose end."

"Believe me, I'm not going to forget that. Thanks, Damon. I'll be in touch."

She set the phone down and then flopped back on the bed, which was amazingly comfortable. Scooting toward the pillows, she stretched out on her back, and gazed up at the ceiling, thinking about what Damon had told her.

At least she knew that Jasmine was still alive. That was the most important thing. There was still hope, and she felt incredibly relieved by that. She suspected the Kumars were feeling the same way.

She still didn't know why Westley and Anika had had a

secret meeting, but at the moment all she could care about was Jasmine and knowing that they had at least until Monday morning to find her and bring her home.

Drawing in several deep breaths, she felt suddenly exhausted. She'd gotten barely two hours of sleep the night before, and the adrenaline wave she'd been riding was starting to wane. Maybe she'd just rest her eyes for a minute...

"So, Jasmine is alive," Jared said, feeling a wave of relief at the report he'd just gotten from Gary, who was monitoring the police investigation through a personal contact. He'd decided to make his own phone call while Parisa was taking hers. "That's good news."

"Better than the alternative. But getting her back in good condition will still be tricky. I also picked up a lead on Sara Pillai."

His pulse jumped. "Seriously?" They'd been tracking Sara since the explosion and had come up with nothing.

"I've been monitoring flights into New York City for days, and a familiar name popped up yesterday—Melissa Holmes. She was one of Sara's former roommates in Paris, but unlike the others, she was an American student."

"I'm familiar with Miss Holmes. I talked to her, as well as Sara's other roommates, right after the explosion. Now, she's in New York City?"

"She's not, but her passport is. I reviewed JFK security cameras and caught a brunette coming off the plane with a New York Yankees baseball cap covering her head and her hair obscuring her features. It made me curious, so I had someone go by Melissa's apartment in Paris, and she's still in France. She looked for her passport and then appeared to be shocked that it was missing. She has very similar features to Sara, and I'm guessing Sara was able to use the passport to come to the United States."

His heart sped up. "If Sara is here, I'm betting Isaac is, too. And Sara arrived yesterday?"

"She got in just after nine a.m. However, that's where the trail goes cold. She hasn't checked in anywhere under her own name or Melissa's name, nor has she used any credit cards that can be traced to her."

"If Sara is in New York, then I have to believe that the Paris explosion and the consulate kidnapping are connected."

"My gut would agree. Any luck getting to Ben Langdon?"

"I'm still working on it."

"Work faster. Daphne called me this morning, asking me where you were. I lied and told her you were probably on a beach somewhere, working on your tan, like she suggested. I don't think she bought it."

"Thanks for the heads-up. Let me know if you get anything else."

"Will do."

As he set down his phone, he blew out a breath, his mind racing with the information he'd gotten from Gary. *Sara was in New York. Was she with Ben?* They really needed to find Ben.

He glanced toward the bedroom door. Parisa had been on the phone a long time. She'd probably heard about the ransom demand. That should give her some relief. Jasmine was still alive—and they had time to find her.

As the minutes ticked by, he began to worry about Parisa. *Why hadn't she come back after her call?* It had been almost thirty minutes. Surely, she wasn't still on the phone.

He walked over to the bedroom door and knocked twice. There was no answer. When he opened the door, he saw Parisa on the bed—fast asleep.

The news about a ransom demand had probably allowed her to let down her guard for a minute, and she had to be tired. He wasn't feeling too energetic at the moment, either. He'd gotten even less sleep than she had the night before, because he'd been watching the building where she'd been hidden away.

Of course, he couldn't lay down next to her. That wouldn't be appropriate in any way.

But as he gazed down at the splay of long, brown hair across his pillow, Parisa's beautiful face, the tender bruising around her eye, and the curve of her lips, he found himself filled with all kinds of terrible ideas. He could still feel the heat of her lips against his, the whisper of her breath on his cheek, the fervor of her kiss. What had started out as a cloaking move earlier had turned into a lot more.

He should not feel this way. He'd kissed plenty of women in his life, some for very similar reasons—to maintain a cover, to get a job done.

But Parisa—she was different. He couldn't put his finger on it. He didn't know why he felt connected to her. They barely knew each other. But he didn't just feel desire; he also felt protective, and that was another unwelcome feeling.

He was on a mission to find the Paris bombers, and even though he was willing to put it on the back burner until Jasmine was safe, he couldn't lose sight of it. It was too important.

Unfortunately, he was out of leads for the moment. He needed a way to get to Ben. Hopefully, Ben's parents would be reachable at some point. They were probably his best bet, unless Gary could pick up Sara's trail somewhere else.

Turning around, he went back into the living room, closing the door behind him, needing that barrier to help him put Parisa out of his mind.

He sat down on the couch and turned on the television, perusing the local news, but it was Saturday and there wasn't much on. He wanted to be doing something proactive, and he was frustrated not to have all of his usual resources available to him, but at the moment he was going to have to wait for something to break.

He settled on a basketball game, hoping for a little

distraction, but as the ball moved up and down the court, he felt his lids getting heavy. He laid down on his side and closed his eyes. A little catnap was all he needed.

Nine

It was dark when Parisa woke up, and she jerked up on the bed, jumping to her feet, as she tried to remember where she was. Then she realized she was in Jared's apartment. The clock on the nightstand said eight fifteen. She couldn't believe she'd slept for five hours.

As she walked across the room, she wrinkled her nose at the appealing smell of garlic.

Opening the door, she was more than a little surprised to see Jared cooking in the kitchen. Something was sizzling in a frying pan on the stove, and there was an open bottle of red wine on the counter.

"You're cooking?" she asked in amazement, as she moved over to the counter.

"I got hungry. I figured you'd be, too, once you woke up."

Guilt ran through her. There was so much to do. It felt wrong to have fallen asleep. On the other hand, she'd desperately needed the rest. "I am hungry," she admitted, her stomach rumbling as she contemplated the steak filets in the frying pan. "It smells good."

"Almost done," he said, popping open the oven and pulling out two baked potatoes and a pan filled with roasted brussels sprouts.

"Hmm, now I know why I smelled garlic," she said.

"I hope you eat meat."

"Definitely."

"Help yourself to some wine, if you like." He pulled a wineglass out of the cabinet and set it on the counter in front of her.

"Looks like you've now familiarized yourself with the kitchen."

He smiled. "I must admit I haven't done a lot of cooking here."

"Where did all the food come from?"

"There's a market downstairs."

"Handy."

She poured wine into a glass and sat down at the counter, watching as he spooned butter over the steaks. He moved with confidence and purpose and he looked sexy as hell, strands of hair falling over his forehead as the heat warmed his face. She couldn't remember the last time a man had cooked for her, and despite the extraordinary circumstances they were living in, this moment seemed remarkably normal.

He glanced in her direction, his green eyes warm and smiling. "How's the wine?"

"It's perfect," she said, even though she had yet to take a sip. "You appear to know what you're doing."

"I do know what I'm doing."

"Are you ever not confident?"

"Hmm, I'd have to think about that," he said with a grin.

She couldn't believe how comfortable she felt with a man she didn't know at all.

"How did your call go earlier?" he asked. "Apparently, you didn't learn anything that made you want to rush out of the apartment and do something."

"I did get some information, but there was nothing for us to do about it."

"What did you hear?" He turned down the flame on the steaks as he gave her his attention.

"The kidnappers made a ransom demand of the Larimers—ten million dollars, to be paid by Monday at ten a.m. The demand came in before we saw Westley and Anika. Maybe they were meeting about that."

"And I assume there's proof that Jasmine is alive?"

"Yes. It was a huge relief to know that there's still time to find her."

"Are there any leads?"

"Not that I was told. I don't know the details of the ransom exchange, either," she said. "I'm just happy that the Larimers are willing to put up that much cash for a woman who is not yet in their family."

"It's a lot, especially when they've already lost a diamond worth five times that."

"Maybe the Kumars will chip in. They're not as wealthy as the Larimers, but they have money."

"I'm sure they will," he said, returning his attention to the steaks. He flipped them over, then turned off the heat.

"Can I help?" she asked somewhat halfheartedly.

"I've got dinner. But if you want to try contacting the Langdons again..."

"I can do that. I should have done it earlier. I was on your bed, and it was so comfortable, I was just going to close my eyes for a minute. I feel guilty I slept so long."

"You were exhausted. You don't have to defend yourself. But if you can talk to Neil or Elizabeth and find out if Ben is staying at the house, maybe we can go by there and see him after we eat."

She pulled out her phone and saw no missed calls. "He didn't call me back. But I'll give him another shot." She punched in Neil's number. She was almost surprised when he answered. She put the phone on speaker, so Jared could hear the conversation. "Neil, it's Parisa."

"Oh, my God, Parisa. We've been so worried about you. How are you?"

"I'm fine. I'm recovered. I called you earlier. Did you get my message?"

"Yes. I'm sorry. I haven't had a chance to call you back, but I'm happy to hear you're well. Elizabeth spoke with Kenisha earlier, and she said you haven't been able to remember anything that would help the police find the kidnappers."

"That's unfortunately true."

"We've heard about the ransom demand and are very happy that Jasmine is alive."

"It's definitely good news. I really want her to be all right."

"As do we. Jasmine and Anika are like daughters to Elizabeth and me, and Jasmine has been so kind to Ben since he came to the city."

"Anika mentioned that." She licked her lips, happy they'd zeroed in on Ben but not wanting to raise any alarm bells. "How is Ben handling everything? Is he staying with you?"

"Not tonight. He told Elizabeth he wanted to stay with friends, get his mind off the terrible events of last night. None of us slept at all."

"I know the feeling. Do you think Ben will be home tomorrow? I want to talk to him about something."

"He should be back sometime in the morning. What did you want to speak to him about?"

She searched her brain for a good and unalarming reason for her to want to talk to Ben. "When Jasmine and I were talking upstairs, she mentioned Ben was feeling down after a romance in Paris that didn't go well. She wanted to give him a book of poetry that had helped her when she'd gone through a breakup, and she thought it might do the same for Ben. She'd actually written a personal note to Ben on the inside cover. I was looking at it when the air went bad and everything went nuts. When I got to the hospital, I still had the book in my hands. It seemed like a sign that I was meant to pass it along. I was thinking it might help Ben get through this, too."

"That's very thoughtful."

"It's Jasmine who was thoughtful. She was worried about Ben. Did he tell you what happened?"

"He hasn't spoken to us about any failed romance, but then he doesn't share his romantic life with us at all."

"I think her name was Sara."

"Sara? Hmmm. He dated someone named Sara back in Bezikstan, but that was a long time ago."

"Perhaps they reconnected."

"Maybe Ben told Elizabeth about it," Neil said. "If you want to bring the book by tomorrow, I'm sure Ben would appreciate having something that Jasmine thought was important for him to read."

"I'll do that."

"Are you sure you're all right, Parisa? Is there anything I can do for you?"

"No, I'm good. I just want Jasmine to come home."

"She will. You must not give up hope or faith. It's what gets us through the hard times. We must continue to believe that all will be as it is meant to be."

"I'm trying to stay positive. I'll see you tomorrow."

"I look forward to it."

She disconnected the phone and looked across the counter at Jared. She'd deliberately avoided his gaze while making up her elaborate story. It was easier to lie without an audience.

"That was impressive," he said, a gleam in his eyes. "A book of poetry that Jasmine had inscribed just for Ben to heal his broken heart. Who could refuse that? How long did it take you to concoct that story?"

"About ten seconds."

"And you think I'm the better liar?"

"I didn't say you were better. I just said you *were* a liar."

"Good point."

"At any rate, it looks like we can talk to Ben tomorrow."

"If he comes home."

"Do you have resources who might be able to find him tonight?"

"My resources have been coming up empty on that front."

"Then I guess we have to wait. Is that steak done, because I'm starving?"

"It's ready. Why don't we eat at the table?"

She nodded, moving over to the table where he'd put out two place settings. "This was nice of you to do. With this being the city of incredible takeout, it would have been easier for you to order something."

"I've done that a lot. I felt like a good piece of meat." He brought their plates to the table and then grabbed the glass of wine he'd been enjoying while he was cooking.

She cut into the filet, and it was a perfect shade of pink. "Just the way I like it," she said.

"I should have asked."

"It's perfect." In fact, she couldn't remember having a steak this good in a very long time. Or maybe she was just that hungry.

As they ate, she couldn't help thinking that Jared hadn't asked a lot of questions about her earlier phone call with Damon. Was that because he'd gotten his own information from some other source? She'd been asleep a long time. Long enough for him to have shopped for food, cooked dinner, and probably talked to whoever he worked for or with.

"So, tell me more about you, Parisa," he said, interrupting her thoughts.

"What do you want to know?" she asked warily.

"I was wondering about your mother and stepfather. You said they were good friends with the Kumars. Why weren't they at the party?"

"They're out of the country. My stepfather retired last

year, and he and my mother travel often for pleasure. They're in Bali now, on a month-long spiritual and meditative retreat."

"That sounds...relaxing."

She smiled at his choice of adjective. "Does it? It sounds stressful to me. Forced quiet is not my kind of thing. But apparently getting in touch with your soul requires structure and rules. My parents seem to love it. This is the third time they've gone on one of these retreats in the last year. I guess it's good they both enjoy it. It would be more difficult if only one wanted to go."

"Sounds like they have a happy marriage."

"They do. Harry married my mom when I was eight years old. My real dad left when I was three, so I barely remember him. Harry has been the only dad I've known. He's a good man, very smart, well educated, well spoken. He cares a great deal about the world. He has lived a life of service, and it has often inspired me."

"What about your mother? What's she like?"

"She was born in India. Her name is Riya. She came to the US when she was eleven with her parents. She's creative and kind, quiet and beautiful."

"Like her daughter."

She smiled at his words. "Nice of you to say, thank you. I'm not that creative. I try to be kind. Quiet—not so much, and beautiful, well, I do look like her, although my skin is a bit lighter than hers, probably because my biological father was blond and pale."

"Does your mother work?"

"She worked in a university admissions office before she met Harry. After they fell in love, she focused on being his wife and my mother. We traveled to whatever post Harry was assigned to. It was a nomadic life, but it was happy." She paused. "My mother and stepfather have had a powerful love story since they first met. They've always been extremely devoted to each other. Sometimes, I felt a little outside of their story, not that they ever wanted me to feel that way. It's just the way it was. It probably would have been different if I'd had a sibling. I wouldn't have felt so alone." She took a sip of her wine. "Now it's your turn. Tell me about your family."

His expression tensed. "There's not much to tell."

"Then it won't take long," she said, giving him a pointed look. "And think about your answer. Make sure it's truthful, like mine just was."

Their gazes clung together, and then he gave her a subtle nod. "All right. I can give you the truth." He got up from the table and walked over to the desk, pulling open the bottom drawer. He came back with a folded piece of paper that had yellowed with age. He sat down and slid it across the table to her.

She felt a bit of nervous trepidation as she unfolded the paper, not sure what she was about to learn, but sensing that it was going to be important.

The paper was a copy of a newspaper clipping. There was a black-and-white photo of a smiling woman with dark hair and light eyes, whose features looked quite similar to Jared's. Next to the photo was an obituary. The date was September 15, 2001. The woman's name was Carol Montgomery.

Her stomach churned as she skimmed through the obit. Carol Montgomery, a loving mother and wife, had died in her office in the World Trade Center on 9/11. She was survived by her husband, Brett, her two sons, Jared and Will, and her father Gilbert.

"Oh, my God," she murmured, glancing over at Jared. He'd lost his normal cocky smirk, his green eyes dark and serious, his expression tense. "This is your mother?"

"Yes. She was an accountant. She spent her days adding up profits and losses for a real-estate firm. She was sitting at her desk when the first plane hit the building, right at her floor. Everyone said she probably never knew what happened, that she was killed instantly. I pray that's the way it went down. I don't want to think about her being scared, knowing she wasn't going to see us again. But the truth is—I don't know. They didn't find her for hours. She was buried in rubble."

A sickening feeling swept through her. "That's terrible. I'm so sorry."

"I was sixteen years old. My brother Will was twelve. My father, Brett, was a high school teacher. He and I were at the same school. I still remember when he came into my classroom with terror in his eyes. And then we ran six blocks to the middle school to find Will. The sky was black. The air was thick; it was difficult to breathe. And there were so many sirens. We lived fifteen blocks from Ground Zero. We could see my mom's office from our rooftop deck."

She shook her head at the horror of his story. "I can't imagine what you went through."

"We didn't know she was dead until two o'clock the following afternoon. We waited up all night, hoping for a miracle, and worrying that the terror wasn't over."

She'd wanted Jared to tell her something true, and he'd certainly delivered, but his story made her sick to her stomach.

Jared cleared his throat and took another sip of wine. "My dad was devastated after she died. He couldn't come to grips with what had happened. My mom was just an ordinary person doing a rather boring job. She wasn't ever supposed to be in danger. She wasn't supposed to go to work one day and not come back."

"No, she wasn't." She glanced down at his mother's smiling face. "I can see you in her features."

"I have her eyes."

"Why is her last name different than yours?"

"She kept her maiden name."

"Is that true or is your real last name Montgomery?"

"It's not important." He drew in a breath and let it out. "After her funeral, my dad finished out the teaching year and then he took me and my brother to a place in Upstate New York, a beautiful piece of property in a rural area where there was a pond and horses to ride, lots of open space, no skyscrapers to remind us of what we'd seen. It was supposed to just be for the summer, but he couldn't bring himself to leave. So, we ended up transferring schools, and we never came back to the city."

"It sounds idyllic."

"It was healing, but, eventually, I wanted more. I went away to college and after that I took a job in Boston for a few years. I've moved around since then."

"Is this apartment your first place back in this city?"

"It is."

"And it has a view of the Freedom Tower. Was that on purpose?"

"Actually, I almost changed my mind about staying here when I saw it, but then I thought it was a good reminder of how easy it is to lose everything."

"Do you need that reminder?"

"No."

"I didn't think so." She gave him a compassionate smile. "That's a sad story, Jared."

"It's my story."

"What happened to your father? Did he ever remarry?"

"He has had women in his life, but he hasn't made it down the aisle again."

"And your brother?"

"He runs a surf shop in Hawaii."

"That sounds chill."

"That would be my brother. Will decided that life is too short to not do what you love."

"That makes sense. Are you doing what you love?"

"Sometimes."

His vague answer reminded her that he was only willing to tell her some of his story, but she did appreciate that he'd opened up as much as he had. "Thanks for telling me about your mom. I know that wasn't easy." She paused, cocking her head to the right as she gave him a thoughtful look. "Why did you decide to share?"

"Because you need to understand my motivation. I know what it feels like to be caught in a terrorist attack, Parisa, even if I wasn't the one who died."

"Which is why you're so interested in the Paris explosion."

"Yes."

"But I'm still not sure what it is about that particular blast that is so intriguing to you. There have been others, some closer to home, some with more devastating consequences."

"One death is a devastation to that person's family."

"I know, but I feel like I'm missing something."

"Let's change the subject. Are you ready for dessert?"

She blinked at the abrupt question. "Uh, yeah, I guess. Do you have dessert?"

"All the fixings for ice cream sundaes: hot fudge, whipped cream, nuts, and, of course, ice cream."

"Sounds delicious."

He grinned, giving her a wicked smile. "Although I can think of a few other ways we might use the whipped cream."

"None of which we're going to do," she said quickly.

"It's not a crime to admit you're attracted to me."

"You're the one who's attracted to me," she countered.

"Well, I can't argue with that, not after that kiss we shared earlier."

"That was expedient."

"It was hot, and you know it."

She frowned. "I don't even know you."

"You don't have to know me to want me. But that bothers you, doesn't it?"

It did bother her, but she wasn't going to tell him that. "What bothers me more is that we lost Westley and Anika. We got distracted."

"So, you can at least admit you were distracted."

She sighed. "Fine. We have some chemistry, but we're not going to do anything about it. We're only together because of Jasmine."

"And because you need a safe place to stay, and for some reason you find it easier to trust me than the person you check in with every few hours."

"Well, as you've mentioned several times, you have saved my life, and the safe house the FBI put me into didn't work out too well. So, let's make some sundaes and then we'll figure out what to do next."

Ten

Parisa surprised him with the awesome magnificence of her sundae: two scoops of ice cream—one vanilla, one chocolate—plenty of hot fudge, a couple of swirls of whipped cream, nuts and a cherry on the top. He'd thought by how slim she was, she might have either foregone the sundae or settled for a small scoop, but she was eating with pure pleasure, her dark eyes lit up, and dollops of whipped cream clinging to her lips with each spoonful.

He was so fascinated by watching her eat that he left his sundae untouched.

"Yours is melting," Parisa told him, as her tongue snaked out to catch a drop of hot fudge.

"You're really enjoying that," he said, scooping up a spoonful of ice cream.

"I love a hot fudge sundae. It's actually my favorite dessert."

"Then I made a good choice. It was this or the cheesecake."

"You definitely made the right choice. I'm going to need

a run after this."

"Are you a runner?"

"I am—which is a good thing, since I also like to eat." She flashed him a guilty smile.

He grinned back at her. "So do I. Have you ever run a race?"

"I've done half marathons. Maybe one day, when I have more time to really train, I'll do the full version. What about you? Do you like to run?"

"I prefer cycling, but I also run and swim."

She raised an eyebrow. "You're a triple threat."

"I did the Iron Man triathlon in Hawaii two years ago."

"I'm impressed."

"Don't be. I finished out of the top 20 percent."

"That's still amazing. Or do you only feel successful when you're the best?"

"I do like to win. Not that I was expecting to win the triathlon, but I was hoping to make the top 10 percent of entrants."

"I like to win, too. I've always been competitive, and I have no idea where I get it from. My mom is the least competitive person I know. I can't seem to shake my drive to win."

"Why would you want to? It's part of who you are. Maybe you get it from your biological father. You really don't know anything about him?"

"I don't remember him, and my mom never talks about him."

"What about your biological grandparents?"

"I know even less about them. They apparently didn't like that their son married an Indian woman."

"Is that why he left your mother? Did he succumb to family pressure?"

"Maybe. My mother has never been forthcoming on that topic. I know he left her in a bad place. Her mother had died a year earlier, and her father had decided to move back to India after that. So, she was alone with a three-year-old. As I mentioned, she worked in the admissions office at a local university during the day, and she picked up tailoring jobs at night. She could sew anything. I did not inherit that skill. She used to lament that I couldn't even hem a pair of pants. But I didn't have the patience. Once she married Harry, however, she found a much easier life."

"How did they meet?"

"It was at the university. He came to a fundraiser. He said he saw her, and he was smitten."

"Love at first sight. Do you believe in that?"

"I do, because I saw it happen with my mom. She fell for Harry hard and fast. She tried to resist, because her first marriage had not gone well, and she'd lost confidence in her instincts. But Harry wouldn't take no for an answer."

"So, you started a new life with a diplomat. Where else did you live besides Bezikstan?"

"Singapore, Brussels, Rome, and Barcelona. It was a wonderful life."

"Where did you go to college?"

She hesitated for the first time, as if she'd suddenly realized they were getting closer to her more current past. He wished they could tear down the barriers between them, but to get her to open up, he would have to do the same, and he wasn't ready for that. It wasn't just about him. He had to think of the bigger picture.

"I went to Berkeley, in California," she said. "What about you?"

"I went to the University of Virginia."

"And what did you study? English? Journalism?"

"Among other things."

"Like..."

"Political science, international studies. I wanted to understand the world that took my mother away."

"Did it help?" She gave him a soft, compassionate look that almost undid him.

Why on earth had he told her about his mom? That had probably been a mistake. But he couldn't take it back.

"Not really," he said shortly, realizing she was still waiting for an answer. He finished off the last spoonful of ice cream and set his bowl aside. "Nothing can really explain away an act of terror. There's no good reason. There's no lesson to be learned from evil."

"I completely understand. I used to try to make sense of an attack that I lived through a very long time ago—the night my parents and I had to leave the Bezikstan embassy while under fire from rebels."

"Tell me about it."

"I was sixteen. I loved our life in Bezikstan. It's a beautiful country, magnificent mountains, clear lakes, colorful people—music, food, and dance. The country is tucked between India, Nepal, and Bangladesh and for hundreds of years it was a peaceful place. We lived at the embassy, and I became friends with the US staffers and also the native Bezikstani people who worked there—the cooks, the housecleaners, the administrative support. I felt like we were all one happy family."

She sat back in her chair, a smile of fond remembrance on her face. "The week before the attack, we'd hosted a party at the embassy. There had been champagne and music, laughing and singing. I wasn't allowed to be at the dinner; it was adults only, but I watched them from behind a heavy curtain. Jasmine and Anika were there, too. We even managed to steal a bottle of champagne. It was almost empty, but there was enough left for us to have a few sips." She laughed. "We thought we were drunk on the bubbles. We were just three silly girls."

"When did you know there were problems?"

"I didn't know most of it until the night we left, but my stepfather had been hearing rumblings for a while. Things were changing. There was income disparity. The government felt elitist to many of its residents. And they didn't like that

America was having what they felt was too big of an influence on political matters. They wanted us gone. My stepfather didn't want to shut down the embassy. He thought he could win the diplomatic war if he could keep people talking. But they didn't give him a chance to talk more. They overran the gates one night. There were guns going off, grenades tossed into the courtyard. One of the Marine guards was killed. His name was Stan Sutherland. I still remember him. He used to give me licorice."

She drew in a breath and squared her shoulders, as if battling the pain of her memories. "Anyway, we had to leave through a tunnel. I know—the irony of another embassy tunnel has not escaped me. We ended up in a school yard. We waited there for the helicopter to come and rescue us."

"You were all together, or did Harry stay behind?"

"We were together until the last minute. The helicopter landed, and we were all running toward it. But I stumbled and fell."

He leaned forward, seeing remembered terror in her eyes. "What happened?"

"My parents were busy getting the staff and their families on board. They didn't realize I'd fallen. And then the rebels found us. They started shooting. I froze. I thought I was going to die. But someone grabbed my hand and pulled me to my feet. He ran me to the helicopter and pushed me on board, just as it was about to take off. He truly saved my life."

"Who was he?"

She stared back at him. "Neil Langdon—Ben's father."

He sucked in a breath. "Really?"

She nodded. "Yes. Neil helped us escape, but he didn't come with us. Neil was a British citizen, and Elizabeth's family lived in Bezikstan, so they felt safe to stay there. It was the Americans the rebels wanted out."

"So, you owe Neil your life." He found that fact to be disturbing. Would Parisa want to protect Neil's son because of what Neil had done for her?

"I do owe him my life," she agreed.

"And you don't want his son, Ben, to be a terrorist."

"I really don't. But..."

He was relieved to hear the word. "But?"

She met his gaze. "I'm not a sixteen-year-old girl anymore. And that bomb blast in Paris killed two people. If Ben knows anything about it, then he needs to share it with the authorities, so the bombers can be brought to justice."

"I'm glad to hear you say that. Because I did get a piece of information while you were sleeping."

She straightened in her chair. "What was that?"

"Sara Pillai used her former roommate's passport to enter the country. She arrived at JFK yesterday morning. She's here in New York City."

"Why didn't you tell me that before?"

"I'm telling you now."

"Neil told us Ben was out with friends. Maybe he's with Sara."

"If they're together, they're in the shadows. I have no idea where Sara went after she left the airport."

Parisa gave him a troubled look. "Maybe we need to put more eyes on her. I think we should call the FBI."

"The FBI and various other agencies have been looking for Sara since the blast."

"Maybe not in New York City."

"Feel free to share that information, but I'd prefer if you didn't say where you got it."

"Fine. What name did she travel under?"

"Melissa Holmes."

She pulled out her phone and sent a text.

"I assume that the reason you decided to text and not call your friend is because you've already discussed Sara with the FBI?"

"Yes. I mentioned there could be a connection between the blast and the kidnapping, especially since the terror group originated in Bezikstan. Do you have a problem with that?"

"No. I figured you shared the information. I don't have a problem if someone else finds Sara and Isaac before I do. I just want them to be found. As for Ben, I think you have a better shot of getting information out of him than law enforcement."

"Possibly. Who are you working with, Jared?"

"I have someone who helps me with research."

"Is that a woman?"

"No, it's a man. Does that matter?"

"Just curious." She paused. "Do you have a woman in your life? This apartment has some feminine touches but nothing that personal."

"The feminine touches are from the interior designer. And I'm currently single. You?"

"I'm also single. And I'm not unhappy about it. I have plenty of time for whatever else I may want."

"I wasn't going to suggest you're unhappy." He wondered about her defensive tone.

"Good, because I'm not, even though my mother thinks I need a man to complete my life."

"Which you don't."

"Damned right I don't." She got up and took her bowl and his to the sink. "Since you cooked, I'm going to do the dishes."

"You don't have to do that."

"It's not a big deal. And it's not like I don't have time."

He smiled. "We do have a rather long night ahead of us. What do you want to do?"

Her cheeks turned pink. "I don't know. Go to bed. I mean, you can use your bed. I'll sleep on the couch."

"All right."

She seemed surprised by his acquiescence. "Okay then."

"But I'm not tired yet, and I can't imagine you would be after your nap," he said.

"We could go on the computer and do some research."

"Sure."

"And then we could watch TV or talk."

"Or whatever," he added, just to see her blush again.

"We're not doing *whatever*. I already told you that."

"Well, if you change your mind—"

"I won't," she said, cutting him off. "Let me finish this and then we'll decide what to do."

—————

Doing the dishes wasn't quite as good as a cold shower, but it was a nice distraction from Jared, who seemed to get sexier and more irresistible by the moment. Parisa almost wished he hadn't told her about losing his mom on 9/11. He'd painted such a vivid picture of that day, she'd felt like she was reliving it with him, and his heartbreak, his anger, had been palpable. His emotions had made him seem much more real to her, much more likeable, because he'd shared his pain with her.

She tried to tell herself that that had probably been the point of his sharing, that he wanted her to like him, to trust him. But that felt too cynical for this situation. While Jared clearly had secrets, his agenda felt patriotic, honorable. *Or did she just want that to be the case?*

Shaking her head, she finished loading the dishwasher and then turned it on, her gaze moving over to Jared. He'd put his laptop computer on the kitchen table and was intensely studying the screen. He always seemed to be simmering…burning to get to an answer or a truth. And she didn't think he ever willingly gave up.

But why was he so fixated on the Paris explosion? Was there something to it that she didn't know?

Jared looked up from the computer and gave her a nod. "You done?"

"Yes." She moved out of the kitchen and pulled a chair up next to him. "What are you working on?"

"Just checking the news," he said, as he closed the

laptop. "Wondering if there would be anything about the kidnapping."

"Was there?"

"Nothing we don't know."

"So, why did you close the computer so quickly?"

He shrugged. "Habit."

"You're used to being secretive?"

"I'm used to guarding my information. You can't break a big story if there are too many leaks."

"Well, I'm not competing with you on a story."

He tipped his head. "Good point."

"At any rate, I was thinking that Brothers of the Earth sounds solidly male. Are you sure Sara is a part of it?"

"I don't know how involved she is. Only men are official members, but there are plenty of women around—wives, girlfriends, siblings. The fact that she worked at the targeted explosion site and called in sick that day leads me to believe she knew what was coming. She could have done something to warn the people she worked with, but she didn't. She's complicit in their deaths."

"Maybe she was scared."

"So what?" he asked harshly. "People died."

"I know it's not an excuse; I'm just trying to get a handle on her. One thing I'm curious about—you were watching Ben at the party. If you wanted to talk to him, why didn't you? Why did you wait?"

"Believe me, I very much regret that. I wanted to see if he was there to meet with Sara and Isaac, but I left it too long. It was a mistake."

She could see the anger in his eyes. "And you don't like to make mistakes."

"No, I don't, not when there are lives on the line. This isn't over, Parisa. They're going to act again. And if they have a fifty-million-dollar diamond, plus another ten million in ransom coming their way, the results could be catastrophic. We have to stop them."

"We will. We'll find a way. Don't give up now, *Mr. Confidence.*"

At her light jab, he blew out a breath, his tension easing at her words. "I'm not giving up. I'm just frustrated, and I hate doing nothing. So, what do you want to do? Watch television? Play cards?"

"Are those my only choices?" she asked.

He gave her a sexy grin. "I have other ideas, but unless you've changed your mind about getting a little closer..."

"I haven't," she said quickly. *Or had she?*

Eleven

-->>>><<--

Parisa forced that silly question out of her head. Of course she hadn't changed her mind about fooling around with Jared. "Let's play cards," she said decisively.

"All right. How about poker?"

"As long as it's not strip poker."

"That would make things more interesting."

"Not going to happen," she told him, even though the idea of seeing Jared without clothes was more than a little appealing.

"I thought you'd be more adventurous." Jared got up from the table and opened a nearby drawer, pulling out an unopened pack of cards.

"I'm adventurous. Want to skydive, bungee jump, climb up the face of a skyscraper, I'm your girl, but sex with a mystery man who could be married, be a criminal, or be gone before the sun comes up—not so much."

He sat down across from her and opened the cards, shuffling them like a well-trained dealer. "I'm not married, and I'm not a criminal."

"What about the last part?"

"I could be gone before the sun comes up—if I had a good reason to leave."

"There you go."

"But I think you could do the same—if you had a good reason."

"Maybe," she admitted. "Which is why playing cards and not having sex is the best decision."

"I'd call it a decision, but definitely not the best one," he drawled.

She smiled, enjoying their charged-up conversation and the fact that she felt more like herself than she had in a long time. As he shuffled the cards again, she said, "Did you by chance work at a casino?"

"For a few months actually—in Las Vegas. I worked high stakes poker."

"Sounds like there's a story there."

"It was interesting to watch what people are willing to gamble, how good they are at hiding their emotions, what makes them sweat, and how they interact with people they think are equals versus those who are clearly beneath them."

"I'm guessing they don't act well."

"That probably wasn't a difficult guess since you have moved in a world of privilege."

"That's true. I have met a lot of people with money, but the ones who impressed me the most were the ones who used their financial status to make the world better. I don't have a lot of patience for materialistic people. Not when I've seen so much suffering. I wish there was more sharing of wealth, more working together, because when people do that, lives can be forever changed."

"Did you see that suffering as the stepdaughter of a diplomat or as a translator?"

"A little of both," she said quickly, realizing how much she was giving away. "So, what are we playing?"

"Your call—poker, Crazy Eights, Go Fish, gin rummy,

blackjack?"

"Let's play blackjack."

"Fine, I'll be the house."

"Great. We both know the house always wins."

"You want to be the house?"

"No. I like bigger odds," she said. "The challenge of beating the house makes it more interesting."

He smiled at her. "Ah, your competitive spirit is kicking in. Shall we play for money?"

"Since I don't have any money at the moment, let's play for something else."

"You already ruled out stripping."

"Yes, I did. Let's play for information. Loser has to answer one personal question about themselves, and it cannot be a lie."

"All right," he said, with another shuffle. "Let's do it." He dealt the cards, one to her, one to him, then another to her face down, while he placed his second card face up; it was a jack.

"Damn," she muttered. She had the terrible feeling he had an ace under there or another face card, and she had a six and a nine for a total of fifteen.

"You want a card?" Jared asked.

She should hit on fifteen. It was a logical move, but Jared seemed to be a man upon whom luck smiled. Still, if she didn't hit, he could beat her with a lot of combinations. "Hit me."

He put down an eight—twenty-three. *Bust.*

Then he turned over his second card—a queen, for twenty. "You lose."

"Fine, what's your question?" she asked with a disgruntled sigh.

"Who was your last boyfriend and why did you break up?"

She was happy the questions were more personal than professional. "That's two questions," she complained.

"Fine, answer the first one."

"His name was Paul. He was a good guy."

"But not good for you?"

She shook her head. "He didn't understand or appreciate the demands of my job. Mostly, because he never wanted to talk about what I did, only what he did."

"Sounds like a loser."

"He was like a lot of men I dated—more interested in themselves than in me."

"I doubt that."

"I'm talking about beyond the bedroom. I haven't met many men who wanted to know the real me."

"Do you show people the real you—even if they ask?"

She stared back at him, knowing that this shadowy, mystery man probably knew as much about keeping secrets as she did. "You'd be surprised how few ask."

"I'm asking."

"Only because you have an agenda."

"Not completely true."

"But partially true."

A slow smile spread across his face. "You've actually made me open up more than I normally do."

"Right back at you, Jared. Is that your real name?"

"Yes. Is Parisa your real name?"

"You know it is. You've done research on me."

"And you've done research on me. Or you've had your friend do it for you."

"There's very little about you on the internet. You clearly are not someone who is posting cat pictures on social media."

"Not a cat fan. Dogs all the way."

"What? How can you say that? Kittens are so cute."

"And completely indifferent. They can love any warm body whereas a dog is loyal, devoted, family."

She thought about that. "You're more like a cat than a dog, so it's interesting that you wouldn't pick that animal for a pet."

"Maybe because I want more in a pet."

"Well, I like cats, and I like dogs, for different reasons. But really, any animal is precious. I never got to have a pet when I was growing up, because we moved all the time. What about you?"

"We always had dogs, mostly Labs, a couple of golden retrievers. They were way too big for our city apartment, but my dad grew up in the country, and he loved having dogs in the house. My mom wasn't nearly as excited about it, but she loved my dad, so..."

As his expression softened, she said, "It sounds like they had a great relationship."

"To me, it looked awesome. They fought, but never with meanness. It was always just small irritations, and usually my dad would end up making my mom laugh, and suddenly they were kissing. She used to say he was a charmer."

"I think you take after him."

He smiled. "Maybe a little."

"Okay, we got off track. Deal the cards."

The next hand gave her blackjack, which made her very happy. "Okay, I'm going to go with your questions—last girlfriend and why you broke up."

"Her name was Carrie. And we broke up because she used me."

"How did she do that?" she asked curiously.

"You already got your two answers."

"But we're still on the topic of Carrie. So, it counts. Go on."

"A friend of mine is a movie producer. Carrie was a model, who wanted to be an actress, and she thought I could get her there."

"I did not expect that to be what she wanted. Who's your friend? Has he produced anything I might have seen?"

"His name is Larry Corker. His latest movie was *Tears in a Bottle,* named after a Jim Croce song."

"I didn't see it, but I saw the trailer. That movie was

super popular."

"Larry is a good producer, and he had a fascination with the singer who wrote the song and then died in a tragic plane crash."

"Where did you meet him?"

"College. First day of freshman year. There was a blowout party in the dorm, and Larry came to school as a rather protected kid. He'd never gone wild, and he made up for it in one night. He actually passed out in the hallway, naked. I found him in the morning, got him some clothes, gave him some coffee. He was mortified. He thought he'd already ruined his college experience, but I got him over the hump. We became good friends. And he continues to pay me back with private screening invites."

"Did you try to get Carrie in to see him?"

"No. I don't use my friends. That pissed her off. She said everyone uses everyone, so what's the big deal? And that if I wanted something, I wouldn't hesitate to do whatever I needed to do to get it."

"Well, she has a point. You're using me right now."

"We're using each other," he corrected. "Although, I still think we could be doing it in a more enjoyable way."

She made a face at his sexy remark. "I think it's time to deal the cards."

They played another hand, and she won again. "Ooh, I'm liking this game."

"Me, not so much," he grumbled. "I thought the house was supposed to win. Okay, what's your next question? And make it an easy one this time."

"What was your most embarrassing moment? You told me Larry's naked-in-the-dorm-hallway story. What about you? What's the experience you wish you could take back?"

"That's not an easy one. I don't believe I have an embarrassing moment."

"Everyone does. You just don't want to say, because you don't want to be embarrassed."

"I don't embarrass that easily."

"Come on, Jared."

"You're a pushy woman, aren't you?"

"Yes, but it's not your turn for a question."

He laughed. "Okay. I was at a community pool in the summer with a girl I'd just started dating."

"Carrie?"

"No. This was during college."

"What happened at the pool?" she asked with interest.

"I jumped out of the water and onto an inner tube and my bathing suit didn't make the trip."

"No way." She started laughing. "You mooned the pool?"

"Oh, yeah, and there were a lot of people around me."

"What did you do?"

"Got back into the water as fast as I could and tried to get my bathing suit up before I had to hoist myself onto the deck. I didn't want a repeat performance, although I'm told I have a very nice ass."

She flushed at the thought of his ass and didn't doubt it was as nice as he'd suggested. The man did triathlons. She could only imagine what kind of muscles his clothes were hiding.

Jared leaned forward, a wicked sparkle in his eyes. "You can see it if you ask nicely."

"I'm not interested."

"Yes, you are."

"You need to deal the next hand."

"Fine, but I better win this time."

As if he'd willed the cards to come up his way, Jared got blackjack, and it was her turn on the hot seat.

"Are you going to ask me my most embarrassing moment?" she enquired.

"I don't think so." He thought for a moment. "What scares you the most? And it can't be about Jasmine. This is about you. What worries you, Parisa?"

"Can I just say spiders?"

"No, because you'd be lying."

She sighed. "True. Spiders don't scare me at all. I don't know. I'm not that fearful."

"Try harder."

"Well, I guess it would be...time."

He arched a questioning eyebrow. "Time scares you?"

"Yes. Too much time to think. Too little time to do what needs to be done. Time that moves too fast, takes me places I'm not ready to go. Time that moves too slow, and I can't get where I need to be. Time that ends before I'm ready."

"So, it's time," he said dryly.

She smiled and gave a helpless shrug. "I can't control time, and I don't like that."

"I get it."

"Do you? Because I sound like a lunatic."

"Does the fear of time come from the night you almost lost your life, almost didn't make it into the helicopter?"

"Probably. I had a lot of nightmares after that." She paused. "But the real problem is that I think too much. My brain is always working. And when I have too much time to think, I worry that I'm not doing enough. I hate to fail, and I hate to waste a second. It's bugging me even now that we're not doing something to save Jasmine or find Ben."

"I can get obsessed like that, too," he admitted. "It sometimes makes me do crazy things...like following a woman from the hospital to a safe house and waiting for her to wake up."

They exchanged a smile of complete understanding, and it deepened the connection between them. "That was crazy," she agreed.

"You're not the only lunatic in this room."

"I guess it's good to have company."

"We'll get back to it all tomorrow, Parisa."

"I know."

"Do you want to keep playing cards?"

"No, I think that's enough truth for tonight. I'm going to

lay down on the couch. You take the bed."

"Not a chance. It's all yours, Parisa."

"It's your bed."

He shrugged. "I'm fine with the couch. I'm not that tired yet. I'm going to catch the news."

Considering how comfortable his bed was, she decided not to argue. "All right. Your call."

He caught her arm as she was about to get up, his gaze boring into hers.

"What?" she asked, her voice suddenly a little too breathless. She trusted him not to force her into anything she didn't want to do, but it wouldn't take much to make her want to do all kinds of things she probably shouldn't.

"This is going to sound strange, but I had fun tonight. I liked getting to know you better."

"I liked it, too."

Probably too much, she thought as she left the table and walked into the bedroom.

Striding over to the window, she crossed her arms as she looked out at the view, thinking about how much she had told Jared and wondering why she'd opened herself up that way. She'd never ever told anyone her feelings about time, but somehow Jared had made her feel like she could trust him with her darkest fears.

She really hoped he wasn't going to abuse that trust, because she didn't usually let down her guard so easily.

Suddenly her biggest fear wasn't time anymore; it was betrayal.

Twelve

—➤➤◄◄◄—

Parisa woke up Sunday morning feeling energized and ready to get some answers. She'd had a good night's sleep and the fog that had been clogging her brain since the kidnapping was finally completely gone. She was also relieved not to have had to wake up and fight for her life. Apparently, her location had not been compromised.

After a quick shower, she dug into her suitcase, happy she'd brought it with her from the safe house. She put on black jeans and a soft pink sweater and headed into the kitchen. She found Jared once again at the stove. He also wore jeans with a long-sleeve gray T-shirt. He must have gone into the bedroom and grabbed new clothes while she was showering. But she didn't care about that right now. She gave him a happy smile. "I was hoping the bacon and eggs weren't a dream," she told him. "I could get used to having my own personal chef."

He handed her a plate and a mug of coffee. "Enjoy."

"Oh, I will." As she sat down at the table, she noticed he wasn't eating. "Where's your breakfast?"

"I ate while I was cooking."

"Very efficient."

"I can multitask. How did you sleep?"

"Surprisingly well. I hope the couch wasn't too uncomfortable."

"It was fine. I can sleep anywhere."

He refilled his coffee mug and brought it to the table, taking the seat across from her. "Your eye looks better today."

"Nothing a little makeup couldn't cover up." She sipped her coffee. "This is good, too. Strong. Just the way I like it."

"I had a feeling you were no-nonsense when it comes to coffee."

"Definitely. I'd rather save my calories for a big-ass hot fudge sundae than put whipped cream in my coffee."

"Good call."

"Speaking of calls, I tried the Langdons again. Neither one answered. I think we should just go to their home. I already told Neil I'd be coming over today, so it won't be a surprise."

"I'm up for that, and I'm glad you said we, because I'm not sitting this one out in the car."

"Is there a chance the Langdons will recognize you from the party or anywhere else?"

"I don't believe so."

"Then I'll just tell them you're my boyfriend."

He grinned. "Perfect. We can hold hands."

"Only if you want me to break your fingers," she warned him.

"I believe you could do that."

"You'd be right," she said with a sly smile, as she sipped her coffee.

"Then I'll keep my hands in my pockets. At least for this trip."

"On the way, we need to pick up a book of poetry. I'll forge a note from Jasmine to lend truth to my story."

"There's actually a bookstore down the street."

"Great. I need something that would heal a broken heart."

"If there's a book that can do that, that author must be rich."

"Have you ever had a broken heart?" she asked curiously, wondering if this mystery man had ever let anyone get that close to him.

He nodded. "Hailey Johnson—fifth grade. She had white-blonde hair and freckles all over her face. I was fascinated by them—by her. I used to walk to recess with her, and then she dumped me for Brad Warren."

"What did Brad have that you didn't?"

"An apartment building with a pool. It was really hot that week."

"I'm beginning to see a pattern of females dumping you for males with more to offer."

"I guess charm isn't always enough."

"I don't think charm is enough, but being a good person is worth a lot. And, this might seem strange for me to say, but I think you're a good person, Jared."

"Why do you think that?" he asked curiously.

"You have a protective streak. You can't walk away from someone in trouble, even when helping them might make your life more difficult. Like you couldn't walk away from me at the party, even though you could have gotten in a lot of trouble for being upstairs. If security had discovered you, then you might be sitting in an interrogation room right now. But you did what was right."

He shrugged, looking a bit uncomfortable with her comment. "It was a gut instinct. I didn't really think about it."

"You should just take the compliment."

"Fine. I'm a good person."

"And…"

He smiled as he sat back in his chair and folded his arms across his chest. "And what? You're a good person, too?"

"I'd rather you didn't make it a question."

"Sorry. I think you're a good person as well, Parisa."

"Because..."

"Because you're trying to help me get to Ben, when all you really want to do is get to Jasmine. It's also possible that getting me to Ben might hurt the Langdons—the man who saved your life. But that's not stopping you. You're a big picture kind of woman. You go for the greater good. I like that."

She was touched by his words. "I'm helping you because the puzzle you're trying to solve is an important one."

"And because you like me."

"I don't think I said that."

His gaze met hers. "But you do—like me."

"That's beside the point."

"I like you, too, probably more than I should."

"I could say the same thing. I don't usually trust people I don't know. In fact, I don't usually trust anyone unless I have a good reason to do so. But for some reason, you're different." She drew in a breath and let it out. "We should get going. We have a lot to do today."

He nodded. "Yes, we do." He got to his feet and grabbed her empty plate. "I'll put this in the sink, and then we'll leave."

<hr />

By the time they stopped at the bookstore and picked up a poetry book, then got into the car and headed uptown, it was almost eleven. Hopefully, Ben would be home from wherever he'd spent the night. Parisa kept a sharp eye out for a tail, knowing that Jared was doing the same.

The Sunday traffic was still busy, not quite as bad as the day before, but it was typical Manhattan: too many people, too many cars.

"While I'm driving, why don't you tell me more about the Langdons, about Ben's parents?" Jared suggested.

She was glad that their conversation was all business now. Back at the apartment, things had gotten a little too personal. "Neil is an intelligent, kind man, very empathetic, and he has a dry sense of humor. He taught French, Spanish, and world history at my school. I, of course, spent a lot of time in his classes as I loved language even then."

"What languages are you fluent in?"

"French, Portuguese, Spanish, and Farsi. I'm pretty good in Russian, Chinese and Japanese, too."

"How do you do it? How do you keep all the words in your head?"

"There's a rhythm to language. It comes easily to me. I think part of why I'm so good at it is that I don't overthink it. So many languages share words that I can piece things together even if I don't know every syllable. It's like seeing five pieces of a nine-piece puzzle and being able to imagine what's missing. With language, I can do that." She gave him a curious glance. "Do you speak anything besides English?"

"I took French in high school and college, but I wouldn't call myself fluent. I can swear in Spanish and Portuguese."

"What about words of passion? Have you never wanted to tell a woman how beautiful she was in another language?"

He flung her a smile. "I usually let my actions do the talking."

She couldn't help but smile back at him. Jared had certainly charmed her with some of his actions. She'd spent too many minutes of the night before reliving their kiss and wondering if it could possibly be as good as she remembered. But the only way to find out would be to kiss him again, and that was not a distraction either of them could afford.

Clearing her throat, she said, "Anyway, we were talking about the Langdons."

"Right. Let's get back to them. You said Neil is British, but Elizabeth is from Bezikstan?"

"Yes. Elizabeth grew up in Bezikstan but went to college in London. She then became a stage actress. Neil said the first time he saw her was when she was in a production of *Cats*. He went to the play four times that week until he found a way to get backstage and ask her out. She thought he was insane. He knew the play so well by then, he could actually recite some of her lines. She said no at first. But Neil was persistent. He kept coming back, and eventually she said yes to a date. A year later, they married, and after she had Ben, they decided to move to Bezikstan to be closer to her family." Parisa took a breath, as she thought about their story. "Elizabeth used to help out in the drama department at the school. She'd run lines with the kids and work on the sets. Both she and Neil were involved in the curriculum. Ben would often hang out at the school with them. He was always toddling around."

"And the Langdons' relationship with the Kumars? How did that happen?"

"Well, I think it started through Anika and Jasmine. The Kumars were very involved in their children's education."

"Did your stepfather and mother get involved with the Kumars through you and your relationship with the girls?"

"Not entirely. Mr. Kumar was the minister of commerce when my father was the ambassador. They often worked on improving trade agreements between the US and Bezikstan. We would have them over for dinner, and they would do the same, and sometimes the Langdons would be there, too. Eventually, we all became close. Everyone felt like family."

"Did you keep in touch with anyone after you left Bezikstan?"

"Anika, Jasmine and I wrote each other the first few years, but that gradually faded away. Before Friday night, it had been fifteen years since I'd seen anyone from Bezikstan, but when we came together at the party, it felt like no time had passed. When I went upstairs with Jasmine, we were the same two girls who'd once spent hours talking together. It felt completely normal. I realized how much I had missed her. We were just getting reacquainted when the air became foul. And then Jasmine was gone." She drew in a hard breath. "I need to find her, Jared. I feel a personal obligation to bring her home. I was the last one to talk to her. I heard her fears about losing herself to Westley, about giving up her life for his. I saw how stressed she was by the weight of that ring on her finger. She was both happy and sad at the same time."

Jared glanced at her, sympathy in his gaze. "I get it. This is personal for you."

"It is, and it really has nothing to do with the fact that I almost died; it's all about Jasmine. She's my friend. And she's a sweet, kind, gentle person. I wish I could be more involved in searching for her. I hate having to hide out."

"You can't help Jasmine if you're dead."

"I know, but I don't like running scared."

"You're not running. You're investigating from the shadows. What was it like living in Bezikstan?" he asked, changing the subject.

"It was wonderful. My mother is Indian, so I wasn't unfamiliar with the culture, although Bezikstan has its own traditions. Knowing Hindi, which is one of the main languages of Bezikstan helped me to blend in. When you can speak to someone in their own language, it is much easier to break down barriers. Harry used to tell me that we're really not so different from each other. When we talk, when we listen, when we try to understand, we realize that."

"I would agree. Unfortunately, some people don't want to listen—they just want to fight."

"Yes. But when there's a chance to win with words, it's important for us to take it. However, I don't go to a gun fight with just a dictionary."

"Good to know." He flung her another smile. "I like how passionate you are about language."

"I'm passionate about breaking down walls, and language can do that. But while I can be idealistic, I am also very practical. So, if language is my superpower, what's yours?"

"Uh, I don't know if I have one," he replied.

"Oh, I'm betting you do. You're not getting shy on me

now, are you, Jared?"

"Maybe I'll let you figure it out for yourself."

"I think one of your superpowers is being able to blend in wherever you go. You're like a chameleon. No one notices you're there, unless you want them to notice. Like at the party—you wanted me to notice you."

"I did."

"But you were not there to flirt with me, so why did you? Why weren't you focused purely on Ben?"

"You looked really gorgeous in that black dress."

She flushed at his words. "I wasn't asking for a compliment."

"You were asking for a reason. That's it."

"Well, thank you."

Jared slowed down, searching the street for a place to park.

Whoever was feeding him information had clearly given him an address. She still wondered who he was working for. *If he wasn't FBI, was he CIA or Homeland Security? Or was he a private contractor—a private investigator?*

The Paris bombing was a global issue. That made her think he worked internationally. If he was part of an agency, why did he seem so isolated?

At some point, they were going to have to put all their cards on the table. But that point wasn't now.

After Jared parked, they got out of the car and walked down the street to the Langdons' building. There was a doorman in the lobby, who asked for their names, then made a call upstairs. After a moment of conversation, he hung up the phone and gave them a nod. "You can go up—912—ninth floor."

"They're home," she said, feeling excited that they were going to talk to someone.

"This is a luxury building and knowing a little about Manhattan rents, I'd have to ask how a teacher from Bezikstan can afford this," Jared commented, as they got into the mirrored elevator.

Her brows knit together at his question. "Good point. I think Neil might come from money, but I don't know for sure."

"Worth looking into," he muttered, thinking he needed to expand his research beyond Ben.

"Let me take the lead with the Langdons," she said, as the elevator doors opened. "They'll expect that."

"No problem. I'll just be your devoted boyfriend, who is incredibly relieved that you weren't kidnapped." He grabbed her hand. "For our cover."

"You're pushing it, Jared."

He laughed. "Not yet I'm not, but who knows what's coming?"

As a flicker of desire ran through his gaze, her gut clenched, and her fingers tightened around his. In truth, neither one of them knew what was coming next, but she was looking forward to finding out.

Thirteen

Parisa knew she should let go of Jared's hand, but she couldn't seem to find the will. They were still holding hands when Elizabeth Langdon answered the door. Elizabeth had short, black hair and dramatic gold-flecked brown eyes that were heavy with liner. Her black slacks and thin, shimmery blue sweater showed off a slender frame. Despite her put-together appearance, Parisa could see the worry in her eyes and the paleness in her skin.

"Parisa," she said. "You're all grown up."

"Yes, I am."

"Neil mentioned you called last night. I'm glad to see you're well."

Parisa let go of Jared to kiss Elizabeth on both cheeks. "This is my boyfriend, Jared MacIntyre." She would have thought using the term boyfriend would have made her stumble, but it had come out surprisingly easy.

"It's nice to meet you, Mr. MacIntyre," Elizabeth said politely.

"You, too. Parisa has spoken very fondly of you and your

husband and your son."

"That's sweet. Neil and Ben aren't here right now, but come in. Would you like something to eat or drink?"

"No, we're good," Parisa said, answering for both of them. She was disappointed to hear that Ben wasn't there, but maybe they could find out where he was.

+As Elizabeth ushered them into the apartment, she was impressed by the designer décor and the stunning views. "This is beautiful."

"We fell in love with it as soon as we saw it." Elizabeth led them into the living room, and they sat down on two adjacent couches. "When Ben moved here for school, we knew we'd be visiting him fairly often. And then Neil took a job at Everly for the year, so it made sense to have a home here."

"Is Ben going to move back to Bezikstan after he graduates? He must be getting close," she said, trying to ease her way into a conversation about Ben.

"He probably has another year. I'm not sure what he's going to do," Elizabeth said. "I'm really glad you're all right, Parisa. You must have been terrified when the kidnappers came in and grabbed Jasmine."

"It all happened so fast, and the fumes were disorienting. I didn't really know what was happening," she said, realizing that Jared had taken her hand again when they sat down. It seemed awkward to pull away now that they were seated so close to Elizabeth.

"You were lucky. We heard the security guards didn't make it."

"I was very fortunate," she agreed.

"Did you see who took Jasmine?"

"I didn't. I was barely conscious."

"That's what Kenisha said. She told me a ransom demand came in yesterday. It's for a lot of money, but hopefully the Larimers will pay it. Kenisha can barely breathe, waiting for tomorrow morning. She's terrified that even if the Larimers pay the money that Jasmine won't be traded back. What do you think?"

"I don't know. I'm worried, too."

"Why do such horrific things have to happen? When we were evacuated from the party, and I saw the ambulances pulling up in front of the consulate, it reminded me of that night in Bezikstan when the embassy was overtaken. I wasn't with Neil when he went to help all of you, of course, but I could see the chaos from my windows. I was so worried for my friends, and I felt helpless, just as I did Friday night." She drew in a breath. "I'm sorry. I'm rambling on. Tell me what you've been doing, Parisa?"

"I'm a translator with the state department."

"You were always Neil's star student in his language class. He said you were a natural." She paused, her gaze swinging to Jared. "What do you do, Mr. MacIntyre?"

"I'm a journalist."

"How long have the two of you been together?"

Jared gave her a smile. "It feels like five minutes, doesn't it, honey?"

"Yes, it does," she said, knowing that despite the very serious circumstances, Jared was enjoying their roles.

"But it's been almost a year," Jared added, as he turned toward Elizabeth. "When I saw Parisa, I fell hard. She was the most beautiful woman I'd ever seen. I could barely speak."

Parisa felt her cheeks warm at his compliment. He was putting on an act, but still, it was nice to hear.

"Parisa has always been a beauty, like her mother. How did you meet?"

"Do you want me to tell the story?" Jared asked her.

"Sure," she said, curious to hear what he would say.

"It was raining, and we were both running for the same taxi. Our hands actually came down on the car door handle at the same time. It was like an electric shock ran through me," Jared told Elizabeth. "Our eyes met, and I thought to myself, where on earth did this stunning woman come from?"

"I think you were more likely wondering how you were going to get me to take a different taxi," she interjected.

He smiled at her. "Not at all. I wanted to get to know you." He glanced back at Elizabeth. "I told her we'd share the taxi. We got into the backseat, dripping wet, and icy cold, but there was so much heat in the car—"

"Jared," she protested, not sure how far he was going to go with the story.

"Don't worry," he said with a laugh. "I'm not going to elaborate. We got lucky enough to be stuck in traffic for almost a half hour, and during that time I convinced Parisa to meet me for dinner that night. The rest is history."

Hearing Jared's tale made her realize how good he was at making up a story on the spot, much like she had been when she'd told Neil about the book of poetry Jasmine had wanted her to give to Ben. How ironic that she would feel so connected to a man who was as good a liar as she was.

"That's so romantic," Elizabeth said. "It's just like one of those romantic comedies I used to act in. And not at all what I would have expected with Parisa. She was always such a cautious, look-before-you-leap, analyze-every-possible-scenario, make-a-pro-and-con-list kind of girl."

He raised an eyebrow as he glanced at her. "You've definitely changed, sweetheart."

"I was a teenager when Elizabeth knew me."

"That's true," Elizabeth said. "You're an adult now, and I'm sure I don't know you at all."

"Speaking of children growing up, I was hoping to speak to Ben."

"Yes." Elizabeth frowned. "Neil said that Jasmine gave you a book, and she wanted Ben to have it, but I don't understand. She didn't know she was going to be kidnapped, so how could she leave you something to give to my son?"

"She was showing me a book of poetry when the fumes came into the room." Parisa reached into the tote bag she'd bought at the bookstore and pulled out the volume of poems that were all about heartbreak. "She said that Ben was heartsick about a girl he was seeing in Paris, and she thought this might help him. She wrote a note to Ben that she thought would encourage him. I was looking at it when the air in the room got bad, and somehow, I hung on to it through everything. Every time I look at it, I feel like I kept it for a reason—Ben needs to have it."

"I can give it to him when he gets back."

"I'd like to do that myself. When will he be home?"

"I don't know. He's having a difficult time dealing with Jasmine's kidnapping. The two of them have become very close. He went to stay with friends."

"Do you know anything about the girl he was seeing in Paris?"

"He hasn't talked to me about her, but I heard him on the phone with Jasmine, and he said the name Sara. He dated a girl named Sara when he was sixteen. I'm pretty sure it's the same girl. Judging from what I overheard, they reconnected in Paris, but things didn't end well. When he came home early from his study program, I was relieved, because there had been an explosion in the city, not far from his hotel, and I didn't like him being so far away from me." She let out a breath. "Not that there's any place that's really safe anymore."

"That's true," she murmured.

"Since he returned, Ben has been depressed. I thought the engagement party would take his mind off things. He adores Jasmine. He was so upset, he tore his room apart, broke a lamp, almost broke a few fingers hitting the wall with his fist. Neil told me not to worry, that he was just blowing off steam, but I'm his mother—how can I not worry?"

Hearing Elizabeth talk about Ben's reaction to Jasmine's kidnapping brought forth mixed emotions. *Was Ben just torn up about his good friend being abducted, or was he somehow a part of it, maybe even a reluctant participant?*

"Do you have Ben's number?" she asked. "I'd really like

to text him, see if we could meet up, so I could give him the book, and maybe my telling him what Jasmine said to me would make him feel better."

"I guess that would be all right," Elizabeth said slowly. "Maybe it would give him a reason to come home." She stood up. "Let me get my phone. Ben just got a new number, and I don't have it memorized."

As Elizabeth left the room, Parisa glanced at Jared. "What do you think?"

"I'm not sure. I don't think she knows much of anything."

"I don't, either. But her motherly instinct has her worrying about her son. She knows something is off with him. And so do we." She pulled her hand away from Jared's. "By the way, that was quite a story you told her about our first meeting. Did you just pull that out of your hat? Or did it happen with some other woman?"

"What do you think?"

"That you made it up on the spot."

"Have you ever done Improv?"

"I have not," she said. "Have you?"

"I took a class in it. It's all about saying yes, going with whatever the prompt is. You'd be good at it."

"Maybe." She crossed her legs, then uncrossed them, a bad feeling running through her. "It's taking her a long time to find her phone."

Jared stood up. "Too long. Clearly, Elizabeth has tremendous love for her son. She could be contacting him right now, warning him not to talk to you."

"Why would she be afraid of me?"

"You asked a lot of questions about Ben. Maybe you ran an alarm bell by your sudden interest in him and determination to speak to him."

She rose, feeling edgy herself. She was starting to trust Jared's instincts as much as her own. Making a sudden decision, she walked out of the living room and down the hall.

Fourteen

Elizabeth was in her bedroom, speaking in low, urgent tones in Hindi. Parisa held up her hand to Jared, who had followed her down the hall, motioning for him to wait.

"Parisa is here and she's asking for you," Elizabeth said. "She wants your phone number. She has a book that Jasmine wanted to give you. She won't leave it with me. I don't know what it's about. She said it's to heal your broken heart. She's acting oddly." Elizabeth paused. "She said she doesn't remember anything about the kidnapping. She didn't see the men who entered the room."

Parisa looked at Jared with a frown. "She's talking about me," she whispered. "About the book and the kidnapping."

She moved closer to the door, as Elizabeth said, "I don't like this, Ben. I'm worried. You have to tell me what's going on, so I can help you. Why don't you come home? What do you mean—you can't? I don't understand." She took a breath. "I don't know where your father went. Yes, yes, I know he sometimes doesn't understand you, but he's your father. He loves you." She paused to listen once more, then added,

"Please, come home, Ben. Whatever is wrong, we can fix it."

"I've heard enough," Parisa told Jared, then pushed open the bedroom door and stepped into the room.

Elizabeth jumped, a guilty look on her face.

"Let me talk to Ben," Parisa said.

"This isn't Ben."

"Yes, it is. I heard you talking, and I'm still fluent in Hindi."

Judging by the expression on Elizabeth's face, the older woman had forgotten that.

"He hung up," Elizabeth said.

"You hung up," she told her, having seen Elizabeth push the button on her phone. "Why? What are you and Ben hiding? Does Ben have something to do with Jasmine's kidnapping?"

"No, God, no! How could you ask that?" Elizabeth demanded, but there was fear behind her vehement denial.

"Because you just told him I don't remember anything about the men who kidnapped Jasmine."

"He was wondering if you'd given the police any helpful information. That's all."

"Give me your phone. I want to talk to him."

"No." Elizabeth put the phone behind her back. "You need to stop ordering me around, Parisa. I don't know who you think you are, but you must leave—now."

"I'm not leaving, Elizabeth. Someone tried to kill me Friday night and again a few hours later. Jasmine is missing, and I believe your son has information on that."

"What? No, he doesn't know anything about it."

"Then why is he hiding out somewhere? Why won't he come home?"

"He's just upset."

"I know you're trying to protect your son, but telling the truth is the best way you can help him. I'm not going to be the only one looking for Ben, Elizabeth. If I go to the police with my suspicions—"

"What suspicions? What did Jasmine tell you?"

At the question, Parisa wondered if Ben had told Jasmine something about the Paris attack. Deciding to improvise, she said, "Jasmine told me that Ben was in trouble, that something bad had happened in Paris, and it wasn't just about a failed romance. She told him he needed to talk to the police, to tell them what he knew, that he might be able to save lives. I'm fairly certain she was speaking about that bomb that went off."

The blood drained from Elizabeth's face. "That's not true. Ben couldn't have had anything to do with that."

"But he knows someone who did—his girlfriend."

Elizabeth started shaking her head. "Please leave. I don't know why you're trying to hurt me, Parisa. Neil saved your life as a teenager. How can you come at our family like this?"

"I'm trying to help Ben. He's in trouble. He's afraid. And the longer he's out in this city alone, the more danger he could be in."

"You think Jasmine was kidnapped because of something Ben did? That's impossible."

Despite her defensive words, it was clear Elizabeth had doubts.

"You're thinking the same thing," she told her. "I know you are. That's why you're worried. You need to tell me where Ben is, or I'll pass my suspicions along to the FBI. They won't take your silence for an answer, and Ben will end up in a lot more trouble."

Elizabeth grabbed the chain around her neck and ran it nervously back and forth between her fingers. "Ben said some people are threatening to kill him and us. He needs to hide. I promised to get him some money."

"What people—Jasmine's kidnappers?"

"I don't know…maybe."

"Does Neil know about this threat?"

"Yes. He spoke to Ben early this morning, and he left in a fury an hour ago. He said he had to get some air. I don't know where he went. He didn't go to Ben. Ben was afraid to tell him where he was."

"But he told you, so you could get him some money, and he could disappear."

"He's a victim in all this. I know my son. He's not a bad person."

"Where is he, Elizabeth?" she pressed.

"You'll hurt him."

"I won't. I'll try to help him."

"How can you help him?"

"My stepfather still has connections in law enforcement," she lied. "I know he'll use those if Ben will come clean. It's his only chance. You know that." She was pulling out all the stops, probably destroying whatever relationship she'd ever had with the Langdons, but she had no other choice. Clearly, Ben knew something.

"You really believe Harry will help Ben?"

"I know he will. You have to trust someone."

"I haven't seen you in years, Parisa."

"Fine. I'll just call the police. I'll be honest, I came here this morning not just because of the book of poetry, but because of the concern Jasmine expressed about Ben. Jasmine loves your son as much as you do."

"Which is why he would never hurt her."

"I believe that, but we both know he's caught up in something, and if people are threatening to kill him and you and Neil that you can't handle this by yourself."

"I don't know what to do?" she said helplessly.

She looked Elizabeth in the eye. "Talk to me. Tell me where he is."

"Ben said he was going to go to the men's homeless shelter run by Sacred Cross. It's by the convention center. He thinks he can blend in and stay hidden until the kidnappers are found. Then he swears he'll go to the authorities and tell them what he knows. He just wants to stay safe until they're caught."

"Thank you."

As they turned to leave, Jared put in a parting remark. "If you're sending us on a wild-goose chase, you'll regret it," he told Elizabeth. "Not just because you may end up in jail on obstruction of justice charges, but you might end up dead. The people who kidnapped Jasmine are playing for keeps. They've already killed two men."

"I know. I'm terrified. Neither of you might believe this, but I really do want Jasmine to be all right. She's my best friend's daughter. I just want to protect my son, too."

"Sometimes, you can't protect people from themselves," Jared told her.

Elizabeth sat down on her bed as tears streamed out of her eyes. "Will you at least try to protect him, Parisa?"

"Yes." Parisa felt compassion for Elizabeth, but she was also angry that Elizabeth had been sitting on information that could save Jasmine's life. "Don't call him, Elizabeth. Don't tell him to run. It won't work. He can't outrun this. He needs help, and I'm his best hope."

"You will remember that Neil saved your life?" Elizabeth asked.

"I could never forget that," she promised.

They headed out of the bedroom and down the hall, letting themselves out of the apartment.

"Do you think she's telling us the truth?" Jared asked, as they took the elevator downstairs.

"I hope so," she said grimly. "But I don't know. Maternal love…it can be pretty damn strong."

When they got into the car, she looked up the address for the shelter, which was near the Javits Convention Center, as Elizabeth had said. She gave Jared directions as he started the engine.

He was all business now—no teasing smile, no sexy humor. He was focused on the job. And that focus made her question again just what it was about the Paris bombing that was so personal to him.

Something else he'd said to Elizabeth had puzzled her. "You told Elizabeth that you can't protect some people from themselves."

"Yeah, so?"

"It felt like you had some experience with that."

He met her gaze for a quick moment, and there was an odd bleakness in his eyes. "I have. It didn't end well."

"Will you tell me about it?"

"Let's focus on finding Ben. Nothing else matters right now."

She couldn't argue with that, but his words only made her more curious and reminded her that while Jared might have shared some personal data about himself, there was still a lot he was holding back.

⟶⟫⟪⟵

Parisa's question triggered some unwelcome memories, and Jared shoved them ruthlessly out of his mind. He didn't want to think about the past right now; there was too much going on. They had their first big break. There was a tie between Ben and the kidnappers. At least, he thought there was. Ben could just be in hiding because of what he'd done in Paris, but since he hadn't been hiding until Jasmine disappeared, his behavior seemed tied to her kidnapping.

He'd been right about Parisa being a valuable asset. She had used her relationship with the Langdons, her debt to Neil, as a way to get Elizabeth to trust her, and it had worked. She had probably destroyed her relationship with the family, but she was determined to save Jasmine, no matter the cost.

"Do you think I should call the FBI?" Parisa asked, interrupting his thoughts. "Ben could have information that will lead us to Jasmine. Should I be sitting on it?"

"Let's find Ben first. See what he knows—get him to talk to us before he calls for a lawyer, or he tries to run. You have the best shot of getting the truth out of him than anyone."

"He might already be running. There's no guarantee Elizabeth won't tell him to do just that."

"I think you convinced her that you're the best chance Ben has at getting a fair hearing. You were very persuasive. You brought in your stepfather, your debt to Neil, pushing all the right buttons."

"Even though they were mostly lies. Harry would never defend Ben if he's truly guilty. But time is ticking away. I did what I had to do. Ben knows something about the kidnapping. If his life is truly being threatened, then he's involved in that at least, maybe Paris, too." She drew in a breath. "But I think he's a side player at best. That's why he's scared, why he's alone."

"I'd agree with that."

"We'll wait to call the authorities until after we locate Ben."

"That won't be long now. We're almost there."

The shelter was two blocks away from the convention center, tucked in between a mix of warehouses, convenience stores, fast-food restaurants, and retail establishments.

Jared parked the car on the first floor of a three-story parking garage about a quarter mile from the shelter. Since it was Sunday, and there were apparently no conventions in town, there was plenty of parking. He took out his gun and put it in the glove box. He might have to pass through a metal detector at the shelter, but Parisa would be armed if they ran into trouble on their way to and from the shelter.

"It's warmer today," she commented, as they walked out of the garage. "With the sun out, it's almost easy to believe spring is not that far away."

"Only about three months," he said dryly. "But I'll take a nice day any time."

"Me, too. I'm a sunshine girl. I always feel better when the sun is out."

He smiled as she lifted her face to that same sun. "There's something to be said for a winter night with a blazing fire and a hot drink."

She smiled back at him. "Sure. That's nice, too. I guess you prefer the cold."

"I like living where the seasons change. Anything gets old after a while."

"Is that why you move around?"

"How do you know I move around?" he countered.

"Good point," she said dryly. "Let's talk about how we're going to approach Ben."

"This one is on me. It's a men's shelter. You won't be going in."

She frowned, not looking at all happy about that. "I don't think Ben will talk to you."

"He doesn't have to speak to me. I'll get him out of the shelter. Then you can work your magic."

"You think you can do that?"

"Wrangle one scared twenty-one-year-old out of a homeless shelter? Yeah, I think I can do that."

"I hope you can back up your confidence, Jared."

"I can."

She caught him by the arm as they neared the shelter. "Hold on one second."

"What's wrong?" he asked, noting a serious gleam in her eyes.

"I know you have your own questions for Ben, but that bomb went off weeks ago, and Jasmine is missing now. She has to take precedence over Paris. Promise me you'll bring Ben out, so we can get the information on Jasmine before you start interrogating him on the explosion."

"I already agreed that Jasmine is the priority."

"Good. I just wanted to make sure we're on the same page."

He glanced down the block, seeing throngs of homeless men gathered outside the shelter. "I don't like the idea of you hanging around the street. Why don't you get a drink in the restaurant next door, and I'll meet you there?"

"All right. Don't be long."

He waited until Parisa was in the restaurant before walking into the shelter.

A man sat behind a counter, tapping on a computer keyboard, while he spoke into the phone resting between his head and shoulder. He appeared to be in his forties and wore a T-shirt with an inspirational quote about finding salvation.

Jared waited until he finished with the call. Then he said, "I hope you can help me. I'm looking for my younger brother." He pulled out his phone. He'd been carrying around a photo of Ben for the past few weeks, and he showed it to the clerk. "His name is Ben, but I'm not sure what he's calling himself today. He's bipolar and suffers from depression. He asked me for help and told me to come down here. My family is really worried about him. I hope he's here."

The older man took a look at the picture. "Yeah, he's here. Came in this morning. Looked like he was coming off a big high, shaking and muttering to himself."

"He sometimes loses track of reality. He doesn't remember where he is or how he got there. Sometimes, he doesn't even remember my name. It breaks my heart."

"Yeah, I know how that goes. My dad is the same way. He's in the gym. I told him he could stay twenty-four hours, then we have to fill out paperwork. Empty your pockets before you walk through the metal detector."

He put his wallet and car keys in a small container and then walked through the detector. The man passed him his belongings, and he moved into the gym.

The large room was filled with cots placed about four feet apart. It was a sea of humanity and the stench was fairly overwhelming. There were probably thirty people in the room. He suspected all the beds would be full come nighttime.

Some of the men were sleeping, a couple of groups were playing cards on the floor between their cots, and a few were reading.

His gaze swept the room until he saw a solitary figure sitting cross-legged on a bed by the wall. He had earbuds on and was looking at his phone, as most kids his age did.

Ben had dark hair like his mother and wore jeans, and a hoodie sweatshirt with Everly stamped across it. Jared felt a wave of relief that Elizabeth had not warned Ben that they were coming.

Fortunately, there was no one particularly close to Ben, which would make conversation easier.

He sat down on the cot next to him and leaned forward. "Ben."

The kid's head jerked, and he pulled the headphones out of his ears, looking suddenly terrified.

"Don't move," he ordered, sensing that Ben was about to run. "Your mother sent me to get you."

"No, she didn't," Ben replied, but he looked a bit uncertain.

"She did. She said you need money and a place to stay. I'm going to provide both."

"Who are you?"

"That's not important. She also told me that you're involved in Jasmine's kidnapping."

Ben's eyes widened. "I can't believe she said that. She's lying. I didn't have anything to do with it. Jasmine was—is— my friend."

He wondered if the stumble meant Ben knew more than anyone else about Jasmine's current condition.

"Your mother is scared. You need to come with me."

Ben vehemently shook his head. "I'm not going anywhere with you. I don't know who you are."

"My name is Jared. We're going to get up and walk out the door. And then we'll go next door and order you some food."

Ben looked confused by his words. "What?"

"An old friend of yours will meet us there. She also wants to help you. Her name is Parisa Maxwell. She was with your mom when your mother called you. So was I."

"Parisa won't help me. She'll hate me for what I did."

"Being involved in Jasmine's kidnapping is hateful behavior, but there is a way out for you, Ben. You can help us get Jasmine back. That will counter whatever you did." A hopeful gleam entered Ben's eyes, and Jared played off it. "You know Parisa is well connected. Her stepfather is friends with the president. She can use her power for your benefit, but you have to help us find Jasmine."

"I didn't know they were going to take Jasmine, I swear."

He wanted to ask who Ben was talking about—if Sara and Isaac were involved. He wanted to ask Ben where he was when the Paris bomb went off, when April died. The questions were right there on the tip of his tongue. But he'd made Parisa a promise—Jasmine first; everything else had to wait.

"Let's go," he said, getting to his feet.

Ben was starting to sweat, and there was more than a little terror in his eyes. "I can't trust you."

"Ben, if I wanted you dead, you'd be dead. I'm trying to save your sorry life. So, get up. And if you feel like shouting for help, remember that I'm not the one you're hiding from, the one who is threatening to kill you. That person is still out there, and right now I'm standing between him and you."

Ben looked unconvinced.

"If you can't trust me, trust Parisa. She used to babysit you. She taught you how to play spades. Your father saved her life. I'm not lying. She's next door. And your mother did send us."

"All right." Ben shoved his phone and earbuds into his pocket, grabbed his duffel and walked out of the shelter. Jared kept as close to him as he could, without looking suspicious.

When they hit the street, he grabbed Ben's arm just in case he decided to bolt and hauled him into the fast-food restaurant next door.

Parisa was waiting in a booth, facing the door. There

were a dozen or so other people in the restaurant, but mostly families or men who looked like they'd come from the shelter next door. Relief filled her gaze when he shoved Ben into the seat across from her and then sat down next to him, so Ben was pinned in the booth.

"Ben," she said with relief. "What's going on? Tell me how you're involved in this."

"If I tell you, they'll kill me."

"I can protect you," Parisa said. "But you have to start talking now."

"I didn't know they were going to take Jasmine," Ben said. "I thought they just wanted the diamond."

"Who's they? Give me some names," she demanded.

Ben shifted as he looked around the restaurant. "Can you guys really protect me?"

"Jasmine's life is on the line, Ben," Parisa said. "You talk. I'll help. Do it now. Every second counts."

"I got into some trouble in Paris. I ran into a girl I used to know in Bezikstan, and we hooked up. I couldn't believe we were together again. I hadn't thought it would ever happen. But her stepbrother, he's not a good guy, and Sara told me that he was making her do things she didn't want to do."

"Like what?" Jared asked, unable to resist the question.

Parisa flashed him a quick look, then turned to Ben. "We'll get back to Paris, Ben. Let's talk about now. Was Jasmine taken by this group? Do you know where they're holding her?"

"Yes. They took her. I don't know where they are. All they wanted me to do was get two guys into the party. I just had to ask Jasmine to hire them as waitstaff. I told her they were friends of mine from Bezikstan and students at Everly, who needed to make some extra cash. I said I didn't know if they were really allowed to work because of their visa status, and she said as long as I vouched for them, she'd tell the kitchen manager to hire them for the party." Ben's gaze filled with anguish. "She trusted me."

"Have they been in touch with you since the kidnapping?" Parisa asked.

Ben shook his head. "No. And even though I don't know anything, I'm afraid they think I know too much."

Parisa tucked her hair behind her ear, her gaze intense as she looked across the table at Ben. "Who contacted you? Was it Sara? Her stepbrother? Someone else?"

"I don't know the person's name. The voice sounded like it was computer generated. He said they'd kill me and my family if I didn't do what they said. I was told that the waiters' names were Victor Salgetti and Ray Bateen, but I don't think those are their real names."

"Where would they stay here in New York?"

"I swear I don't know."

"But you know Sara is here, right?" Jared put in. "She arrived in New York Friday morning."

"No, she didn't. She couldn't get into the country. Everyone is looking for her."

"So, you know she's in hiding," Parisa said. "Where would she go if she came here? Does she have friends, family?"

"Her only family is her stepbrother. Everyone else is dead. But she's not here in the city. She can't be," Ben said in confusion.

"She is here. She used her roommate's passport, Melissa Holmes," Jared said.

"I don't know anything about that."

"Is Isaac here, too?"

"Maybe. Probably. I think he's the one who's setting me up. He knew I was connected to the Kumars, that I go to the consulate a lot. He has to be the one behind this."

"How did he use you, Ben?" Jared asked. "Is the group going to pin the Paris bombing on you?"

Ben's eyes widened. "What do you know about Paris?"

"Ben," Parisa said, drawing Ben's attention back to her. "We have to find Isaac. Did he talk about New York? Does he have friends here? Are there students at Everly involved in the group? We need a lead. It's the only way we're going to find Jasmine."

Ben drew in a breath and let it out. "The only place here that Isaac ever mentioned was a comedy club in Hell's Kitchen. It's called the Stone Cellar. He said his friend was a bartender there, so he used to get in for free. I don't know the guy's name."

"When did they contact you about getting the men into the party?" Parisa asked.

"On Tuesday, three days before the party. I told Jasmine not to wear the ring. I told her it was too much. She said Westley was insistent, that she had to wear it. I suggested she put it on for the announcement and then take it off right away." He paused. "Look, can you give me some money? Can you help me get out of town? I'm really scared, Parisa. I never meant for any of this to happen. You have to believe me. I love Jasmine."

"I love her, too," Parisa said. "And I'm terrified for her—and for you. I don't think you're safe, Ben. You're a loose end that needs to be tied up. I'm going to do you a favor. I'm going to make sure you're protected." She lifted her gaze and looked toward the door.

Jared was shocked by her action and quickly turned his head as three men came through the door, wearing dark suits and badges at their belts. *Parisa had called in the FBI.*

"You tricked me," Ben exclaimed, as the men surrounded their table.

Jared's mouth drew into a tight line, feeling the same sense of betrayal.

Parisa had called the feds while he was in the shelter. *What the hell had she been thinking?* They'd had an agreement—a plan. They would question Ben first, and then they would turn him over.

Clearly, Parisa had had a different plan.

"The safest place for you is in custody," Parisa said to

Ben as she slid out of the booth. She pulled her phone out of her pocket and handed it to the tall, dark-haired man with the blue eyes, who had driven her home from the hospital after the first attack, the same one who'd put her in the safe house, and probably the person she'd been in contact with the entire time.

"I recorded everything," Parisa told the agent. "He's all yours."

"Thanks," the man said shortly, giving him a sharp look.

Jared slid out of the booth, allowing the agents access to Ben.

Parisa gave him an apologetic look, but he wasn't interested in her apologies.

He'd made a big mistake playing this all her way. He'd let her get everything she needed before he'd gotten anything he needed. But it was too late to change that now.

He headed out the door, waiting outside until the agents brought Ben out and put him into a waiting black SUV.

Then he started down the street, needing to burn off the anger and frustration running through him.

Parisa had to jog to keep up with him, but he didn't give a damn.

"Jared, I had to do it," she said.

He stopped walking and glared at her. "You didn't have to do it right then. I wanted to talk to Ben about the explosion. You knew that."

"We agreed that Jasmine is the priority. And every minute counts. You can talk to Ben later."

"Oh, yeah, sure. The FBI won't have a problem letting me in to do that."

"I'll make it happen."

"You think I'm going to believe you now? I thought we were a team."

Anger flared in her eyes. "I didn't betray you, Jared. I didn't turn *you* in to the FBI."

"What basis would you have to do that?"

"Oh, I don't know—the fact that you snuck into the consulate party and followed me to an FBI safe house."

"Hardly crimes worthy of the FBI."

"The point is—I didn't sell you out."

"You did sell me out—on Ben. You don't think I couldn't have had my own conversation in the shelter? But I'd promised you that I would bring him out first. And I kept my promise. You did not."

"I wasn't looking at it that way. Jasmine is in danger. Everything else can wait."

He ran his hand through his hair and gave her a hard look. "Do you work for the FBI, Parisa?"

She stared back at him. "Yes. But I don't work here in New York. My job as a translator in the state department is my cover. I am fluent in many languages. I didn't lie about that."

"Well, that's great. I'm so glad you didn't lie about what languages you speak," he said sarcastically. "You have no idea what letting Ben slip out of our control could mean."

"Then maybe you should tell me. What agency do you work for?"

As he thought about whether or not he wanted to come clean about everything, he saw a white work van driving down the street in their direction. It seemed to be moving too slowly for the flow of traffic, and it would be directly across from them in seconds.

The driver's window came down. Something glinted in the sunshine.

"Gun," Parisa shouted, shoving him toward the door of a nearby boutique as a spray of bullets shattered the glass windows next to them.

Fifteen

———➤➤◄◄◄———

As screams followed the gunshots, he and Parisa ran through the shop, asking the startled clerk if there was a back door. She pointed toward the dressing rooms.

"Come with us." Parisa waved her arm frantically at the woman. "You need to get out of here."

The woman ran through the hallway, past the dressing rooms and pushed open the back door. They entered the alley, and the clerk looked around in panic.

"Go to the massage parlor," Jared said, spying a nearby door off the alley. "Tell them to lock the doors and call the police."

Parisa had her gun out, watching the door of the shop they'd just come through as well as the innocent woman running down the alley and into the massage parlor.

Once she was out of sight, they headed in the opposite direction.

They were a hundred yards away when a shot rang out. Parisa dashed behind a dumpster, and he followed. Then she peered around the container and fired off three shots, before ducking back down. He really wished he had his gun now.

A hail of gunfire followed, bouncing off the metal dumpster.

"There's at least two of them," she said, breathlessly.

He picked up a rock and broke the glass on the locked door next to them. Then he reached inside and opened it. "Let's go."

Parisa rose, taking two more shots to keep the gunmen away, and then ducked into the room after him. They appeared to be in a printing facility, which was dark and empty, for which Jared was extremely grateful. They ran past large printing machines, reams of paper, and boxes of supplies, before ending up in the front lobby.

They charged out the front door, setting off an alarm and ran down another crowded New York City sidewalk. They didn't talk, but they were in complete and utter sync, Parisa following his lead as he ducked in and out of stores and around corners. They ran for another fifteen minutes, taking a fire escape to the top of a building, before taking a brief rest on the roof.

He looked over the ledge at the street they'd just run through. From this vantage point, he could see everything, and after five minutes, he started to breathe a little easier. "I think we lost them."

Parisa was also studying the street below, and she slowly nodded. "We're about six blocks away from the garage where we parked the car. Do you think they followed us from there or from the Langdons' apartment?"

He shook his head. "No. I think they followed the feds to the restaurant after you called your pals."

A startled light ran through her eye.

"That clearly didn't occur to you," he said.

"No," she muttered, sinking down on the ground beneath the ledge.

It was then he realized there was blood on her neck. "Were you hit?" He squatted next to her. "You're bleeding."

She put a hand to the side of her neck and winced. "I think it's glass from the window."

"Let me see." He gently lifted her hair out of the way and saw a sliver of glass sticking out of a bloody patch of skin on her neck. "I think I can get it," he said, pulling the glass out as gently as he could. "We need to get you to a doctor."

"Too risky."

"There could be more glass in there. It could get infected."

"We'll pick up some antibiotic ointment when we get the car."

She was tough—that was for sure. And why wouldn't she be? She was an FBI agent. That fact was still sinking into his brain.

"All right." He knew as well as she did that a hospital or urgent care visit would become public record, and Parisa needed to stay off the grid.

He stood up and took another look at the street below. There was no sign of the van, and no men moving through the crowded block of tourists and shoppers. "I don't see anyone."

"Is your car registered to you? Can they trace it? Because I gave your name to the FBI. They know we're together, and if the attacks are coming from the bureau, they could trace me through you."

"The car was rented by George Carmichael. He has a Brooklyn address."

She stared back at him, and he could see the questions in her eyes, but all she said was, "Okay."

"Let's go back to the garage," he said. "We need wheels, and I really don't believe we were followed to the parking structure. If we had been, they would have taken us out there. The drive-by came after you called the bureau in."

"I can't believe that my own agency is trying to kill me."

"It's certainly not an ideal situation," he said dryly. "Come on." He got to his feet and extended his hand.

She reluctantly took it, even as she said, "I can stand up

on my own."

"I know you're a badass, Parisa. I just had a front-row seat to your skills. But, just so you know, we're still not even. I saved your life twice. You only saved mine once. And I saw the gun the same time you did; you just yelled first."

"It still counts as my save. I just hope neither one of us has to do it again," she murmured, as they headed back down the fire escape.

It was a nice thought, but he didn't believe it for a second.

They took a circuitous route to the car, finding it exactly where they'd left it. There was absolutely no one around, with only two other cars on the parking level, and both appeared to be empty. After another minute of assessment, they approached the vehicle. By force of habit, he checked around the car, including the undercarriage, before opening the door and getting behind the wheel.

Parisa put on her seat belt, wincing as it hit her neck.

"We'll take care of that soon," he said, hitting the gas. "Right now, we need to get somewhere else." He drove out of the garage and away from the convention center, making his way onto Riverside Drive, then heading over the George Washington Bridge into New Jersey.

He made a quick stop at a drugstore for first-aid supplies, then drove past Fort Lee, and into the Palisades Interstate Park, where he found a parking spot near the Hudson River. From here, they had a great view of Manhattan, but he wasn't as interested in the cityscape as he was in taking care of Parisa.

He pulled antiseptic and bandages out of the bag as well as a pair of tweezers and a small flashlight.

"You're prepared," she said. "Quite the boy scout."

"I want to make sure all the glass is gone." He turned the light on her wound, happy to see that the bleeding had mostly stopped and that the cuts didn't appear to be big enough to need stitches. "Does it feel like anything is still in there?"

"Not really. It's much better since you got the glass out."

He leaned in close to her, trying not to be distracted by her sweet breath on his cheek, the curve of her neck, the silky texture of her hair as some of it brushed against his forehead. He saw one tiny little sliver of glass and he gently pulled it free with the tweezers. Everything else looked good. "This next part is going to sting."

"I can take it."

He dabbed her wound with a cotton-soaked antiseptic pad, hearing her swift intake of breath as he did so. But she remained perfectly still as he finished cleaning the cut and then put a large Band-Aid over the area. "You're good," he said, sitting back in his seat. "You might have a little scar."

"I can live with that. Thanks." Her gaze grew troubled as it met his. "I need to apologize to you, Jared."

"I'm not stopping you."

"I shouldn't have called the bureau without telling you first, without giving you a chance to interrogate Ben. To be perfectly candid, I wasn't thinking about you when I called Damon; I was only concerned about Jasmine. I didn't believe there was any way you and I were going to chase down the kidnappers without more help. It seemed irresponsible and dangerous to keep the information about Ben to ourselves."

"All I needed was ten more minutes."

"Maybe Jasmine needed those ten minutes more."

He hated that she had a point. "So, who's the guy you called?"

"Special Agent Damon Wolfe. He's not just a fellow agent; he's a friend. I went to Quantico with him. I trust him completely."

"Even though he took you to the safe house where you were attacked?"

"Yes. He felt sick about that."

He shook his head at her stubborn belief in her friend. "He's the most likely person to have betrayed you, Parisa. Look what just happened."

"I know Damon. He wouldn't do that. There's another leak at the bureau. But that doesn't matter now. We need to figure out what's next."

"What's next?" he asked in surprise. "You gave away our best lead. There's no *next.*"

"I don't believe that's true. We can check out the Stone Cellar—where Isaac Naru's friend works."

"I'm sure he'll run as soon as the feds show up, and they're probably already there. You gave Damon your phone with the information Ben gave us about the Cellar."

"Then they'll get him, and hopefully he'll be able to tell them where Isaac is."

"Let's hope so. Because there's no guarantee Ben will talk to the agents. It was different with you. He thought you would protect him. Now, he knows you won't."

"That's true, but I still think I made the right move, Jared. I'm sorry I didn't tell you first. But the bureau will be in a better position to track the calls to Ben's cell phone and determine who contacted him. Ben is the best connection to the kidnappers we have, and maybe the only person who can help find Jasmine before it's too late."

"Let's just hope the mole at your agency doesn't get to Ben before that can happen."

She stared back at him. "Damn."

"Yeah," he said, seeing the realization spread through her eyes.

"I need your phone. I have to tell Damon what just happened to us."

He reached into the bag and pulled out a prepaid phone. "I got you a new one in the drugstore." As she reached for it, he pulled it away. "On one condition—you make this call on speaker."

"Fine." She took the phone and punched in a number.

A male voice answered a moment later with a simple, brisk hello.

"Damon, it's me, Parisa. We have a problem. I was shot

at after we left the restaurant."

"What? Are you serious? Are you all right?"

"Yes. There were two gunmen. They were in a white work van. I didn't get the license plate number." Parisa paused, glancing over at him.

He shook his head, wishing he had gotten a number or even a good view of the gunmen. All he'd noticed were two men in jeans and hoodies, probably thirties, but who knew?

"They chased us, but we were able to lose them," Parisa said.

"By we, I assume you're still with your mystery man."

"Yes. Look, Damon, someone at the bureau sent the gunmen to the restaurant to take me out. There's no other way they would have found me. There's a mole."

Damon blew out an angry breath. "I can't believe this."

"You need to protect Ben. If they're working this hard to shut me up, they'll be even more determined to make sure Ben doesn't talk."

"I understand," Damon said in clipped tones.

"Did you get any more information from Ben?"

"No. He asked for a lawyer as soon as we put him in the car. His parents showed up at the office a few minutes ago. They're advising him not to speak to us. We're going to bring the Kumars down and see if they can talk their good friends into taking another position. We also sent a team to the Stone Cellar, but we couldn't locate anyone who admitted a friendship with Isaac Naru. The owner told us one of the bartenders has been sick this week—Colin Jansen. That name familiar?"

"No."

"We'll track him down. The cops are going to sit on the Cellar and see if anyone of interest shows up there."

"Good."

"I need to get back to Ben. Are you going to have this number for a while?"

"I don't know. I'll check in with you in a few hours. You

need to get Ben to talk about the Paris bombing, too. The events are probably connected." She paused, mouthing the word *Sara* in Jared's direction, a question in her eyes.

He gave her the go-ahead nod.

"There's something else," she said. "Sara Pillai is in New York. She came into the country under a fake ID, name of Melissa Holmes. She arrived on Friday morning at JFK. No trace of her since then. I'm guessing her stepbrother Isaac is here, too.

"You have better resources than I do," Damon said grimly.

She didn't comment on that. "Is Vincent still hanging around?"

"He has been here all day."

"Did he know you were meeting me?"

"Yes. I'd like to keep him out of this, but he and Director Hunt are good friends, and I can't go to the deputy director without proof of something."

"I know. Just make sure Ben stays alive long enough to talk."

"You stay alive, too. Take care of yourself, Parisa."

"Thanks."

"Who's Vincent?" Jared asked, as she set down the phone.

"That's a long story."

"At the moment, we've got nothing but time, so start talking."

Sixteen

Parisa drew in a breath, knowing that she needed to tell Jared everything, not just because he was in danger, too, but because he might be able to help her figure things out. He could be more objective, bring a new perspective.

"Vincent Rowland is Westley's godfather," she said. "He was at the party. I actually spoke to him right after I first caught you staring at me. You probably saw him."

"Sure. I remember him—older man, gray hair, looked like he was someone familiar with money and power." Jared's gaze narrowed. "Why did you ask Damon if he was hanging around the FBI offices?"

"Because he's former FBI. He was an agent for over twenty years, one of the best. His son, Jamie, was in my training group at Quantico. The first week, they put us in teams of six. We did all of our training assignments together. We interviewed each other, analyzed each other, put ourselves through lie detector tests, stripped ourselves bare of our secrets, and became really, really close. But a few weeks before graduation, we were on a training mission, a hostage situation in a high-rise building. During the extraction of the hostages, Jamie fell and died. No one really knew what happened. Jamie was out of sight from all of us when he fell. In the end, the investigators determined that it was human error. Vincent was not happy with that conclusion, but there was a very thorough review of every detail. And Jamie was known for taking risks. He was fearless and probably a little overconfident. But he shouldn't have died. I know we've all felt guilty and wondered if we could have done something differently."

"I'm sorry, Parisa," Jared said quietly.

"It was tragic."

"So, why are you suspicious of his father now?"

"Vincent has kept in touch with all of us since Jamie's death, having us over for a memorial celebration every single year for the last four years. We thought it was because we were the last links to his son. But at the most recent celebration, I thought Vincent was acting strangely. He seemed more obsessed with the details of the accident than ever before. He kept asking me questions about it. And I started to feel really uncomfortable. I didn't think much about it after I left, but in the past year things have been happening to our remaining group of five that we can't quite explain. Three of my friends have had to run for their lives, and during each situation, there has been some problem at the bureau, some leak, some information disseminated that should have been kept secret. It's nothing particularly noticeable. There's usually a way to rationalize it. But some of my former classmates are starting to think that Vincent might be responsible, that he might be trying to get back at us by messing up our assignments."

"That sounds a little out there," he commented.

"I thought so, too, but when you look at the pattern of what's going on, it starts to make more sense. Anyway, when I saw him at the party, I was surprised. But then he explained he's Westley's godfather, and it made perfect sense that he would be there."

"But now you're wondering if he's the one leaking your whereabouts at every turn."

"He doesn't work at the bureau, but he has a lot of friends in the New York field office who do work there, including Deputy Director Peter Hunt. As Westley's godfather, it's not surprising to anyone that Vincent would be spending time in the office trying to help with the investigation. But it does make me wonder."

"Okay. What about Damon Wolfe? What's his story?"

"Damon was in my Quantico group. He's part of the original six, and I trust him completely. He's not selling me out. He had his own problems with the bureau less than a year ago. He almost died. After his case was resolved, they cleaned house in the New York office, but maybe a new mole has sprung up or has been there all along."

"Let's say you're right. Vincent is looking to get some sort of payback where you're concerned. When did he put his plan into motion?"

"What do you mean?"

"Before or after the attack at the consulate? Was Vincent behind your invitation to the party? If he was, that would mean he knew the kidnapping was coming."

"That's interesting. Maybe he did want me at the party. Maybe he set that up." She considered that scenario for a second. "It would tie in with the fact that I never asked for an invitation, but the family thought I did. But how would he have known I'd go upstairs with Jasmine? Unless, he's the one who told Jasmine I wanted to talk to her privately. That actually makes sense, too. But what doesn't make sense is Vincent's motivation to hurt his godson. I can't see why he'd pick Westley's engagement party to get revenge on me."

"I can't, either. Unless we're completely off base on who is behind the kidnapping. We've been focused in on Bezikstan and the rebel group that was involved in Paris."

"Because of Ben's involvement," she pointed out. "He's

the link."

"But that diamond would be worth a lot to many people. Even Anika had a theory about Westley wanting the diamond," he reminded her.

"True. And Vincent probably has connections who would be able to help him unload it," she said slowly, pondering that possibility. "Vincent and Westley could have been working together to steal the diamond. Westley could have convinced Hutchinson to hire the shady security company."

"Or Westley could have told Hutchinson to ask Vincent who to hire. With Rowland's FBI connections, that might have made sense."

"But those guards died because of those toxic fumes. Would Vincent kill other people to get to me?"

"Maybe you were just the icing on the cake. He might have been willing to kill to get his hands on a fifty-million-dollar diamond, and getting you involved was just a bonus."

"And the fumes might not have been meant to be that deadly." She paused. "Vincent did speak to me about the value of the diamond at the party. He also mentioned the curse, which is fairly irrelevant, although I suppose people might think the diamond is cursed after what happened to Jasmine." She glanced at Jared. "But let's back up and say that Vincent had nothing to do with the theft. How else could he be involved?"

"Well, getting back at you could simply be a crime of opportunity. Vincent figured you were already a target, because you were the only witness to the kidnapping. If you died, everyone would assume the kidnappers had taken you out. But that assumes the fact that Vincent wants to kill you. It seems that your other friends are very much still alive, no matter what else they've gone through."

"Which is why we don't know what's going on. Are we that good at surviving, or is Vincent that bad at killing us? Or is there some other plan in the works, and this is all just a warmup, a form of personal torment?" She sighed. "I don't think I can come up with an answer with the facts I currently have."

"Probably not."

"And I'm more concerned about Jasmine than myself. I'm also worried about you. Today, you were clearly seen with me, Jared. And I did give your name to Damon when I first spoke to him yesterday, which seems like a million years ago now. He ran your name through our database; there's a record of that. Because of me, you're probably not as invisible as you thought you were."

He shrugged. "I'm not concerned about that."

"You should be. You could have been shot today."

"But I wasn't."

"They'll try again."

"We'll be ready."

"Does that mean we're still partners?" she asked, happy to see that his earlier anger had dissipated.

He frowned as he turned his gaze back on her. "I don't like what you did, Parisa. We were working together, and you went behind my back. How can I trust you?"

"It was an impulsive decision, Jared. When I was waiting in the restaurant, I started thinking about how much needed to be done, how many boots were required on the ground, how many people might need to be investigated, places to be searched, and how little time there was before the ransom payoff. That overrode everything. All I could think about was that I didn't want Jasmine to die."

"People died in Paris, too."

"I know that," she said, noting the depth of emotion in his voice. "But Jasmine is in danger now. And you know how critical it is to find her as soon as possible." She tilted her head, giving him a long look. "I told you who I am, Jared. Now, you need to tell me who you are. Let's put all our cards on the table. No more secrets. Who do you work for?"

He gave her a long, hard look and then he said, "CIA."

She let out a breath, a little surprised he'd actually told

her, but not really shocked he was CIA. "So, you're a spy."

"I prefer operative."

"Were you in Paris at the time of the explosion?"

"Yes."

"When did you come back to New York?"

"Two weeks ago. When I realized Ben might be involved, I followed him back here."

"So, your apartment is really new."

"I rented it furnished."

"Why are you working alone, Jared? Or are you working alone? What is the CIA's involvement in this?"

"The agency is not involved in the investigation into Jasmine's kidnapping, unless someone on some level is working with the bureau, providing information on Bezikstan radical groups. But that person is not me."

"But the CIA is looking into Paris."

He hesitated. "Yes, but not with as much intensity as I would like."

He was answering her questions, but he still wasn't giving her much. As she studied the shadows in his light-green eyes, it all clicked in to place. "You knew one of the Paris victims, didn't you?"

"Yes."

"Why didn't you tell me that before?"

"Because you didn't need to know."

"You're not going to give me that CIA bullshit, are you?" ·

"It's true. You didn't need to know."

"Well, I do now. Who died in Paris? Was it a friend, a girlfriend, a relative?"

"It was a coworker, a fellow operative. Her name was April." He turned away from her, staring out the front window, as he tapped his fingers restlessly on the steering wheel.

"You and April were working a case in Paris?"

"It actually started in London."

"Tell me about it."

"We started tracking the Brothers of the Earth after they took credit for a bombing on the outskirts of London, at a concert venue."

"I remember that."

"That's when Isaac Naru came up on our radar, and his stepsister, Sara. Sara traveled to Paris, and April thought she was our best shot at getting someone with access to the inner circle, so April followed Sara to France. I was still working on the London angle, so we split up for a time."

"Did April make contact with Sara?"

"Yes. April got a job at the Café Douceur where Sara worked. She and Sara hit it off right away. But then Sara got a visit from an old friend and was suddenly caught up in a love affair with a former boyfriend from Bezikstan—Ben Langdon. April took a wait-and-see approach, wondering if Ben was also part of the group. But as the days passed, April began to wonder if Sara would be of any use at all. She and Ben just seemed to be having a romance. Sara wasn't meeting with Isaac or doing anything that tied her to the radical group. April told me she was about to call it and come back to London."

"What changed?"

"Isaac showed up in Paris. April met him at the café. He was friendly, flirty. She decided to make a play for him. While the group only allows men to be official members, there are lots of women around to support the men."

"I'm assuming it worked. She caught Isaac's interest."

"Yes. She went out with him several times. One night she heard Isaac talking to someone in Hindi about an opportunity to stop time, which is what they claim their bombings are about—to stop time and make everyone realize that there is only one right way." He paused. "April knew she was getting closer to some valuable information, so she turned up her romance with Isaac. She was thrilled when he wanted to introduce her to some of his friends, who had recently arrived from London. He thought she would like them and appreciate their values."

She drew in a breath, knowing where his story was going. April had been acting just like she would have acted in a similar situation. April had been trying to get inside the circle, so she could bring down the terror group. "What happened?"

"She told me to come to Paris—that the London group I'd been following was already there. I had one more meeting with a friend working for British intelligence, so I didn't leave right away."

Parisa was beginning to realize that Jared's motivation probably came from guilt as well as a lot of other emotions.

"The next day, April texted me, saying that the group was taking orders from someone else, and that person was either in Bezikstan or the US; she wasn't sure. She had a hunch, but she had some questions to ask Isaac. They were going to meet at the café that afternoon. I was supposed to be there, too. But I ran late. I was half a block away when the bomb went off."

Her pulse jumped. "Oh, my God. You saw it happen." She put her hand on his leg, feeling the need to touch him, to comfort him in some small way. "I am so sorry, Jared."

"I found April. There was so much blood..." He drew in a breath. "Her eyes were open, but she was shaking all over. I knew she wasn't going to make it. She told me to tell her parents that she loved them, and that she'd been happy in Paris, doing exactly what she wanted to do."

"I told them she could tell them herself, that she was going to be all right. I lied to her."

"You were trying to be comforting."

"I could have used that time to ask her what she'd found out, but I didn't. I probably had two minutes to get a name or two. Instead, I told her to imagine going to her favorite place—which was Yosemite. She was an avid rock climber. This dreamy expression came into her eyes, and it was the last thing I saw."

"You gave her some peace."

"I should have gotten the information."

"She might not have had a name. It seems to me that April was the kind of woman who would have made sure you had a lead if she had one."

"I don't know. I think she was just too far gone."

"Who else died at the café?"

"The manager. The bomb went off in the kitchen area. Some guests were injured, but they survived. And as I mentioned before, Sara called in sick that day. She had to have known what was going to happen."

"You think April was the target?"

"Yes. I believe that Isaac made her as CIA or something, and he decided to stop time and stop her with one fatal blow."

She stared into his eyes, seeing the pain and the anger. "I hope I'm not being insensitive, but I just want to know the whole story. Were you and April in love? Were you involved?"

"No. We were friends and partners. We had worked a lot of missions together. We'd saved each other's life. We'd had each other's back. But it was always about the job for us. April was in love with a guy back home—where she grew up in Montana. He was a rancher, a homebody. She'd had a chance with him, but she'd chosen the CIA instead. She'd wanted to see the world. But there was a part of her that thought that one day she'd go home and marry him and have babies."

"She thought he'd wait for her?"

"I don't know if she really believed it, or if it was just a story she told herself." He paused, gathering his thoughts for a moment. "I cared a lot about April, and I want to get justice for her. I also want to stop the Brothers of the Earth from blowing anyone else up. It's what she wanted more than anything, and the best thing I can do for her is to make that happen."

She nodded. "I get it, Jared. April sounds like an amazing

person."

"She was tenacious. Sometimes she got tunnel vision—a little like you."

"I can be guilty of that."

"It's not the worst trait in the world," he said with a sad smile.

"You didn't let April down, Jared."

"I didn't say I did."

"But that's what you think." She could see the shadowy truth in his eyes. "You blame yourself for not getting to Paris sooner, for letting her get in too deep without backup. But clearly you had a target that you were working in London. And she was a skilled operative. Right?"

"She'd actually been at the agency two years longer than I had."

"There you go. She knew what she was doing. She knew the risks."

"She was good undercover. I don't know how Isaac figured out she was an agent. But I do know I'm going to bring him and his band of brothers down."

"Maybe a sister, too," she said lightly.

"Oh, yeah, Sara is also on my hit list, and if Ben belongs there, too…"

He didn't have to finish his statement. "Then he should also be punished," she agreed. "I know his father saved my life, and I let Elizabeth believe that I would let that debt guide my actions, but I have my priorities straight."

"Glad to hear it."

"Thanks for telling me about April. It must be incredibly difficult for you to have lost two people you loved in terrorist attacks."

"I have to admit that the explosion in Paris set off a lot of triggers for me. But all of it just makes me more determined to do what I can to prevent other people from having to live through those moments."

"Okay, but why does it feel like you're acting alone,

Jared? Or is that just my impression? Does the agency want you to work me? Do they think I'm the one who will lead you to Isaac and Sara? Because of my ties to Bezikstan?"

"No. The agency put me on leave for ninety days. After Paris, I got a little heated with one of the deputy directors."

She raised an eyebrow. "What did you do?"

"Slugged him. He had it coming. He prevented me from following a lead that might have gotten me to Isaac before he disappeared."

"Why would he do that?"

"Because unbeknownst to me and April, the agency had had an asset in Brothers of the Earth for months, and the company wanted to protect that asset."

"Who is the asset?"

"Apparently, I don't need to know. I was shut out of the investigation, told to take a mandatory leave and get my head together."

"But you're working with someone."

"A longtime friend here in New York. He's feeding me what information he can without completely jeopardizing his job. But after what happened today, it's possible the agency is going to find out what I've been doing."

"Could you lose your job?"

"Possibly. But if I can bring down the group, I'll take the win and leave."

"You're putting everything on the line."

"That's the only way I know how to work."

She completely understood that. She was exactly the same way. "Leave everything on the field, right?"

He smiled. "Go big or go home. I'm sure your competitive drive would appreciate that."

"Yes. And I'd do the same thing if someone I cared about had died. I'd want what you want—justice. So, are we still working together?"

"Until you pull the rug out from under me again."

"I won't do that. And I trust you won't, either."

He tipped his head. "Deal. Now, I have a very important question for you, Parisa."

"What's that?" she asked warily.

"Do you like tacos?"

"Does anyone not like tacos?" she countered.

"I'll take that as a yes. There's an amazing food truck stop just up the road, and one of those trucks has the best tacos you will ever eat."

"I'm in."

"Why don't we both turn off our phones? I don't think anyone is tracking us through them, but just to be sure…"

"Done," she said, pulling out her phone. "It's just you and me, Jared."

"Let's try to keep it that way."

Seventeen

—➤➤➤◀◀◀◀—

Jared didn't know if he could trust Parisa. In fact, all evidence pointed to the fact that he *shouldn't* trust her. But in spite of what had happened earlier, he found himself unable to pull away from her, especially since he'd just spilled his guts about everything.

She might get him killed, or, at the very least, make it impossible for him to reach his objective, but for now he was going to keep her close. He wanted to believe he was making that decision because she could still be useful to him, but that didn't begin to touch on the real reason.

The truth was he liked her, respected her, connected with her. Maybe it was because they were in the same line of work, or maybe it was just because she was interesting, attractive, intelligent, and challenging. He liked her competitive fire, her drive to win, but also the fact that she balanced all that out with caring and kindness.

He'd seen the way she'd talked to Ben, handling her emotions while she did the job she needed to do. And he'd seen the way she'd reacted to his story about April, showing compassion and empathy for a woman she'd never met, but a woman she probably would have liked a lot.

They'd only known each other a few days, and they'd only shared their secrets five minutes earlier, but he felt like he'd known her for years.

It was a dangerous feeling, one he wasn't at all comfortable with. In his line of work, there were always too many secrets, too many lies. The call of duty could come at any moment. So, he'd kept his relationships light and easy, with women who didn't want more.

Frowning, he didn't know why he was thinking about Parisa and a relationship at the same time. They were agents from rival agencies. They were working a case. They were not having a romance.

Except that there was something simmering between them, something they'd been dancing around since that first look, something that had taken on new life with their impulsive kiss the day before.

But that *something* needed to stay on the back burner.

He doubted he'd have trouble convincing Parisa of that fact. She had her priorities straight. *Find Jasmine. That was all that mattered.*

And he did want to find Jasmine, but he also wanted to find April's killers. It was beginning to look like they might be one and the same, which would make it easier. Neither he nor Parisa would have to choose their target over the other. At least, that's the way he hoped it worked out.

Maybe Ben would tell the FBI something that would be useful, and since Parisa was an agent and had Damon Wolfe as her inside eyes and ears, they would be able to stay in the loop.

But for now, he was going to put all that on hold. His stomach was rumbling, and he always thought better when he wasn't hungry.

Concentrating on the road, he drove down the Palisades Interstate Highway until he got to another river park and headed into the parking lot, where the taco truck was one of six trucks serving up food.

It was two o'clock on Sunday afternoon, past the lunch hour, but there were still plenty of people buying food. After ordering an assortment of tacos, they sat down at a picnic table with their food and two cold beers. The sun was still bright, the air warming to the mid-fifties.

He faced the parking lot, giving Parisa the view of Manhattan on the other side of the river. He wanted to make sure he was ready in case someone found them again. He felt confident that they hadn't had a tail on their way out of the city, but he didn't want to underestimate whoever was after Parisa.

The tacos were just as good as he remembered. They'd opted for fish, chicken, and beef, and he couldn't help smiling as Parisa worked her way quickly through two of them. She ate almost as fast as he did, something else they had in common.

She gave him a pointed look. "You're staring at me."

"Appreciating your enthusiasm," he said, thinking that wasn't all he was appreciating. The pink in her sweater brought out her eyes and her smile made him feel warm all over.

"I'm always enthusiastic about food," she said with a more relaxed expression than she'd had earlier. The tacos were clearly doing the trick at easing her tension.

"Me, too," he admitted.

She finished her last bite and took a long swig of beer. "I don't love beer, but today it tastes exactly right. This was the perfect choice, Jared."

"I'm glad it didn't disappoint."

"Have you been here before?"

"Many times, especially when I was in high school."

"It's been around that long?"

"I'm not that old."

She laughed. "You're at least on the other side of thirty."

"By a few years. You?"

"A little less than a few. But the fact that you might be a tad older does not make you wiser."

"You think you're smarter than me?" he challenged, resting his forearms on the table.

"I'd say I'm as smart."

"Is that really what you want to say?" he teased.

She laughed. "No, but I'm sticking with it. And you're getting to know me a little too well."

"Playing cards with you made some facts inescapable." He paused, wanting to know even more about her. "When did you decide to join the FBI?"

"When they asked me. It wasn't even on my radar. I'd always planned to work for the state department as my stepfather did, and I was working as a translator in DC when the FBI recruited me. I was intrigued by their offer. I was a little bored just translating and transcribing. I wanted to make a difference in a bigger way. And, as we've just discussed, I have a competitive drive and a thirst for achievement. I like pressure and big moments. I like putting it all on the line for the greater good. And the FBI gave me a chance to do that, so I signed on." She paused, giving him a knowing glance. "You like that, too."

"Adrenaline can be addicting," he agreed. "How long have you been an agent?"

"A little over four years."

"Has the bloom worn off the rose?"

"That happened awhile ago, but I've enjoyed my different assignments."

"What were you doing in San Francisco?"

"Classified."

He tipped his head. "Got it. What about your family? Do they know you're an agent?"

"No. My stepfather would handle it well, but my mom would just worry about me, and I don't see the point of putting her through that. They are thrilled that I get to travel as a translator and don't ask too many questions. Sometimes I think Harry knows, but he hasn't said anything."

"What about extended family? Do you have any?"

"Harry has a sister and a brother-in-law and a couple of kids who are older than me. They live in various parts of Connecticut. They are all married with children. But we see them on some holidays. On my mom's side, my grandfather went back to India a long time ago, and I don't even know him. I think my mother speaks to him occasionally, but probably no more than once a year, if that. There's still bitterness between them, because she felt like he abandoned us, which he did."

"I can see why she'd feel that way—why you'd feel that way, too."

"Their estrangement made it more difficult for me to relate to that side of my family. My grandfather has some siblings in India, and they also have children, but I've never met any of them. As for my biological dad's family, I haven't seen him or them since I was three years old. I'm connected by blood to a lot of people I've never met. It's strange. But I've learned over the years that family is really the people in your life you can count on—at least for me." She took another sip of beer. "Now, it's your turn, Jared. What's your story? How did you come to be in the CIA? Was it because of 9/11?"

"Yes. Before that, I wanted to be a basketball player or a sports writer or maybe work in film."

"Okay—those are all different choices."

"The sky was the limit, until I realized it wasn't. After 9/11, everything in my life changed. Things I thought were important were meaningless. Every problem I'd ever had seemed incredibly trivial. I knew I had to do something that would honor my mother's death and make her proud. I wanted to stop the terrorists before they got to US soil. The CIA, with its global perspective, seemed the best place to do that."

"Do you still think so?"

"I don't know," he admitted. "There are a lot more politics than I ever expected and so many gray areas. The best way for the agency to get intel is to work with people who are doing terrible things and try to turn them. I sometimes have a problem with who we're protecting and at what cost."

"Like the asset in Brothers of the Earth."

He nodded. "Exactly. I don't know who that person is, because it's above my pay grade. But I do know that they're still alive, still working with the terrorists, while April is dead. I understand it on a purely logical, strategic level, but…"

"But your heart hurts," she said simply, meeting his gaze.

"Yeah, it does. I can't stop wondering if the asset knew that April was being targeted, and if they stayed quiet, if they let her die."

"And no one will tell you that?"

"I don't have a need to know."

"That's a popular phrase at the agency."

"Too popular and used to conceal more than it should."

"Didn't anyone else go to bat for you, Jared? There must be other people at the CIA who would want to see April get justice."

"As I said, I made a few mistakes after April died, and that shut down my pipeline of information. Besides slugging a deputy director, my boss is afraid I'm too personally invested. She thinks that will lead to mistakes. She assures me that everything that needs to be done is being done."

"But you don't believe her."

"No. I think they'll sacrifice justice for April to get more intel from the asset."

"Maybe that's not a horrible thing," she said slowly.

He frowned. "Really? You don't think that's a horrible thing?"

"I'm just wondering if the justice can come later—if preventing future attacks isn't the more important goal. And I think you've wondered the same thing."

He shrugged, not wanting to admit that. "Here's what I think—we can get justice and take down the group at the same time. We can go on offense, instead of continuing to play catch-up, to work some asset, who clearly couldn't prevent what happened at the Café Douceur or chose not to."

"Do you think there's a sympathizer in the CIA who is protecting this asset for another reason?"

"I can't rule it out."

"Well, I hope you can achieve your goals, Jared, but let's face it, it's a big ask. This terrorist group is spread across a couple of continents. Tearing down the entire organization is going to take a lot of manpower."

"Right now, I just want to take down Isaac and Sara, and I'm betting Isaac is in the city, too. I also think they're connected to Jasmine and the diamond. It's all part of a big play for a tremendous windfall. And you know what they're going to do with all that cash—wreak havoc on the world."

"You're starting to kill the glow of my taco happiness," she murmured.

"Sorry."

She rested her arms on the table and gazed into his eyes. "What are we going to do now, Jared?"

"I honestly don't know. Do you have any ideas?"

"We could go back to the Kumars. They should be happy to see me again. I'm sure they've been notified of Ben's involvement by now, and the fact that I found him and turned him over to the bureau would put me in a heroic light."

"True, but I'm not sure what there is to gain by talking to the Kumars. They're not going to know anything until tomorrow at ten when the ransom is supposed to be paid."

"There has to be something we can do. I can't just do nothing."

"I'm not thrilled with the idea, either. Hopefully, your pal Damon will come up with some good information."

"I should turn my phone back on in case he tries to reach me."

He pulled out his phone and turned it on as well. He didn't believe anyone was tracking their burner phones, but it would probably be better if they picked up a new set after they left their current location.

"No missed calls or texts," Parisa said. "He's probably tied up with Ben's interrogation."

He didn't have any calls from Gary, either. "I don't think we should go back to the apartment."

"I don't, either. Why don't we find a hotel on this side of the river and regroup?" she suggested.

"I have a better idea."

"What's that?"

"You'll see," he said, getting to his feet.

"I thought we were done with secrets," she complained.

"This is just a small one." And one he hoped he wouldn't regret. "If you don't like it when we get there, we can go somewhere else. But I need to clear my head, and I know the perfect way to do it."

As they got into the car, he sent a quick text. Then he turned off his phone.

Eighteen

---⟫⟫⟪⟪---

On the way to wherever Jared was taking her, they stopped to pick up two new prepaid phones and tossed the ones they'd been using previously into a dumpster behind a restaurant. She knew Jared had another phone that he seemed determined to hang on to, but he'd turned it off, so hopefully it was untraceable. She had to trust that a spook knew how to stay off the radar.

As Jared headed toward Upstate New York, she became increasingly more curious as to where they were going, but she had to admit the quieter highways, the thick canopies of trees, the houses set back from the street, and the landscape dotted with horses and barns and long driveways made her feel calmer. She liked Manhattan with its energy and pace, the amazing food, art museums, and plays. But this more rural part of New York also had an appeal. They weren't that far from the city, but it felt like they were in another world.

Jared turned off the highway and entered a narrow lane that wound past a couple of houses, ending in a circular drive in front of a two-story house, with a big, rambling porch.

There was lots of open space around the home, including a border of trees that created a wall of privacy, and a creek that meandered across the property.

As she stepped out onto the loose-pebbled drive, she said, "Whose place is this? And if you tell me it's a safe house, I'm going to have to suggest to the bureau that they step up their game."

He smiled. "It's not a safe house. It's the home my family moved into after 9/11."

"What? Wait a second. You're bringing me to your dad's house?" She was more than a little surprised.

"He's not here. He lives in Hawaii now. I bought the house from him three years ago, and I put it in a trust that cannot be traced to me."

"Not even by a rogue FBI agent?"

"Nothing is foolproof, but this place is as close to that as you can get. Let's go inside."

She followed him up the steps and into the house.

"It's a bit musty," he said, as they stepped into the entry.

The small foyer had dark hardwood floors and a staircase leading up to the second floor. Off to the right was a wood-paneled living room. On the other side of the hall was a dining room, and she presumed there was at least a kitchen and maybe a bath on this floor.

Jared walked into the living room, pulling dustcovers off the couches and chairs. The style of décor was more rustic farmhouse than the modern contemporary pieces he had in his Manhattan apartment.

"My dad left his furniture behind when he moved," Jared said. "At some point, I probably need to pick up some new pieces."

She walked into the room, pausing by a series of photographs on the wall. She felt a tug on her heart as she stared at a family of four: mother and father and two boys of elementary school age. The picture had been taken in front of a Christmas tree. Everyone was dressed in red and black.

Jared's dad was a mirror image of his son, with brown hair and light eyes. His mom had dark-red hair and the kind of smile that drew you in, much like Jared's. Jared, who appeared to be about twelve, was making a goofy face at the camera, while his brother appeared more well-behaved.

"My mom loved that photo," he said, coming up next to her. "Even though I was making trouble. She said it captured the moment perfectly."

"Sounds like she thought you were a troublemaker most of the time."

"I liked to have fun," he admitted.

"And your brother—does he have the same mischievous personality?"

"No. He's very chill, laid-back. He doesn't move too fast, doesn't think too hard, doesn't worry at all. I envy him. He takes after my dad. I'm more like my mom." He paused, glancing back at the photo. "Those were happy times. I really had a great childhood. I took it for granted."

"Most people do," she murmured.

He looked back at her with his penetrating green eyes, and she caught her breath, fighting the urge to kiss him again, to take this small quiet moment and make it even more intimate, to give him comfort, to share his pain, to bring him pleasure.

But then Jared stepped back.

She felt an absurd wave of disappointment. *Had she just misread the moment?*

"You want the tour?" he asked, digging his hands into his pockets. "Or do you want to have a little fun first?"

"I'm leaning toward fun," she said warily. "But what does that involve?"

"A trip next door."

"That was not the answer I was expecting. Especially because a second ago...never mind."

"There's time for that kind of *fun* later. I have something else in mind, something that will clear your head. If you're game. And I'm betting you are."

"Of course I'm game. Lead on," she said, feeling an irresistible pull to join in whatever adventure Jared had in mind.

He took her out the front door, around the back of the house, through a thicket of trees and a wooden gate.

"Is this your property, too?" she asked, as they moved down a narrow path.

"No. It belongs to my neighbors, Pam and Carl Hale. They've been family friends forever, and when my dad moved to Hawaii, they got custody."

"Custody of what?" she asked, getting her answer as she heard a soft neigh from the barn they were approaching. "Horses?"

He nodded and led her into the barn, stopping by the first stall, where a chestnut horse gave a whinny of approval as Jared stroked her nose.

"Hey, Honey," he said. "Have you been a good girl?"

It felt odd to hear Jared speak in a soft, husky voice to a horse. "Do you two want to be alone?" she asked dryly.

He grinned. "Jealous?"

"Of you calling a horse honey?"

"That's her name." He stepped back and waved his hand toward the dark-gray horse across from Honey. "That's Barnabas, and next to him is Colette."

"You know all their names?" she asked in surprise.

"He should. He named them," a man said, coming into the barn.

For a moment, her heart leapt into her throat, and she almost reached for her gun, but Jared was walking forward, his arms extended, as he gave the older man a bear hug.

"It's good to see you, Carl. And I only named Barnabas and Honey. It was your wife who named Colette. How is Pam?"

"She's fine. She's out shopping with her sister. Wish I'd known you were stopping by a little earlier. Pam would have liked to see you."

"Sorry about the short notice. I want you to meet my friend, Parisa. This is Carl."

"Nice to meet you." Carl shook her hand with rough fingers. He had a curious glint in his gaze as he added, "About time Jared introduced me to one of his girlfriends."

"I'm not his girlfriend," she said quickly.

"Well, that's a pity." Carl gave Jared a pointed look. "What's wrong with you?"

"Hey, I'm working on it. But I might need some help from Honey and Barnabas."

"They're all ready to go," Carl replied. "You ever ridden before, Parisa?"

"A few times," she admitted, inwardly thrilled that Jared's plan involved horseback riding. "But not in the last ten years."

"It's just like riding a bike," Jared told her.

"We're really going riding?" she asked him, as Carl pulled Honey out of her stall.

"It's the best way I know to clear my head. I know you want to get back to everything, but we have some thinking to do, and there's a path that winds through the hills and around a small pond."

"It sounds perfect."

Jared helped her onto Honey's back, and then hopped on to Barnabas with an easiness that suggested he'd spent a lot of hours in the saddle. They walked the horses away from the barn, and she was happy to have a few minutes to get used to riding again.

When they hit the broader path, and Jared urged the horses into a trot, then a gallop, she was ready for a faster speed. With the wind in her face and the powerful animal beneath her, she felt like she was flying, like she was invincible, and it was a glorious feeling after the past few days of feeling helpless and out of control. Reality would eventually catch up, but for now, she was just going to enjoy the moment.

They didn't talk as they rode, but every now and then, Jared flung her a smile that made her stomach clench, and she realized she was falling for him, which was a really bad idea. She just didn't know how to stop it from happening. They kept getting closer, and the more she knew about him, the more she liked him.

There was a chemistry between them that felt like it was going to blow her mind if she ever gave in to it. But as much as she liked adrenaline, getting closer to Jared seemed a little too dangerous.

It wasn't like it had to go somewhere, but it felt like there was nowhere it could go.

They worked for competing agencies. They traveled the world. They lived their lives in the shadows, and they were almost always alone. They might be together now, but it wouldn't last.

They were truly two ships passing in the night, sharing the same space for just a very short time. It would be better if they didn't get any closer. It would be safer...

On the other hand, since when did she ever choose safe?

Sighing as her mind spun around once more, she told herself to stop thinking and just enjoy the moment.

When they got to the large pond, they circled it once, then Jared motioned for her to stop. He hopped off his horse and helped her down.

"That was amazing," she told him.

"I'm glad you're enjoying yourself. You ride well."

"I actually learned to ride in Bezikstan with Anika and Jasmine. Isn't that ironic?"

"It is. We'll let the horses graze."

"They won't run away?"

"These two appreciate rest." He led her toward a pile of large rocks. As they sat down on the boulders, he said, "This is one of my favorite spots. When I was a teenager, I used to come out here and think for hours on end."

"It's beautiful. Although, I have to admit I don't see you as a thinking-for-hours-on-end kind of guy."

"Maybe not hours. Let's call it minutes."

"Did you used to think about your mom when you came here?"

"I did. I also thought about my future, what I wanted to do, where I wanted to go. When my dad first bought the house and took my brother and me out of the city, we were both unhappy. We liked being away from the tragedy, but we didn't care for the fact that we weren't with our friends anymore. We had to start at a new high school where everyone knew each other. We were not just sad—we were city kids, completely out of place."

"I doubt you had any trouble making friends. You have the kind of personality that allows you to fit in anywhere."

"I suppose. But I had a lot of anger in me back then. Gradually, over time, and after a lot of horseback rides, and some extra nurturing from Carl and Pam, who have been a second family to me, I started to let go of some of that anger. I came to love this place. And whenever I had a break, I found myself coming home."

"So, someday you want to live here permanently? Is that why you bought the house?"

"I don't know if I'm a permanent kind of guy, Parisa. But I just knew I couldn't let the house go. What the future holds, I don't know." He cocked his head to the right, giving her a thoughtful look. "What about you? Where is home?"

She had to think about that. "I don't really have one. My mother and stepfather have a townhouse in DC now. They bought it a few years ago. I've never lived there, so while it's where they are, it doesn't feel like my home. The photos on their walls are from their recent travels. I'm sure my mom has a photo album somewhere with photos from my childhood, but I haven't seen it in years. I have an apartment in San Francisco, but the assignment I had there is over, and I'm not sure where I'll go next." She let out a breath. "It's weird. I've never thought about how rootless I am. I'm glad you bought your family home, Jared. I think someday you'll be really glad you have it."

"It's not like my mom was ever here. The memories are limited to after her death, but it does represent...peace. It's where we came to terms with our new normal."

She held out her hand to him, and he wrapped his fingers around hers. "I've always thought normal is overrated," she said.

He smiled back at her. "Me, too. Good thing—since my life isn't normal now."

"Mine isn't, either. I have to admit that lately I've been feeling a little restless. The night of the engagement party, I was thinking to myself that it was the first event I'd gone to in as long as I can remember where I was actually myself. And being there, talking to Neil and Anika and Jasmine, made me feel like the girl I used to be." She shook her head, feeling a little foolish by the admission. "It's hard to explain."

"But easy to understand," he told her, tightening his hand around hers. "I know what it's like to live in the shadows, but you can come into the light, can't you? The FBI operates out in the open far more than the CIA does."

"I know, and I've thought about it. I just haven't made any decisions. I'm good out in the field. I may not blend into situations as easily as you do, but my language skills have given me opportunities to get close to people no one else can access."

He looked out over the pond, then glanced back at her. "Is that really why you do it?"

"You think I have another motivation?" she asked warily, not sure she liked him digging into her psyche.

"I'm just wondering, in light of your gypsy background, and your lack of a real home, if you're not sure who you are if you're not undercover—if you can't be someone else."

"That's an insightful comment."

"Is it true?"

"I don't know. Maybe a little. It can be easier being someone else."

"I agree. When you're undercover, the only expectations are for the job performance. If you fail, it was your character who failed, not you. If people don't like you, it's not the real you. At the end of the day, if you achieve your objective, that's your victory. The fake persona takes all the failures. The real person takes all the wins."

"I never thought of it that way, but you're right." She paused. "You know what's really weird, Jared?"

"What?"

"I never thought I'd have this much in common with a spook."

"Or I with a fed."

They exchanged a warm smile that sent a shiver down her spine. She didn't know where things were going between them, but she sensed they were heading into reckless territory. "We should probably go back. It will be dark soon."

"Okay." He stood up, then pulled her to her feet, and against his chest.

She caught her breath at the purposeful look in his eyes. "What are you doing?"

"Fulfilling a very old fantasy. I used to dream about bringing a beautiful woman here, sharing a kiss as the sun went down. Want to be that woman?"

"More than I should," she whispered, sliding her arms around his waist as she lifted her head to his, as his mouth covered hers with delicious heat.

It was the kind of kiss that could have gone on forever. Everything about it was sheer perfection—slow, purposeful, tender but simmering with unexplored passion. In Jared's arms, she felt like she'd found the happiest place in the world. His presence surrounded her, but it didn't overwhelm her, didn't make her feel any less important; it actually made her feel like she was more important than she'd ever thought.

A whinny from Barnabas and a gusty breeze, brought

them back to chilly reality. The sun was slipping past the horizon, and it was time to go home.

Which was a really odd thought...because she didn't know where home was...except that maybe it was starting to feel like anywhere Jared was...

That was a disturbing thought.

Nineteen

—➤➤◄◄◄—

Parisa sprinted ahead of him on the ride home, and Jared had a feeling her quick pace had more to do with what had just happened between them than a desperate desire to get the horses back to the barn before dark.

He wasn't as excited to return as she was, because he didn't believe they could outrun whatever was brewing between them. He'd felt a connection to her the first time he'd seen her. In his gut, he'd known she was going to be important in some way. It was probably the real reason he hadn't tried to talk to her at the party. It wasn't just his mission that had kept him away; it was his internal alarm system that had rung all kinds of bells when his gaze had landed on her.

Now that he actually knew her, the tie between them had only grown stronger. She was both a perfect match for him and the worst possible person he could fall for. They were alike in so many ways. They shared a passion for justice, a desire to live life on a big stage, a desperate need to make the world better, and a love of the shadows.

But where did two people who were rarely themselves end up?

He'd thought for some time that being a CIA operative and having a personal life was impossible. There were too many secrets. *How could he ever lie to someone he really loved? And not just once, but over and over and over again?* It wouldn't be fair to the other person.

But would it be different with someone who understood that lies about the job were a necessary evil?

He didn't really think so.

But kissing Parisa after they'd both finally shared who they really were had felt different. There had been an honesty to their intimacy, a deeper desire to connect that went way beyond the physical.

But it didn't have to be that way, he told himself. They could keep things light as long as they both were on the same page.

And, surely, they were on the same page.

Parisa had a job that she loved. She wasn't planning on leaving the FBI any time soon. Her job took her undercover and wherever the bureau wanted her to go. She didn't want a relationship that would make that difficult. And he felt the same way. Maybe it could work.

Or was he just being ridiculous?

He frowned at the crazy direction of his thoughts. He'd never thought so hard about whether or not he wanted to have sex with a beautiful woman as he was right now, another reason why Parisa was different.

They were together for a reason that had nothing to do with their personal feelings or desires. They had a mission to accomplish. *Find Jasmine. Stop the terrorists. Anything and everything else would have to wait.*

He just wished there was something they could do right now, because it was the waiting part that made him think too much and want too much. And the night loomed long and large in front of them. He was starting to share Parisa's greatest fear of having too much time…

-━➤➤◄◄━-

Parisa wondered what thoughts were keeping Jared so quiet. He usually had a lot to say, but on the ride home, and while putting the horses away with Carl's help, he didn't have a lot of words.

They'd finally made their way back to Jared's house, and after a quick tour of the home, they'd ended up in the kitchen. Carl had insisted on giving them a bag filled with sandwiches, chips, and cookies as well as water and coffee, guessing they hadn't had time to stock up on any provisions.

"Are you hungry?" Jared asked, as he unpacked the goodies.

"I'm still full from the tacos we had earlier, but you go ahead."

"I'm fine. I'm going to make some coffee." He put the sandwiches and bottled waters in the fridge, then moved across the room to the coffeemaker.

She took a seat at the table, pulling out one of the new phones they'd picked up earlier. "I want to check in with Damon."

"Good idea. Would you put the phone on speaker?" he asked. "Then we can both get the update."

Years of being secretive and deceptive made her want to say no, to keep the call private, but she and Jared were in this together, and she trusted him even more now that he'd opened up to her. It almost surprised her to realize the depth of that trust.

His gaze sought hers. "Is it that tough of a decision?"

"No, it's not a difficult decision at all. We'll call Damon together."

A smile entered his eyes. "Good. But…"

"There's a *but*?" she asked warily.

"You can't tell him who I am."

"He already knows your name." She stopped abruptly. "Is Jared MacIntyre really your name? Because he ran a check on you after we first met, and you did not come up as CIA."

"Jared is my first name."

"And I suppose I don't need to know your real last name."

"It doesn't matter at the moment. He thinks I'm a journalist?"

"Yes. Your cover is still intact."

"Good. I don't need the CIA getting involved, and I'm not just saying that because I'm worried about getting fired. I don't want them to throw up barriers that not even the bureau can get over."

"I get it. But at some point, someone from the agency is going to figure out you're still involved in the case."

"By then, I hope to have found April's killers."

"I'd ask if finding April's killers is worth losing everything, but I already know the answer."

He met her gaze. "It is worth it."

"There's a chance you could end up with no justice and no job."

"We're going to make sure that doesn't happen."

"I don't know if I can help save your job, but I will definitely do my best to find April's killers."

She punched in Damon's number, then set the phone on the table, as Jared sat down across from her.

"Hello?" Damon said a moment later, his voice hushed.

"It's Parisa. Is it okay to talk?"

"One minute." Silence followed his answer, and then he came back on the phone. "We're good now. Are you all right?"

"Yes. What's happening with Ben? Did he start talking?"

"No. But Raj Kumar is speaking to him now. We're hoping he might be able to persuade Ben to say something of value."

"I hope so. Are Ben's parents still there?"

"They left when Raj showed up. They wouldn't even speak to him."

"Raj must be really confused and feeling so betrayed by both Ben and his father right now. Maybe it was a mistake for me to turn Ben into the bureau so quickly," she muttered. "I might have been able to get more out of him."

"You did the right thing. He probably would have shut down with you, too."

She wasn't so sure about that, and judging by the expression on Jared's face, his thoughts were running close to hers.

"We did find the bartender at the Stone Cellar, who admitted to knowing Isaac," Damon continued. "In fact, Isaac was in the club Thursday night."

Her heart sped up. "So, he's here in the city."

"Yes. The bartender claims he has never seen Isaac outside the club, but he gave us a couple of other locations Isaac mentioned that he likes to go. They're mostly other clubs, but it gives us somewhere to start. He also said that the night Isaac was in the club, he was talking to two guys, who appeared to be Indian. We're looking through surveillance tape from the club."

"Those could be the kidnappers."

"Unfortunately, the club is frequented by a lot of young men who fit that description. We also chased down the IDs of the two waiters that Ben got into the party. Both men were deceased. The identities were stolen."

"That's not unexpected."

"No. We've gone through Ben's phone. There were three calls from a number that is now disconnected. We traced it to a phone purchased from a convenience store a week earlier. It was a cash transaction, and the team is going through security footage obtained from the store and neighboring buildings to see if we can pick up any familiar faces. That's going to take time."

"Time that Jasmine doesn't have. I could take a shot at the Langdons again. Make them see how important it is for Ben to keep talking," she suggested.

"I doubt it would help. You're not Mrs. Langdon's favorite person. She said you owed the family your loyalty, and you betrayed them."

She felt a twinge of guilt at Damon's words. She had betrayed the Langdons, but she'd only done it to save Jasmine's life. She supposed that didn't make a difference to them, since she'd put their son's life on the line to do that.

"I think it's best if you stay out of this, Parisa," Damon continued.

"What about the ransom? Have the kidnappers contacted the Larimers again?"

"No. The drop is set for tomorrow morning at ten o'clock at Shell Park. Now you know what I know. One last thing. Vincent has been pressuring me to bring you in. He claims to be very worried about you. I told him that you are staying off the grid until Jasmine is found. I'd suggest you do just that."

"I want to do more than hide, Damon."

"There's nothing you can do that we're not doing."

"I'll check in with you again later." She ended the call and sat back in her seat. "Looks like you were right, Jared. We might have gotten more information if I hadn't turned Ben over."

"There's no point in looking back. Regrets get us nowhere." He got up. "Do you want coffee?"

"Sure."

He filled two mugs and returned to the table.

She sipped her coffee, immediately appreciating the kick of caffeine. "At least we know Isaac is in New York, although that only makes me worry more. The city is a target-rich environment. And that diamond could buy a lot of explosives."

"It could also buy a lot of weapons to overthrow the Bezikstan government, which is one of the goals of Brothers of the Earth."

"That's true."

"But I'm not discounting a New York target. The group wants to be noticed. They want recruits and the more attention they get, the more people who sign up. We have to stop them."

"I want to do that; I'm just not sure how." She thought for a moment. "Maybe I should call Neil. I didn't speak to him earlier. I could make a case for Ben cooperating with the FBI. He's a reasonable, intelligent person, and I know he cares about Jasmine." She paused. "You still have his phone number, don't you?"

"I do," he said, pulling out his second phone. "It's worth a shot." He read off the number to her, and she punched it into her phone.

She put the call on speaker again. The number rang four times, and then Neil answered. Her heart quickened. She hadn't really thought he'd pick up.

"It's Parisa," she said. "Please don't hang up."

"Do you know what you've done?" Neil asked, anger in his voice.

"I know that Ben is probably the only one who can save Jasmine, and you're not letting him talk to the FBI. I don't understand why."

"As I told Raj, Ben doesn't know who took Jasmine. He was being threatened by an unknown person. All the information he had, he gave to you."

"He knows more, Neil. He knows about an explosion in Paris that's tied to a group called Brothers of the Earth."

"I'm aware of the group. It started as a peaceful group of protesters in Bezikstan, who were working toward changing policies that would be beneficial for the country. Unfortunately, extremists took over and turned it into a terror group. Ben is not a part of that."

"But the girl he was seeing, Sara Pillai—her stepbrother, Isaac Naru, is in the group. And they are both in New York

City. They're probably involved in Jasmine's kidnapping, and Ben may know where Sara and Isaac are."

"He doesn't know."

"When I asked about Ben's romance in Paris, you acted like you didn't know, but you do know, don't you?"

"Ben gave me a bit more information after I spoke to you," Neil said. "He told me that Sara had gotten into some trouble, and he might be caught up in it as well."

"That's why he needs to talk to the FBI. There may be some small detail that he knows that can help."

"My lawyer has advised against it."

"Your lawyer?" she echoed. "Why are you letting a lawyer tell you what to do when you already know what's right? You taught me to think for myself, to stand up for what I believe in, to risk everything for a friend. And you didn't just tell me, you showed me, when you saved my life at great peril to your own. Please, Neil, help Jasmine. She doesn't have much time left."

"I want to help her," he said, his voice filled with pain. "But my son—I have to protect him."

"If Ben helps find Jasmine, everything will be easier for him. And I'm pretty sure Ben wants to do the right thing. When I saw him earlier, he was scared, but he was also torn up about Jasmine. He genuinely loves her. And, so do you."

Neil didn't say anything for a moment. "You're very persuasive, Parisa. No wonder Elizabeth told you where Ben was."

"I'm only telling you what you already know. Give your son a chance to prove he's the man you know him to be. Save him the way you saved me."

"I'll think about it," he grumbled. "I have to go."

The call disconnected, and she turned off her phone, feeling like she'd failed. "Well, that's that."

"You might have gotten through to him."

"I doubt it. He can't see past Ben. He's afraid for his son."

"But his son has more to fear than just the FBI."

"I know. Neil said the Brothers of the Earth started out as a group of peaceful protesters. I wonder what turned them from wanting a better life for people in Bezikstan to wanting to end the lives of people they don't even know."

"Greed—and not just for money: for power, for control, for respect."

"I should have asked Neil if he knows any members of the group still in Bezikstan."

"That's a good question for another day. The players we're interested in are already here. We just have to find them."

"I wish we could do that before tomorrow, but I don't see how." She let out a sigh.

"Tired?"

"And frustrated. There are too many missing puzzle pieces." She paused, giving him a speculative look. "Why haven't you checked in with your contact at the CIA?"

"I sent him a text when we were riding back. He hasn't answered yet."

"Interesting that you did that on the sly while I've been putting every call on speaker."

"It was just the easiest way to do it. I promise if I get a text back, I will read it to you."

"Or let me see your phone," she said.

He tipped his head. "Sure."

"Do you think we should go back to the city, Jared?"

"No. I think your friend, Damon, was right when he told you to stay off the grid."

She frowned. "I didn't join the FBI to be safe. And I can take care of myself."

"What would you do if we went back to Manhattan?"

"I don't know. I just hate waiting."

"Believe me, I share your impatience. I've been running through all the things I could have done differently so that we didn't end up here, but like I said before, regrets don't change anything. We can only move forward. Tomorrow we'll do that."

"I was really hoping we could find Jasmine before the ransom drop."

"The FBI might still find her. It sounds like there are a lot of people working around the clock."

"I hope so. At any rate, I want to go to the consulate in the morning, before the drop. If I can't be a part of the operation, I can at least stay with Anika and Kenisha."

"We'll go back to the city when the sun comes up."

"That's a long time from now."

He gave her a sexy smile. "We can play cards again. I'm sure there's a pack around here somewhere."

"Maybe." As she rolled her neck around on her shoulders, she felt a twinge of pain in her neck.

Jared's gaze narrowed. "Let me check your wound."

"It's fine."

"I want to make sure of that." He got up from his chair and switched on the light.

"You keep the lights on even though you're never here?"

He shrugged. "I like knowing the house is ready in case I need a place to go." He grabbed the bag he'd picked up from the drugstore earlier and brought it over to the table.

She took off her coat, already feeling warmer, and he hadn't even touched her yet. "When were you last here?" she asked curiously, as he pulled a chair close to her and lifted her hair off her neck.

"When I transferred the property into the trust three years ago." He paused. "I'm going to change the bandage."

"I'm sure it's fine."

"Well, I don't want you to get an infection on my watch."

"I promise not to sue you."

He smiled as he gently removed her bandage. "It looks good. No more bleeding. I'll just put a little more antiseptic cream on it."

"That stuff stings," she complained, as he opened the tube.

"You're a badass FBI agent. You can take it."

"Well, now I have to take it."

She winced as he applied the ointment but knew it was the best way to keep the wound clean. He applied a new Band-Aid, his fingers stroking the area around her neck a few seconds too long, stirring up all kinds of other feelings. He was so damn close to her. It wouldn't take much to fall into another kiss.

But where would that lead?

She didn't want to give herself permission to answer that question. Clearing her throat, she tried to get back to what they'd been talking about. "So, three years—that's a lot of utility bills to pay for a place no one lives in. It's not just that you want to have a place to stay in if you need it, it's because you need the lights to be on at home. You need to imagine this place as it was, filled with family—your family."

He gazed into her eyes. "Maybe that's part of it."

"I told you I don't have a place that's home anymore, but there was one Christmas a year after my mom married Harry when we went to a cabin in Aspen for the holidays. And it felt like I was living inside a holiday card. There was a roaring fire, a live Christmas tree that smelled amazing, presents under a huge tree, and hot chocolate with marshmallows. But it wasn't just all those things that made me smile—it was that my mom was so happy. She and Harry would kiss under the mistletoe, accidentally getting caught there dozens of times." She smiled at the memory. "I hadn't seen her smile or laugh like that in years. I felt the love between them and also the love they had for me. It still stands out in my mind as the perfect holiday. And sometimes when I'm far from home, or I haven't talked to my mom in a while, I let myself go there in my head."

"Have you ever actually been back?"

"No. I'm afraid to ruin my favorite daydream. I guess what I'm saying is that I can understand why you want to keep this place as it is, or as it was, even if you never come back."

"I don't want to ruin the daydream, either," he admitted.

"But you brought me here. Why?"

He thought for a moment. "Because I wanted to show it to you. And don't ask me to explain that."

She smiled as she impulsively brushed a strand of hair away from his eyes. "You don't have to explain. I know why. I'm just a little...afraid, Jared."

"The woman who never backs down from a challenge? You're afraid? Of what?"

"I don't want to hurt you."

"Or you don't want to get hurt?" he countered, his knowing gaze clinging to hers.

"Maybe a little of both. You and I—we have nowhere to go."

"I've been telling myself that since I met you. It doesn't seem to make me want you less." He paused. "But the real question is—what do you want?"

She licked her lips and knew she had only one answer to give, one response that was honest and true and terrifying. "You, Jared. I want you."

Twenty

—➤➤❤❤◄—

Parisa expected Jared to react with a kiss, not a long, contemplative stare. "Maybe the real question is what do you want?" she said, turning things around.

"I want you, too."

"Then why are you just staring at me..."

A smile slowly spread across his mouth. "I'm building anticipation."

Relief ran through her that she hadn't completely misread him. "We've had enough anticipation." She stood up and held out her hands.

He slipped his hands into hers as he rose.

"I think you'll like this even more than anticipation." She pulled him closer, then let go of his hands, so she could wrap her arms around his neck and pull his head down to hers.

As soon as their lips touched, she felt as if a thousand firecrackers went off in her head. Her blood thundered through her veins. Her heart pounded against her chest and tingles of desire ran through every nerve ending. It was like a giant ocean wave had swept her up, and she might either wipe out or have the ride of her life.

She wanted that ride. She wanted Jared with a need that was thrilling and terrifying.

With the physical connection would come emotions, and those emotions could make her vulnerable. But she wasn't thinking about what would come later, only about what would come next.

She wanted to be with Jared. She wanted to know this man even more intimately than she already did.

And Jared seemed to want the same. His hands ran under her shirt, bringing more delicious heat, as his fingers stroked her spine, sending shivers through her.

His tongue swept into her mouth, a beautiful, joyful, intimate dance.

They tasted and took what they pleased, until they both finally had to come up for air.

"Damn," he murmured, gazing down at her. "You're something else, Parisa."

"We're something else. This—*us*—it feels different."

"I know. I want to go fast and slow—at the same time."

She felt much the same, but right now need was driving her actions. "Take off your jacket and your shirt."

"I see we're heading for fast," he teased. He took off his black leather jacket and pulled his shirt up over his head and tossed it on the table.

She swallowed hard at the stunningly broad, flat, muscled chest in front of her, with just a smattering of dark hair. He was tan, too, as if he'd spent quite a bit of time without a shirt on. What a gorgeous man he was, but the long scar running under his right rib cage and another across his shoulder reminded her that he was also a man of many layers.

She ran her fingers along the rib cage scar. "How did you get this?"

He shrugged, as she met his gaze. "Does it matter?"

"It looks like it was serious."

"I survived."

"It doesn't look as old as the one on your shoulder."

"It was last year. I'm hoping the scars make me sexier."

"I'm not sure you could get any sexier," she said with a laugh, loving how easy it was to be with him, how real and honest it felt.

"Your turn, Parisa. I'd like to see some of the curves you're hiding under that sweater."

She licked her lips, then took off her sweater, shaking out her hair as she did so. She threw it on top of Jared's shirt, watching his gaze narrow on her breasts, as she played with the front clasp of her lacy, cream-colored bra.

"You're killing me," he said, a somewhat tortured note in his voice.

"Oh, I don't think so. We're nowhere near that."

He put his hands on her bare waist, and the heat sent another thrill of desire through her. She flicked open the clasp on her bra and then pulled it off, tossing it on the growing pile of clothes.

Jared's gaze on her breasts was filled with pure male pleasure, and whatever shyness she might have had evaporated under his hot, needy look. She took his hands and lifted them to her breasts.

Jared didn't have to be told twice what she wanted him to do, his fingers spreading across her skin, his thumbs teasing her nipples as another surge of heat swept over her. And then he kissed her again, and she felt like her insides were melting away.

"Let's go upstairs," he murmured.

"Too far away," she returned, pressing him back against the counter. "I like it here." She looked into his eyes. "In the light. I want to see you, Jared. No shadows for us tonight. You and me, out in the open, who we really are, scars and all."

His gaze darkened. "I haven't been who I really am in a long time."

"I haven't, either. But I want to be tonight. I feel like I

can be myself with you. No judgment."

"No judgment," he echoed. He followed his words with a kiss, and then his lips slid down the side of her neck.

She sighed with pleasure, wanting his mouth, his hands on every part of her body.

As they kicked off their clothes, she realized the rest of Jared's body was also magnificent. He was honed, fit, powerful and very, very male.

She caught her breath as his gaze made the same appreciative trip down her body.

"Lucky me," he muttered.

"Lucky me," she said.

And then there was no more time for words, only for touching, tasting, loving...

It was wild and raw and honest—exactly what she needed. She'd been in the shadows too long, but the light was glorious, freeing...earth-shattering.

Jared made love the way he did everything: with intensity, enthusiasm, confidence, and generosity. They fell into a pace, a rhythm, that seemed as if it was theirs alone, the perfect symphony, the perfect climax, the perfect everything...

At some point, they made their way into the living room, sinking into the soft pillows of the couch, talking and laughing, and then kissing again as desire sparked once more.

Jared woke up with two thoughts: he had a beautiful woman in his arms, and the couch was damned uncomfortable. But as he tightened his arms around Parisa, the discomfort faded away. He was exactly where he wanted to be...maybe even *needed* to be.

He frowned at that thought, not liking the serious weight of it. He didn't want to think beyond right now. He just wanted to enjoy being in the moment.

Parisa was a mix of toughness and tenderness, cautiousness and fearlessness, optimism and pragmatism. He very much liked how she thought, how her hopes overrode her fears and her passion for her job, her friends, what was right, what was just, drove her actions. She was a force of nature, a whirlwind of beauty, and he couldn't imagine not seeing her every day, not talking to her, or laughing or competing—not sharing...everything.

But time was running out...in so many ways. The lights of the room still bathed them in a brilliant glow that had been so important to Parisa and surprisingly important to him, too. But there was also sunlight coming in through the window blinds. Morning was rapidly approaching, and their escape from reality was almost at an end.

As if Parisa had read his mind, she moved against him, her dark eyes flickering open. She gave him a sleepy, happy look, another expression he'd like to see every morning.

"Is it morning?" she asked.

"Not quite, but soon."

"Good. I'm not ready to get up yet." She snuggled back against him.

He wasn't ready yet, either. He didn't want to move, didn't want to let her go, because he didn't know if he'd ever get her back. It was strange to be worried about that. He was usually the one who didn't know when or if he'd return. But with Parisa...she was just like him. She could be gone in the blink of an eye and that was disturbing.

"Jared?"

He looked down at her and caught her questioning gaze.

"You just got stiff," she said. "And not in a good way."

He smiled. "It's all good."

"Better than good. Last night was...real."

He nodded, knowing that he'd needed it to be as real, in the light, completely honest, because he couldn't remember the last time it had been like that. "Unfortunately, there's a lot more *real* stuff coming in a few hours."

"I know. But we're not there yet."

"You want to catch another hour of sleep?"

"Or..." she asked with a lift of her brow.

"Or we could test out the new mattress I have upstairs that I've never slept on."

"I like the second option."

"Me, too," he said, pulling her off the couch.

"By the way," she said, as they ran naked up the stairs. "Having seen what those pool-goers saw all those years ago, I'd have to agree that you really do have a very nice ass."

He laughed as she reminded him of the story he'd told her. "Good to know."

"You know what else I know," she said, as she pulled him down on the bed with her.

"What?"

"I'm about to blow your mind."

"Again?" he asked. "And I thought I was the cocky one."

"Well, you already had your turn. Now, it's mine."

"I do like the way you think. And the way you kiss," he added, as her mouth touched his. "And yeah, that, too," he said, as she moved down his body.

———————

While Jared was showering, Parisa got dressed and went downstairs to make coffee. It was seven fifteen, so they had a few hours to drive into Manhattan and get to the consulate before the scheduled ransom exchange.

She felt a twinge of regret as her brain focused back on the job at hand. It had been more than a little nice to let it all go for the night. Especially since the night had turned out so fantastically amazing.

She smiled to herself at her use of double adjectives. She didn't really have enough words, or maybe the right words, to describe her night with Jared. And it wasn't even all about him; it was about herself, too. She'd felt free for the first time in forever. Unfortunately, she suspected the emotions Jared had helped her unleash were not going to go back into the box she'd put them in a long time ago.

But that was a problem for another day.

Opening the refrigerator, she pulled out the sandwiches they'd gotten from the neighbors the day before. Unwrapping the first one, she bit into turkey and Swiss with sliced tomato and pesto sauce. It was delicious, and she'd definitely worked up an appetite. She was just swallowing the last bite when Jared entered the room.

His dark hair was damp from the shower, and his cheeks were cleanly shaven. He smelled good. He must have found some aftershave somewhere.

He walked straight to her and gave her a long, deep, minty kiss. "It's been too long since I kissed you," he said.

"It's been about an hour. You taste like toothpaste."

"And you taste like pesto."

"I saved you a sandwich. They're delicious."

He grinned. "Not as delicious as you."

She flushed at the look in his eyes. "You're going to need to rein it in, Jared."

"Is that what you want me to do?"

"Not really. It's kind of nice to have a man so boldly interested in me."

"That's a change for you?" he asked in surprise.

"Well, they might have been interested—but not in the real me, which I didn't show them, so I guess I can't complain."

"I get it," he said, taking a sandwich out of the fridge.

"Do you want some coffee?"

"I'd love a cup."

She filled a mug and brought it over to the table, as they sat down. "Have you had a lot of relationships out in the field?" she asked curiously.

"I wouldn't call them relationships. What about you?"

"Same," she admitted. "I've done far more flirting than

anything else, you know? It's a lot of smoke and mirrors."

"I agree. If we need a change in career, maybe we should just become magicians."

"You could be my pretty boy," she said with a laugh. "The one I put in the box and cut into pieces."

"I was thinking of you as my pretty assistant."

"See, that's the problem with us. We both like to be on top."

"We actually both had fun on the bottom and on the top and on the side…"

"Like I said, we need to start reining all this in," she said, feeling more heat run through her. "The night is over."

"Is that all we get—a night?"

"I don't know, Jared," she said, telling him the complete and utter truth. "Do you?"

He met her gaze. "No."

"Until we do, let's table this kind of talk."

He nodded as he unwrapped his sandwich. "All right. You told Damon you wanted to be at the consulate this morning. I assume that's where we're headed when we get into the city."

"Yes. I may not be able to be at the drop, but I can at least talk to Anika and Kenisha. Maybe I can get their take on Ben. Anika might know more about Ben's relationship with Sara than his parents do."

"Good point," he said, as he devoured his sandwich. "There's something else I've been wondering about. I've gone over in my head what April told me right before the explosion a million times. She said the head of the group was in Bezikstan or the US, someone who had a lot of connections, someone no one would ever expect to be a supporter of their cause, which allowed him to move freely without suspicion."

"Okay. But that could be any number of people."

"It could be Raj Kumar."

"Jasmine's father?" she asked in astonishment. "No way."

"Why not?"

"Because…just no way."

"It could be his director of security, Mr. Bhatt, the man who conveniently didn't vet two men who joined the waitstaff at the last minute, the one who hired a guard on the back stairs, who disappeared."

"You make some good points."

"Or…" he continued.

Her gut twisted at the look in his eyes. "Or who?"

"Neil Langdon."

"Why would you suspect Neil?"

"Because his reactions are off. Why wouldn't he do everything he can to help find the daughter of one of his best friends?"

"To protect his son."

"But like you told him, the more Ben cooperates, the better it will be for him."

"He's not thinking clearly. He's worried."

"He's also a teacher, a professor now, a man who has access to a lot of young, passionate, ideologic people."

"Okay, you're going in a lot of different directions."

"I agree. Raj and Neil are long shots, but I like to consider all possibilities. I know those two people are not who you would want to be suspects."

"No. But let's get to the city," she said. "The sooner we start talking to people, the sooner we'll get some real answers."

As they stood up, Jared caught her by the arm. "Before we go." He gave her a long, tender, loving kiss, made even more personal by all the intimacy they'd shared. "It's still you and me, Parisa. Partners—even if we disagree."

She gazed into his eyes and felt a rush of affection. Actually, it felt like love, but she was afraid to call it that, even in her own head.

Instead, she said, "Partners—definitely. And I'm not angry. I just want to get to the truth, wherever it leads."

"I do, too."

The buzzing of a phone startled her. "Is that yours?"

"Yes, sorry. I turned it on to text Gary again—my contact at the agency." Jared pulled out his phone and read a text, his jaw turning to stone.

"It doesn't look like good news. What's happened? It's not Jasmine, is it?" she asked, suddenly terrified by the look in Jared's eyes.

"No, it's not Jasmine. It's me. The agency found out I was present at a shooting near the convention center yesterday."

"How would they know that?" As soon as she asked the question, she realized she knew the answer. "The FBI mole. They know who you are. They want you off the case."

"So does the agency. They want me at Langley today. They've arranged for me to catch the company plane. I need to be at the airport at eleven."

"Then that's where you'll be."

He shook his head. "No."

"Jared, you have to go. This is your job, your life."

"Let's go to the consulate first. I'll make a decision after that."

She couldn't imagine what other decision he could make. "Maybe the agency just wants your information, so they can put together a bigger investigation."

He gave her a short smile. "If that was the situation, they wouldn't call me to Langley. They want me out of New York. They want me off the case. That's not going to happen."

"You're really going to risk everything, aren't you?"

"Yes," he said, no trace of doubt in his voice. "Help me make it count?"

"I will," she said, really hoping she could keep that promise.

Twenty-One

$\leftarrow$—➤➤◄◄—$\rightarrow$

It was almost nine when they got back to the city and parked near the consulate. The sun had disappeared behind dark clouds, and it was now a cold, gloomy day, with a storm approaching. Jared hoped that wasn't a precursor of what was to come.

He'd gotten a couple more texts from Gary, pleading with him not to throw away his entire career for this quest, that April wouldn't want that. And Gary was right—April wouldn't want him to do that. But he'd already disobeyed orders to stay out of the case, and when he got to Langley, there was a good chance he'd find out his job was already over or that he would be sent to a desk, which was not something he was interested in.

He was going to play things out for a while longer. He still had a couple of hours before he had to decide.

"Are you okay?" Parisa asked, giving him a thoughtful glance, as they neared the consulate. "If you want to go to the airport—"

"I'm good. Let's see what's happening here."

They went up the steps to the consulate, where they were detained by two guards. They gave their names, then waited as one of the guards went into the building. A moment later, Kabir Bhatt came to the door, nodding at Parisa.

"Miss Maxwell. What can I do for you?"

"Mr. Bhatt. This is my boyfriend, Jared MacIntyre. We'd like to see Anika and Kenisha."

"They're not taking visitors."

"Well, I'm not just any visitor, and I want to wait with them," she said. "I know what's happening this morning. Please tell them I'm here. I'm not leaving until you do."

He frowned at her words. "One moment." He left them on the step as he stepped into the building.

"He better let us in," she murmured, tapping her foot impatiently as she looked around.

He followed her gaze, feeling a bit exposed. There was still danger in the city for Parisa, and they couldn't forget that.

The front door opened again, and Mr. Bhatt waved them inside. "Mrs. Kumar and her daughter ask that you join them in the salon," he said, motioning toward a room off the main living room.

Jared wasn't thrilled with being relegated to the sitting room when he could see FBI agents, Westley Larimer, and Raj Kumar in the main living room, but maybe he'd have a chance to slip inside once Mr. Bhatt moved on to his other duties.

Anika and her mother were seated together on a gray sofa, coffee mugs in front of them, as well as a plate of untouched pastries and fruit. As Anika stood up to greet them, he couldn't help noting her immaculate appearance, the dark-green dress that clung to her frame, the high-heeled black boots, the made-up face. Kenisha, on the other hand, looked like she hadn't slept since her daughter had been taken. Her face was haggard, and her black pants and sweater were wrinkled as if she'd been wearing the same clothes for days.

"Parisa, thank you for coming," Anika said, giving Parisa

a half-hearted kiss on each cheek. Then she turned to him. "We haven't met."

"Jared MacIntyre," he said, extending his hand.

"Jared is my boyfriend," Parisa put in.

"I hope you don't mind my presence," he added. "But since Parisa was attacked yesterday, I don't want to let her out of my sight."

"You were attacked?" Anika asked in surprise.

"Yes. Since the kidnapping, there have been a couple of attempts on my life. Someone is obviously concerned that I saw something."

"Which clearly you didn't," Anika said. "Or you would have told someone by now, right?"

"Of course," Parisa replied.

"I thought you said you were single," Anika continued, giving both of them a hard, questioning look.

"I wasn't sure if I wanted to get serious with Jared, but after what happened Friday night, I started wondering why I was pushing him away when life can change so quickly," Parisa explained, giving him a loving look.

She really was a good liar. But he also knew how truthful she could be.

He moved past Anika to avoid more questions and also to speak to her mother. "Mrs. Kumar? I'm very sorry about all this. I am praying that Jasmine comes home safe."

"As am I," Kenisha said, dabbing at her eyes with a well-used tissue. "Please sit down. Do either of you want something to eat or drink?"

"We're fine," Parisa said, as they settled on the couch across from the two women. "Is there anything we can do for you?"

"There's nothing to do but wait," Kenisha replied. "You heard about the ransom demand?"

"Yes, that's why I came by. I wanted to offer my support. I also heard about Ben."

"Ben," Anika said scornfully. "I can't believe he betrayed

Jasmine. He let the kidnappers into the house. He knew something was going to happen to her. I hope he rots in jail for the rest of his life."

"Anika, please," Kenisha said. "We don't know the whole story."

"We know enough. And I don't know how you can defend any of the Langdons." Anika turned back to them, fury in her gaze. "Neil and Elizabeth hired an attorney and won't let Ben talk to the FBI."

"I heard that," Parisa muttered. "I was hoping they'd changed their minds. I actually spoke to Neil last night. I thought maybe I'd gotten through to him."

"I haven't heard that anything has changed," Anika said, crossing her arms. "But then, Mother and I are being kept out of the loop. Apparently, the women have no place in any of this."

"Anika, don't do this. Your father and Westley are focused on getting Jasmine back. They're not trying to punish you," Kenisha said. "And I just can't take any more anger or unhappiness today."

"I'm sorry," Anika said quickly. "I'm just terrified, Mother."

"I know," Kenisha said, putting her arm around Anika.

While the two women were consoling each other, he rose. "Do you mind if I use the restroom?"

"It's down the hall on the right," Anika told him.

"I'll be right back," he said, hearing Parisa ask a question about Westley as he left the room.

They hadn't discussed what they'd do when they got inside the consulate beyond finding a way to get whatever information they could. Now that he'd made his move, Parisa would keep Anika and Kenisha distracted.

As he made his way down the hall, his memory of the layout of the consulate came in handy. There were two doors leading into the living room: one from this hallway, and one from the front foyer.

He paused by the bathroom, glancing around. There was no one in the hall, no one paying attention to what he was doing, so he moved closer to the living room door, which was partially ajar.

From his limited view, he could see Westley and his father Phillip, Agent Wolfe, Mr. Bhatt, the NYPD detective who'd been at the hospital with Parisa the first night, and the older man she'd spoken to at the party, Vincent Rowland. Maybe it was a good thing they'd been sent to the smaller sitting room. Vincent didn't need to know Parisa was here.

"Just do exactly as we've practiced," Damon told Westley. "No deviations. Do you understand?"

"Yes," Westley said tersely. "I've got it. We've gone over it a hundred times. I don't hand over anything until I see Jasmine. But I'm afraid they're going to realize there are cops all over the place and not show themselves."

"We already have people in place," Damon said. "They've been there for over two hours. When the kidnappers get there, they won't see anyone new arriving on the scene."

"I hope that's true."

"This will work," Vincent reassured Westley. "The bureau knows how to run this."

"That better be true. I can't even think about what Jasmine has been going through the past few days."

"Don't think about it," Damon advised. "Stay focused on what you need to do."

Hearing footsteps, Jared quickly backed away from the door and dashed across the hall into the bathroom. He heard heels clicking down the marble floor and peeked out to see Anika walking toward the kitchen. This might be the perfect time to get a moment alone with her, ask her what she was doing with Westley the day before.

When he entered the kitchen, he saw a male chef at the stove and a woman chopping vegetables. *Where had Anika gone? Had she simply headed toward the back stairs?*

Then he felt the rustle of a breeze and realized the door

to the basement was open.

His heart jumped against his chest. He knew better than anyone what was in that basement—a way out of the consulate. *Why would Anika be leaving her family now?*

"Can I help you?" the woman who'd been handling the vegetables asked.

"I was just looking for some water," he said, improvising a cough.

She reached into the fridge and pulled out a bottled water.

"Thanks," he said, as she handed it to him. He made his way quickly back to the salon.

Parisa gave him a speculative look. Kenisha was on the phone. He motioned for Parisa to get up.

She moved across the room, and he leaned down to whisper in her ear. "We need to go—now."

A dozen questions filled her gaze, but she simply nodded. They walked down the hall and out the front door. Neither of the guards seemed interested in their departure, and the law enforcement personnel were still in the living room.

Once they were out of sight, they jogged the rest of the way to the car.

"Where are we going?" Parisa asked, as he fired the engine and pulled into the street.

"To the end of the tunnel," he replied, turning quickly at the next corner. "I'm pretty sure Anika is using it to get out of the house unseen."

"She said she was going upstairs to make some calls."

"She didn't. She went down to the basement."

Parisa grabbed at the door handle as he sped around the next corner, and then he slowed down as he saw Anika walking toward a small silver Prius by the park. She had a duffel bag over her shoulder now, and his pulse leapt once more.

"Oh, my God," Parisa said, putting her hand on his leg.

"That duffel bag..."

"Filled with cash, I'm guessing."

"Anika is making the drop. Westley is going to be a decoy."

He flung her a quick look. "I think so, too. Maybe that's what she and Westley were setting up the other day. But I don't think the switch is sanctioned by law enforcement. I heard your pal Damon going over the rules with Westley, and there was no mention of Anika's involvement."

"The kidnappers must have contacted Westley separately."

"And he enlisted Anika's help."

"Which is crazy, because she won't know what to do, how to handle a situation as volatile as this."

"I don't know about that. Anika seems like a pretty cool customer to me."

"Cool, yes, but she's not a hostage negotiator."

"I don't think there's going to be a negotiation." He stayed several cars behind Anika as she drove away from the park. The last thing he wanted was for her to spot them.

"I should call Damon," Parisa said.

"Let's play this out a bit longer, just in case we're wrong. Plus, Vincent Rowland was in the living room with Damon. If you call Damon, and Vincent is involved, you could be putting Jasmine's life on the line—"

"Got it," she said crisply, pulling her gun out. "We've got this."

The FBI agent in Parisa had just come to life. He could see the determination and focus in her eyes, and he felt exactly the same way. If Anika was meeting the kidnappers, they might have only a split second to make a decision that could save Jasmine's life.

As he stopped at a light, he saw Parisa drilling her fingers against her thigh. He covered her hand and met her gaze. "We're going to do everything we can to save her. We're as well trained as anyone."

"I know. I'm glad you're with me, Jared. We're stronger together."

"I agree." They were better together in a lot of ways. He just didn't know if they could stay together.

Twenty-Two

———→≫≪←———

"Where do you think Anika is going?" Parisa asked as they took the Midtown Tunnel, heading toward Queens.

"I'm guessing a house," he said. "It makes sense that they'd keep Jasmine in a single-family home—no doorman, no nosy neighbors to hear anyone yelling or crying."

She checked her watch. "It's 9:20—forty minutes to the official drop. Westley will be leaving in probably ten minutes. Maybe we're wrong. Anika could be going to a friend's house."

"Then why didn't she say she was leaving when you were in the salon? And why did she exit through the tunnel? And what's in the bag?"

Jared asked a lot of good questions. Her gut told her that Anika was going to make her own drop. *But would Jasmine be there?* She straightened in her seat as Anika's car slowed down. "She's looking for an address. Don't get too close."

"I won't." He reduced their speed, lingering at a stop sign for an extra beat.

The homes in this neighborhood were modest in size, and

rather run-down, with overgrown weeds sprouting through cracked sidewalks and chain-link fences around some properties. Parisa caught her breath as Anika turned in to the short driveway for an old, narrow, two-story colonial with peeling yellow paint. It was between an empty lot and a house that had been boarded up. There were homes across the street, but no one too close.

Jared crossed through the intersection and pulled over behind a parked truck several houses down from the one Anika was at. He cut the engine.

She gripped her gun tightly as she watched for some sign of movement from the residence. There was no one out in this working-class neighborhood on a Monday morning, which could be good. She didn't want to deal with innocent bystanders if things went south.

"What is she waiting for?" Jared questioned.

"I don't know, but we need to get closer."

"Agreed. There's a bus coming down the street behind us. If Anika or anyone in that house is looking in this direction, we'll be out of sight for a second. I'll cross the street. You take this side."

"Got it," she said, her hand on the door.

She split her gaze between Anika and the bus coming up behind them. As it lumbered past them, she jumped out and ran down the street, hiding behind a large tree, two houses down from Anika's location. On the other side, she could see Jared squatting behind a parked car, even closer to the house than she was.

She forced herself to breathe as seconds passed. She really hoped no one was watching her or Jared from one of the other houses. The last thing they needed was a neighbor coming out to investigate.

She was beginning to wonder if anything was going to happen when Anika suddenly opened her car door. She stepped onto the driveway but didn't make any attempt to close her door. In fact, she seemed to be using the car as a barrier between her and the house.

The door to the home slowly opened, and a woman stepped out on the porch. Her dark hair was pulled back in a ponytail and tucked under a Yankees baseball cap. She had dark glasses covering her eyes and wore jeans and a New York Yankees sweatshirt.

There was no weapon visible, and the woman didn't look at all threatening, but Parisa had learned a long time ago that appearances could be deceiving. The woman motioned to Anika to come to the porch. Anika shook her head. It didn't appear that they knew each other. They were both wary.

Was Anika waiting to see her sister?

She turned her head at the sound of an engine. A minivan was coming down the street. She used it once again for cover, jogging down to the next house, the next tree. She could hear Anika speaking now.

"My sister or I leave," Anika said.

Her heart raced at Anika's words. *Jasmine had to be in the house.*

The woman walked over to the open door and said something to someone inside.

While the woman had her back turned, she saw Jared move behind the short brick wall that lined the driveway. He was only a few feet from Anika now.

Her gaze returned to the front of the house. Another woman was shoved through the door, her hands tied behind her back.

Jasmine! Her heart leapt with joy. *Jasmine was alive!*

She seemed to be crying, her shoulders shaking, her long hair tumbling around her face. She was still wearing the dress she'd had on at the engagement party. A man stood in the doorway behind Jasmine, holding her arm with one hand, a gun in the other.

"Put the bag on the porch," the man ordered.

Anika grabbed the duffel bag from the passenger seat and then walked around the front of the car. She set the bag at the bottom of the steps.

"Open it," the man said. "Show me what's inside."

Anika unzipped the bag and pulled the sides open. "It's all there. Let go of Jasmine."

"Get the bag, Sara," the man told the woman in the baseball cap.

Sara, Ben's girlfriend. The man holding Jasmine was probably Isaac Naru.

She could only imagine what Jared was thinking right now. He'd want to act. He'd want to take down Sara and Isaac, two people who were responsible for the death of his friend. But Jasmine needed to be out of the line of fire. She trusted Jared would wait.

As Sara moved toward the bag, Anika suddenly grabbed it, holding it like a shield in front of her. "Let go of my sister," she said. "Then you get the money."

Parisa frowned. Anika was acting with a lot of courage, but the kidnappers could shoot her, grab the bag, and kill Jasmine.

"Hand the bag over," the man ordered. "Or you both die."

"Do what he says," Sara said, a pleading note in her voice. "He will kill you."

"Let my sister go," Anika said again. "You don't need her anymore."

"Isaac, please," Sara said, giving the man a pleading look. "She's right. We don't need Jasmine."

Isaac suddenly shoved Jasmine forward—so hard she stumbled, falling to her knees and then halfway down the stairs, knocking Sara backward against the rail in the process. Anika dropped the bag of money and reached for her sister.

The duffel bag was in the clear. All Sara had to do was grab it. But that didn't seem to be good enough for Isaac. He raised his gun, pointing it at the Kumar sisters.

He was going to kill them.

Parisa came out of hiding, running across the street. Her presence swung Isaac's attention in her direction.

At the same time, Jared rushed toward Anika and Jasmine.

Isaac fired at her as she jumped behind a tree. Then she got off her own shot. Isaac fell back into the house. She ran toward the structure, but Jared was closer.

"Stay with the women," he yelled, as he ran into the house, with his gun drawn.

Sara had disappeared, so she grabbed the duffel bag and urged Anika and Jasmine to the other side of the car.

As they knelt on the ground, Anika had her arms around a shaking and sobbing Jasmine.

She squatted down next to them, putting a reassuring hand on Jasmine's shoulder. "You're okay, Jasmine. You're safe now."

"Home...I want to go home," Jasmine said, gulping for air.

"I know. Soon."

"Are they gone?" Anika asked, her face white, her dark eyes shocked.

She looked toward the house. It was quiet—too quiet. She silently willed Jared to be okay.

"Parisa?" Anika asked. "Should we leave? Before they come back?"

"One second." She glanced around. No one had come out of their house at the sound of gunshots. It was clearly an area where people weren't home during the day or didn't want to get involved. "We'll stay put," she said decisively. "I can protect you until help comes."

She pulled out her phone and punched in Damon's number. He didn't answer. He was probably on his way to the other drop site.

She sent a text: *I've got Jasmine. Westley's drop is a decoy. Call me.*

"Parisa," Jared said, as he came out of the house with hurried strides.

She stood up, relieved to see him, but he was furious.

"They're gone," he said. "Isaac must have gone out the back door. I don't know how he got away. He was bleeding."

"He must have had a car somewhere. What about Sara?"

"Didn't see her, either. Dammit!" Anger and frustration ran through his eyes.

"I texted Damon. I haven't heard back yet. I was about to call 911."

"Try Damon again," he advised. "This isn't the end. I found bomb-making materials in the house. But what was more terrifying was what wasn't there—the bombs."

"They were making bombs?" Anika asked, her eyes widening even more.

"Yes. You took a hell of a risk coming here on your own," Jared told her. "What were you thinking?"

"Westley said it was the only way to save Jasmine," Anika replied. "They told him they'd kill her if I didn't bring the money here. I didn't know what to do. If I told anyone, I'd be putting my sister's life on the line."

"Jasmine, do you know anything about the bombs?" Parisa asked.

"I heard them talking about an attack. I don't know where or when."

Her heart went out to Jasmine. More than anything, Parisa wanted to just hold her and hug her, but they needed information.

"We need to get Jasmine to the hospital," Anika said, tightening her arm around her sister.

"I'll call 911," Parisa replied, but before she could do so, her phone rang. It was Damon.

"What the hell?" Damon shouted. "You have Jasmine?"

"Yes. We're at 427 Allen Street, Queens. I followed Anika to Jasmine. Westley knew all along he was a decoy. Sara Pillai and Isaac Naru were here when we arrived. Unfortunately, they got away. I shot Isaac. I don't know how badly he's injured, since he managed to run away, but he may need to find an urgent care facility."

"Got it."

"Sara is on foot, I think. She's wearing a NY Yankees sweatshirt, jeans, and a matching baseball cap." She paused, hearing Damon relay the information to someone in the car.

He came back on the line. "Alerts are going out right now. The local cops will be at your location soon, along with an ambulance. Is Jasmine hurt?"

"I don't think so, but she needs to go to the hospital and get checked out. One more thing—Jared is here with me, Damon. Make sure the cops know we're armed."

"Understood."

"And Damon, there are bomb-making materials in the house."

"We'll be there in ten minutes," he said tersely.

She put the phone into her pocket and gave Anika and Jasmine a reassuring look. "Help is on its way."

Jared pulled out a pocketknife and cut the tie off Jasmine's hands.

Jasmine made a grimace as she moved her arms. Her face was pale, dark shadows under her very wide eyes, a few bruises across her jaw. She'd been through hell, but thank God she was alive.

"Did they hurt you?" Anika asked her sister.

"Not—not really," Jasmine said, tears coming down her face. "But I—I thought they were going to kill me."

"You're going to be okay," Parisa reassured her.

"I've never been so scared. I thought I was going to die."

"Who took you out of the consulate?" Jared asked.

"Two men," she said, her eyes pained. "They said Ben set me up. Is that true?"

"Was one of those men the guy who was in the house with you?" Jared continued.

"No. Isaac came later."

"You know him?" Jared asked.

"No. But I heard Sara call him Isaac. I remembered her from school in Bezikstan. I used to tutor her and some of her friends." Jasmine sucked in a breath. "I asked her why she was doing this, and she said she didn't have a choice. I begged her to help me, but she said they'd kill her if she went against them, that Isaac was obsessed with Brothers of the Earth throwing over the Bezikstan government, making sure everyone in the world knows their righteous cause. I guess the diamond will fund their efforts."

Jared squatted in front of Jasmine. "Did you hear any other names? Did they talk about what they were planning? Did anyone else come to the house?"

"Sometimes I heard male voices. Once, they were arguing, but I don't know what about. Other times, it seemed really quiet. They kept me in a closet most of the time. They'd open the door to give me food or water or let me use the bathroom a couple times a day. I never saw anything but the bedroom, the bathroom and the closet." Jasmine shuddered. "I didn't think I was ever getting out of there."

Anika squeezed Jasmine, then gave them a ferociously protective glare. "Stop asking her so many questions. She's traumatized."

"We need to find the kidnappers before they hurt anyone else, before they set off a bomb somewhere in the city," Jared said grimly. "Jasmine, you said they brought you food. What was it?"

"Uh, it was Indian food."

"Did it always come from the same restaurant?"

"Roti," she said. "The wrappers said Roti."

"Good, that's good," he told her. "Can you remember anything else?"

"They said *kaala kaua* several times."

"They said the word *raven* in Hindi?" Parisa cut in.

Jasmine nodded. "I don't know what they meant by it."

"Do you?" Jared asked her, as he stood up.

"I don't know," she muttered, the word feeling familiar in a way she couldn't quite explain.

"I'm going to run through the house again before the cops

get here," Jared said. "You're okay?"

"Yes. Go," she said, hearing a distant siren. Turning back to Jasmine, she said, "Was there anything else that might help us identify them or figure out where they are?"

Jasmine shook her head. "I'm sorry. I want to help, but I don't know."

"It's okay. You're doing great."

"Ben asked me to let his friends work the party. I never imagined he'd set this up," Jasmine said, more tears welling up in her eyes. "Ben is like my little brother. Where is he?"

"He's in FBI custody. But he's not talking," Parisa answered.

"What do you mean?" Jasmine asked in confusion.

"Neil and Elizabeth hired a lawyer, who advised Ben not to speak."

"Which is breaking our mother's heart," Anika said bitterly. "Elizabeth was her best friend."

"Ben must be in trouble. He wouldn't have done all this if he wasn't being threatened," Jasmine said.

Parisa wondered how Jasmine could still defend Ben after what she'd been through. "Maybe you can talk him into helping us find your kidnappers," she said.

"I will do anything," Jasmine replied. Turning to her sister, she said, "How is Westley?"

"He's going to be really happy you're all right," Anika said with a tearful smile. "He's been completely distraught. The man adores you."

"His parents must hate me for all the trouble."

"They don't blame you. They were willing to pay whatever the kidnappers wanted to get you back," Anika said. "The Larimers love you, Jasmine. And, most importantly, Westley loves you. I don't think I realized how much until all this happened. I'm sorry if I ever gave you doubts about him."

"You were being a protective sister," Jasmine said. "But I should have spoken up about the ring. I never wanted to wear it. I should have made Westley understand that."

"Well, you won't have to wear it again," Parisa put in. "I doubt the Larimers will ever see that ring again."

"Maybe it was cursed," Jasmine said.

She nodded, thinking that it felt like a hundred years since she and Jasmine had first spoken about the ring in Jasmine's bedroom at the consulate.

She straightened as two police cars and an ambulance pulled up in front of the house. Four uniformed officers walked up the driveway. She put her gun on the hood of the car and moved around the vehicle to speak to them, as the EMTs attended to Jasmine.

As she identified herself as an FBI agent to the officers, Jared came out of the house. He gave the officers a brief explanation of what was inside. Two of the officers went into the house to investigate, while the other two went to speak to Jasmine and Anika.

"Did you find anything else?" she asked Jared.

"A lot of food wrappers from the restaurant Jasmine mentioned," he muttered. "It's a few blocks from here. We need to check it out."

"Damon is on his way with every other agency in the city."

"Send them over when they get here," he said shortly.

Seeing the determination in his eyes, she knew she wasn't going to stop him, nor did she really want to. Jasmine was safe. It was Jared's turn now to call the shots.

"You're supposed to be at the airport in..." She checked her watch. "An hour."

"We need to find Isaac. That's all that matters."

She made a quick decision. "Go. I'll catch up."

He gave her a hard look. "This isn't good-bye."

"I know," she said, really wanting to believe that. "I'll talk to the police. You do your spook thing."

She moved down the sidewalk, planning on distracting the officers from questioning where Jared was going, but two neighbors had finally come out of their house from across the street and were now conversing with the police, so she left them alone.

"Thank you, Parisa," Anika said, moving over to her as the EMTs sat Jasmine on the back of the ambulance. "You saved Jasmine's life and mine, too. Who are you?"

"You know who I am."

"I don't think I do. Are you a police officer?"

"No."

Anika gave her a sharp look. "You're not going to tell me, are you? Well, it's fine. I'm still grateful."

"What you did was very risky, Anika. You should have had backup. You should have told someone what you were doing."

"Westley and I didn't think we had a choice. But for a moment there, I thought I'd probably made the stupidest decision of my life—until you showed up. Why did you follow me?"

"Because I saw you and Westley meeting in secret the other day. I wondered if you and Westley had something going on."

Her eyes widened. "Really? You followed me the other day, too? I certainly raised your suspicions. Why?"

"Because you lied to me when you got the text from Westley and told me it was from your boss. I knew you were up to something. I'm just glad it was about saving Jasmine and nothing else."

"I guess I'm not a very good liar. But I would never be interested in Westley. He is far too arrogant and controlling for me. However, he does really love my sister. He only asked me to help because the kidnappers told him it had to be me."

"You're very brave, Anika."

"I have a feeling I'm going to start crying as soon as the adrenaline wears off." She paused as a stream of black SUVs came down the street.

Damon was one of the first people to hit the sidewalk,

followed by a dozen other agents. Police detectives and other law enforcement personnel were close behind. But it was the car that pulled up next that made her heart fill with emotion.

The Kumars—Raj and Kenisha—and the Larimers—Phillip and Westley—ran toward the ambulance. Anika went to join them.

"That's a happy scene," Damon said, as he joined her.

"It could have very easily gone the other way."

"Thanks to you, it didn't. What made you follow Anika?"

"I had a hunch," she said lightly, knowing that Damon would have a lot more questions.

"We'll get into all that later. What has Jasmine told you? Start with the bombs. Is there an attack forthcoming?"

"She doesn't know what their plans are. I haven't been in the house, but I heard there was evidence of bomb-making materials. Jasmine said she'd speak to Ben. Maybe she can get him to tell us more. She still seems to believe he has a good heart. I don't know why she's not blaming him for what happened to her, but she's not."

"I'll try to make that happen as soon as possible. Anything else I need to know?"

"We need to find Isaac and Sara as soon as possible."

"Local police just picked up Sara at a bus stop."

Relief washed over her. "That's the best news you could have given me. What about Isaac?"

"No sign of him, and Sara claims she doesn't know where he is, but we've got every agency in New York looking for him, and I think we have a good chance of getting her to talk. I need to get inside the house. Are you sticking around?"

Before she could answer that question, she saw Vincent Rowland come down the street with another FBI agent. "I don't think so," she said. "Jared told me there were a lot of food wrappers inside the house from a local café. He went to check it out. I'm going to catch up with him. I'll call you if the lead is worth anything."

Damon gave her a hard nod. "Stay in touch."

"I will. I don't think this is over yet."

As Damon went into the house, she retrieved her gun and managed to slip away without drawing anyone's attention. Jared's car was gone, but he'd said the restaurant was only a few blocks away. Pulling out her phone, she checked for the address and then started jogging down the street.

Twenty-Three

Jared noticed the drops of blood while he was standing in line at the Roti Indian Café to talk to the young male clerk. There was one female customer ahead of him, and two men in the kitchen filling orders. He followed the blood trail down a back hallway, past two bathrooms to a staircase.

He pulled out his gun, moving quietly up the stairs. There was more blood on the landing and on the knob of a closed door. He listened for a moment, hearing what sounded like muffled groans. He had no idea who was on the other side of that door, but his gut told him it was Isaac. The blood was fresh and judging by the number of food wrappers from the café downstairs, clearly the kidnappers had been at this location numerous times.

He tested out the knob. The door was locked. He didn't really want to kick it in and alert anyone, either in the room or downstairs, as to his presence. He pulled out his wallet and removed a lock-picking tool.

It took him only a minute to turn the lock.

He slowly opened the door, raising his gun as he did so.

He saw a man lying on the couch, a towel pressed to his gut, a gun on the coffee table in front of him.

Isaac!

His heart jolted with a rush of adrenaline. The man he'd been hunting for weeks was right in front of him. He didn't see anyone else in what appeared to be a studio apartment. He strode forward, his gun on Isaac.

"Don't move," he said, as Isaac tried to sit up and get his gun.

The man stared back at him, as if weighing his options. If he hadn't been bleeding so badly, he probably would have come at him, but it didn't appear as if Isaac had much strength left. His face was ashen. Sweat dotted his face, and his breathing was fast. He was obviously in pain.

Jared walked over to the coffee table and grabbed Isaac's gun. "Where's Sara?"

Isaac shrugged.

"You're not going to make it through the day, Isaac. You talk, and I'll get you help."

"I'm not afraid to die," he said, his voice laced with a British accent.

"That's good, because that's where you're headed, unless you decide to help. Where's the bomb?"

Isaac stared back at him. "What bomb?"

"The one you and your pals made. What's the target?"

"You think I'd tell you?"

"If you want to live, you will."

"Who are you? Why are you alone? Where's your badge?" Isaac asked, his gaze narrowing.

"I'll tell you who I am. I'm April's friend. Remember her? The woman you killed in Paris?"

"The CIA bitch?"

His gut tightened at Isaac's despicable words. "You killed her."

Isaac gave him a brash, unrepentant look. "So what?"

"You'll pay for what you did."

"The CIA won't let me pay. I'm their asset," he drawled. "They'll protect me, or they get no more information."

"They won't protect you, not for killing an agent."

"You're wrong," Isaac said, a mocking expression on his face. "They already know what I did. They don't care. I'm useful to them."

Anger and fury ran through him, as he wondered if he was wrong, if the agency would protect Isaac.

He'd never felt such overwhelming rage, such an intense desire to kill someone. This man, with his evil grin did not deserve to be on this earth. It would be easy to pull the trigger, to make sure April got justice. She deserved that. His hand tightened on his gun.

"Jared, don't."

He turned his head to see Parisa in the doorway. She had her weapon out as she came into the room.

"Don't kill him," she said, her gaze on his. "Not because he deserves to live, but because you will never be the same."

"I don't care about myself."

"Well, I do," she said. "I care about you."

"He thinks the agency will protect him."

"They will," Isaac put in.

"We'll make sure that doesn't happen," Parisa said. "We'll get justice for April and for Jasmine."

"Is the FBI right behind you?" he asked.

"I told Damon I was following a lead, that I'd call him if it panned out. It's just me and you…and him."

He looked back at Isaac, at his smug smile. He wanted so much to take this man's last breath, to avenge April's death. *But if he did—what difference would there be between him and Isaac?*

He saw Isaac's gaze darting around, looking for an escape, or maybe another weapon. "Don't move," he warned him.

"You're not going to kill me," Isaac drawled. "You're going to save my life."

"I don't have to kill you. I can just let you die. At the rate you're bleeding, that won't be long."

"She won't let you." Isaac tipped his head at Parisa. "She's a woman. Women are weak."

"Not this woman. I'll let him do whatever he wants," Parisa said. "And I won't mind watching." She turned to him. "It's up to you, Jared. This is your call. Whatever you say happened here will be what happened."

He felt a rush of amazement at her words of unconditional support. He knew what he had to do. "Call Damon."

She pulled out her phone and made the call.

"You're a coward," Isaac said, spitting onto the ground. "All of you Americans are cowards."

"What's cowardly is killing an innocent person," Jared returned.

"The CIA bitch wasn't innocent. She was using me. I used her."

"If you knew she was CIA, and you're an asset, why the hell would you kill her?"

"Because she thought I was playing both sides." Isaac paused, then uttered a short, harsh laugh. "She was right."

He shook his head, wondering how his agency could have protected this terrorist as long as they had. That ended now. He would make sure of it. "You won't be playing any sides anymore. You'll be sitting in prison."

"It won't matter. I am but one person. My brothers will change the world. We will bring our righteous cause to everyone. Today, *Kaala Kaua* will fly and inspire others to do the same."

"What are you talking about?" he asked.

Isaac's cold grin chilled his soul. "You'll find out soon enough. We are going to educate the world. Everyone will know our name."

"Where's it going to happen?"

"You can't stop it. It's too late, and you don't know where

to go."

"I know where to go," Parisa said suddenly, a note of shock and anger in her eyes. "I have to leave, Jared."

"What? Where are you going?"

"I don't have time to explain. It's going to happen at noon." She looked at her watch. "That's in thirty minutes. Give me the car keys. I'll text Damon on the way."

"How do you know it's happening at noon?"

"Because of the story," she said cryptically. "*Kaala Kaua*. The raven. I can't believe I didn't remember before. It's going to happen at the college."

"What the hell? What story? What college?"

"Everly. The bomber is going to be on a roof or a ledge, someplace high."

"That's not much to go on," he said, as he handed her the car keys.

"It's all I have."

"Why Everly?"

"Because the person who told that story works there." She ran to the door.

"Parisa, wait!"

But she was already gone. He had to trust Parisa could take care of herself until he got there.

"She won't be in time," Isaac said. "I wish I could be there to see it. Perhaps the Raven will take her with him." His eyes took on a fevered glow. "And soon I will join the Raven as well. We will soar together with the souls who have gone before us and will come after us. Then we will be free."

"Who is the Raven?"

Isaac didn't answer. Instead, he started chanting in a language that Jared couldn't understand. At the sound of footsteps pounding up the stairs, he backed up, keeping his gun on the door.

Damon came into the room, gun drawn as well, followed by six other agents.

"MacIntyre?" Damon said, his gaze sweeping the room.

"I take it this is Isaac Naru."

He lowered his gun. "Yes. He's all yours. I need to get to Everly College."

"I'll take you," Damon said briskly, as the other agents secured Isaac. "I got Parisa's text that Everly is the target."

"That's what she said. It's happening at noon. The bomber will be on a roof or a ledge, which doesn't narrow it down much. How big is the college?"

"I don't know. I haven't been there. But I'm sure there are at least five or six buildings," Damon replied.

As they moved through the café, they had to make their way through a half-dozen more agents interviewing the restaurant staff. If the café was a meeting place for the terrorist cell, hopefully, they'd get even more leads.

As he got into the SUV with Damon, he called Parisa, but she didn't pick up. "She's not answering." He sent her a text: *Where are you? What building?*

"How does she know it's Everly College?" Damon asked. "Did Isaac tell her?"

"No. He said the *Kaala Kaua* will fly today, and apparently that translates to the Raven will fly today. Parisa said she knows it's Everly, because the person who made up the story works there."

"Jasmine Kumar teaches at Everly. Ben Langdon is enrolled there. And Neil Langdon is a guest lecturer," Damon said.

"It has to be Neil." His stomach turned over at that thought. *Would Parisa have to kill the man who had saved her life?*

Damon took out his phone and punched in a number, then said shortly, "We need all agencies at Everly College to evacuate classrooms and dorms. Suspected bomb or bomber on a roof or a ledge. I'll be there in ten minutes." He set down his phone, then gave Jared a hard look. "Police, FBI, and Homeland Security, as well as campus police, will respond to the threat."

"Good."

"So, let's get to you. Who the hell are you?"

"I'm CIA," he admitted. "At least for now. I've been operating off book."

"I figured it was something like that. You've been after Naru since Paris?"

"Yes. He killed a fellow agent."

"Sorry. Why is that off book?"

"Because a key suspect was also a CIA asset."

"What?" Damon exclaimed.

"I didn't know Isaac was the asset until just now. But it finally makes sense why the agency wanted me off his tail."

"This is going to be a bureaucratic nightmare."

"Definitely," he agreed. "I'm happy that Naru is in FBI custody."

"Because you don't want the CIA to protect him."

"I don't," he said, meeting Damon's gaze.

"I get it," Damon said with a nod. "You want him to pay."

"Yes. But making him pay won't mean anything if this bomb goes off, if Parisa..." He couldn't finish the sentence, because the thought was unthinkable. "I can't lose her."

"You're in love with her," Damon said, making it a statement and not a question.

"I might be," he admitted.

"Well, you're not going to lose her. She's my friend, too."

"She told me. She also told me about Vincent Rowland. Would he be aware of what's going on now?"

"Oh, yeah," Damon said tightly.

"Then Parisa might have more to worry about than just the Raven." Fear ran through him, and he prayed that this time he'd get there in time.

Twenty-Four

—➤➤◄◄◄—

Parisa had never been to Everly College before, but she was guessing the Raven would be near the language arts building, if her supposition that Neil Langdon was involved was correct. Although, she couldn't stand to think Neil could be a part of any of this. But he was the one who had made up the story about the raven. He was the one who had told it to every student who came through his classroom.

As she ran between buildings, the story ran around in her head.

It was a stormy day when the hawk came down from the sky and went after the baby ravens, tearing their tree nest apart, attacking the mother, and forcing the babies to flee to a nearby ledge along the window of a classroom.

For days, the children pushed twigs and grass onto the ledge, so the baby ravens wouldn't starve. They waited and prayed for the mother to come back, but she never did.

The ravens huddled there in the wind and the rain, enduring storms that never seemed to end. They were trapped, too afraid to move.

But there was one raven who grew impatient, every day flapping his wings just a bit more. He didn't want to leave the others, but he also knew he couldn't stay on the ledge. He had to try to fly.

The clock in the bell tower was ticking off twelve bells for the noon hour when the children inside the classroom saw the raven strut back and forth along the ledge. He looked down, then up. They watched with bated breath.

And then he was gone, soaring into the heavens. At first, he was flapping his wings like a madman, but then he realized he could fly.

The skies opened up. The sun beamed down on the rest of the ravens, and one by one they followed the raven's lead, finding a new day, a new world—peace.

The hawk no longer controlled their destiny. They could be whoever they wanted to be. They had finally found the courage.

Everly didn't have a bell tower, but the tallest building she could see overlooked a large courtyard where students were eating, studying, talking at tables and benches. No one had any idea there was danger lurking.

She wanted to scream at all of them to run—but run where? She could be sending them into danger instead of away from it.

She had to find the Raven first. She ran into the lobby of the tallest building and dashed up seven flights of stairs, finding a door that led on to the roof. She pushed through it, coming to a crashing halt as she saw her former mentor, the man who had saved her life, standing near the edge of the building, wearing what appeared to be a vest filled with explosives.

He whirled around and put up his hand. "Don't come any closer, Parisa."

"What are you doing, Neil?" She stopped about ten feet away from him, shock still running through her that it was really him, that he was the bomber.

"Saving my family."

"What are you talking about?"

"I created a monster, and it is now devouring me. The storm will not lift until I fly."

"You're the Raven," she said. "*Kaala Kaua.* Isaac said the Raven would fly today." She looked into his tortured gaze. "I knew it was you all the way over here, but I kept telling myself I had to be wrong. I couldn't imagine that you were behind Jasmine's kidnapping, that you're a terrorist. My God, Neil! You're a terrorist?"

"It didn't start out like this."

"You need to take off that vest now."

"I can't. Stay back," he added hastily. "Or you will die, and I don't want that to happen."

"I don't understand, Neil. How did you turn into this?"

"It started about six years ago, when I began to teach at the university. The students would come to my house for study group. Elizabeth would feed them. And I would offer them help. Sometimes I told them stories in different languages to increase their skills. The raven was one of those stories. It inspired them to dream, to want more, to trust in themselves and their ability to change their circumstances. They were so energized, so full of hope. They wanted to make changes in Bezikstan; they wanted to be politically active, they wanted to make their country better. I thought it was good to encourage them. I didn't like what was happening with the government, either. Things got bad after you left. Bezikstan changed. There was more poverty, less opportunity."

"Are you telling me that Brothers of the Earth was founded in your living room?" she asked in astonishment.

"I didn't know what they would become. I tried to steer them back to their true path, but a few years ago, I started losing control. There was an explosion in Bezikstan, a car bomb, and they took credit for it. I told them they had to stop. They told me that Elizabeth and her mother would die if I ever said a word."

"Why didn't you leave? Why didn't you tell someone?"

"Elizabeth's mother was ill. She couldn't travel. I sent Ben here, to New York City. I wanted him far from the group. I thought he was safe. They said out of honor to my bringing them all together, they would leave me alone as long as I stayed quiet, which I did. But then Ben went to study abroad. I had no idea he would run into Sara in Paris, that he would fall in love, and that he would become a part of the horror I had tried to protect him from."

"He didn't know you started the group?"

"He knew nothing. He still doesn't. He's innocent."

"And Sara—how involved is she?"

"Sara doesn't want to be involved, but Isaac is her only living relative. And he is one of the leaders now, one of the most radical."

"Who set up the kidnapping? Who contacted Ben?"

"I believe it was Isaac. He knew of Ben's connection to the Kumars, to the consulate."

"Did you know what Ben was going to do?"

"I didn't even know about him and Sara until the day after the kidnapping. When Jasmine disappeared, Ben confided in me. He said only the diamond was supposed to be stolen, but Isaac got greedy. He wants more control, more money. I went looking for Isaac. Ben said he might be at a café in Queens, but he wasn't there. While I was gone, you found Ben and you turned him in."

"And you wouldn't let Ben talk—even with Jasmine's life on the line. That café could have been raided by the cops days ago. Jasmine could have been rescued earlier."

"Elizabeth's life was also on the line, and Ben's, too. There were no good choices."

"There were a lot of choices better than the ones you made. What is the plan now? Are there others here on the campus—wearing explosive vests? Are there more bombs? More targets? You have to tell me, Neil. Was the diamond stolen to finance a massive bombing here in the city?"

"Not here—Bezikstan. The diamond paid for weapons. The group is on their way back home. Isaac and Sara stayed behind to squeeze more money out of the Larimers."

She was relieved that the action was not going to be here in the city. There was still time to head off an attack in Bezikstan. "If everyone is gone, then why are you doing this here?"

"It's the price I have to pay for Elizabeth's life. If I don't die, she will. The men who put this vest on me said Isaac has her."

"What men?"

"I don't know their names. They showed up at my office an hour ago. They brought me up here to the roof and told me what I had to do."

"Isaac does not have Elizabeth. Isaac is in FBI custody and so is Sara. We found Jasmine. She's alive. It's all over, Neil. You don't have to do this."

Neil turned his head to look over the roof. "The police are here. You called them. The students in the courtyard are being evacuated."

"I told you—it's over. All you have to do is take off the vest. If you turn evidence against the group, you can be put into protective custody. No one will find you."

He turned back to her. "You don't understand, Parisa. I don't control the bomb. It's on a timer. It's going off in..." He checked his watch. "Six minutes."

She swallowed hard. "We'll get a bomb squad up here."

"They won't get here in time. I will stand on the ledge, give the students a chance to see me, and they will run faster. I don't want to hurt anyone. You need to leave. I'm going to jump so that the bomb goes off in the air, and, hopefully, no one else will die."

She couldn't believe what he was saying. "I can't let you die, Neil. You saved my life when I was sixteen."

"If you want to repay me, take care of Elizabeth and Ben.

That's what you can do for me." His gaze filled with sadness. "This is all my fault. I liked the adulation, the kids looking up to me. I wanted to be their mentor, their guru. It was my ego that brought me here. And now they are in control."

"Which is why we need you alive to help us stop them."

She pulled out her phone and punched in Damon's number.

"Parisa, where are you?" he yelled. "Jared and I are in the parking lot."

"It's the language arts building, the tallest building on campus, right by the courtyard. I'm on the roof with Neil Langdon. He's wearing a suicide vest. It's remote controlled. It's going off in about five minutes. Where are you?"

"Running in your direction. We should be there in five. The buildings are being evacuated. Get the hell out of there."

"Is there any way we can defuse the bomb?" she asked, already knowing the answer.

"Not in the next five minutes. Get off that roof, Parisa," Damon said, pausing, as he yelled, "Dammit, give me back the phone."

"Parisa," Jared interrupted, obviously having grabbed the phone from Damon. "Don't let him take you down with him."

"He saved my life, Jared," she said, logic and emotion colliding inside her. "I have to try to save his."

"There's nothing you can do, is there?"

"He says there's not. He wants me to leave."

"Then do it."

"Three minutes," Neil said. "Get out of here, Parisa. We're running out of time."

She heard shouting coming across the phone she still had in her hand, and she knew that both Jared and Damon would be entering the building soon, probably at the same time the bomb was going off. They would try to save her, and they would die trying.

She put the phone next to her ear once more. "You have to stay away, Jared—Damon. I'm coming down now. Don't come into the building. Don't get too close." She looked at Neil, giving him a sorrowful look. "I wish I could help you— the way you helped me."

"I'm sorry I wasn't the hero you thought I was, Parisa. Please, help Ben. He's a good kid. He's not part of any of this. His only mistake was to fall in love with the wrong woman." He looked at his watch. "One minute. Go, Parisa. I don't want your death on my conscience, too."

She hesitated one last second and then turned and ran toward the door. She took one look back and saw Neil get on to the ledge. He looked down at the ground and then up at the sky—just like the raven in his story. He checked his watch one last time.

"No," she screamed.

Jared and Damon ran toward the building. They could see a man standing on the ledge of the roof. The police stopped them when they reached the perimeter.

While Damon flashed his badge and stopped to explain who they were, Jared dashed past security and entered the building. The door had barely closed behind him when the bomb went off. He was knocked off his feet, his head bouncing off the wall, as plaster rained down around him.

Stunned, it took him a moment to stumble to his feet. There was a ringing in his ears that was shockingly painful. He scrambled to his feet, terror in his heart.

Where was Parisa? Had she already left the building?

But he hadn't seen her standing by the police, and she wouldn't have gone far.

He raced toward the stairs, leaping two steps at a time as he made his way past some minor damage, hoping that this would be as bad as it got, that the main explosion had occurred outside and far from Parisa.

She had to be all right.

The prayer went around and around in his head as fear rocketed through him.

This wasn't like the last time. Parisa wasn't April. Parisa wasn't...dead.

She had to be alive.

But he'd said those same words before, to no avail.

Finally, he burst through the door leading onto the roof. He stopped abruptly, unable to see more than a foot in front of him. There was a thick, dark, burning smoke in the air— the same smoke that had surrounded April, the same kind of smoke that had swirled around the World Trade Center when his mother had died. He could not lose another person he cared about like this.

"Parisa," he shouted, coughing as he inhaled too much dust. "Where are you?"

"I'm here."

Her voice rang through his heart. And then she appeared in the swirling dust.

"I'm here, Jared."

He threw his arms around her, holding her as close as he could, burying his face in her hair, needing to really feel that she was alive.

"I'm okay." She pulled back, looking up at him with her heart in her eyes. "But Neil's dead."

He nodded, his gaze sweeping her face, searching for any sign of injury, but thankfully she appeared to just be a little scratched up. "I figured."

"He jumped off the roof. There was no way to stop the explosion. Hopefully, his action caused the least amount of damage."

"I'm just glad he didn't take you with him." He framed her face and gave her a hard, grateful kiss. "You should have left as soon as you saw him."

"I was trying to think of a way to save him, the way he saved me. I couldn't come up with anything."

His heart tore at the guilt in her eyes. Parisa could be

fearless and ruthless, but she also had the biggest heart of anyone he knew.

"I know I shouldn't care, but I do," she said.

He gave her another tight hug. "It's okay to care."

"It's not. Neil started the Brothers of the Earth. He said it was just going to be a peaceful, political activist group with idealistic students in it. But it took on a life of its own. When he tried to stop it, they threatened to kill him and his family. He said he couldn't leave Bezikstan because Elizabeth's mother was ill. But he sent Ben away for college, so he wouldn't get swept up in it."

"That makes sense. What happened today?"

"Two men came to Neil's office. They told Neil that Isaac had Elizabeth. Neil believed them. That's why he didn't fight the vest. He was trading his life for hers. I told him Isaac and Sara were in custody, that Elizabeth was all right, but I don't know if that's true. I was trying to give him a reason to live, until I realized it wasn't going to be his choice. The bomb was going to detonate, and we didn't have enough time to defuse it."

"We'll find Elizabeth. He said there was only this bomb, right?"

She nodded. "Everything else is happening in Bezikstan. There's going to be a coup. It's imminent. The diamond financed a lot of weapons."

He blew out a breath. "I'm not saying that's good, but..."

She met his gaze. "I know. It's at least more of a fair fight between the rebels and the government versus innocent lives being taken at random."

"Parisa?" Damon yelled, interrupting their conversation as he came out onto the roof with two other agents.

"I'm all right," she said.

Jared was reluctant to let her go, but he sensed Damon needed reassurance that his good friend was alive.

Parisa and Damon exchanged a heartfelt hug, while the agents made their way across the roof, presumably looking for evidence and clues.

"You scared the hell out of me," Damon told her.

"I'm sorry. Everything was happening so fast, I didn't know what to do. Is anyone else hurt?"

"No. Because of you, the courtyard was evacuated before he took his dive."

"He said he was going to stand there for a minute, let everyone see him, so they could get away."

Damon shook his head in bewilderment. "I have to admit, I never considered Neil was involved in any of this. I just thought he was being a protective father."

"He was. He didn't know that Ben had even met Sara until after Jasmine was kidnapped. Then he realized that the group had used Ben to get into the consulate. The diamond is financing weapons to overthrow the Bezikstan government. That's the big plan. But apparently Isaac got greedy. He decided to take Jasmine as a hostage, so he could get more money, so he could run his own schemes."

"He won't be running anything," Damon said. "Isaac is in surgery now. His condition is critical. Hopefully, he doesn't die before we get more information out of him."

"He better not. That's the main reason I kept him alive," Jared muttered.

"I'm going to pretend I didn't hear that," Damon told Jared.

"I guess you guys have gotten acquainted." Parisa's questioning gaze moved from Damon to him.

"We have," he said. "Damon drove like a maniac to get us here in time."

She smiled. "Any excuse to drive fast, right, Damon?"

Agent Wolfe shrugged. "It was all for you, Parisa. You should have left this building, though. You took a huge risk."

"I know. I wanted to save him. But it was too late. It was too close to noon." She started, her gaze swinging to his. "Jared, you missed your plane."

"This was more important."

"What plane was that?" Damon asked curiously.

"I was supposed to report to Langley on my activities here in the city, but I was a little busy."

"You'll sort it out," Parisa said confidently. "You captured a terrorist and helped save innocent lives. The city is safer because of you."

"I think we all had something to do with that," he replied. "I was only able to find Isaac because you shot him, and he left a blood trail."

"But you were smart enough to follow the food wrappers to the restaurant," she pointed out. "Which got you to the blood trail."

"That's true."

"Hey, what about me?" Damon said dryly.

Parisa sent a warm, thankful smile in Damon's direction. "I can't thank you enough for all your support."

"You were our lifeline," Jared added. "I just hope Parisa will be safe now. We still don't know who ordered the attacks on her, or how her location at the safe house, and again at the men's shelter, was compromised."

"There's going to be a thorough internal investigation," Damon said. "And I know where to start. At any rate, let's go downstairs."

"We're right behind you." Parisa slid her hand into his as Damon headed for the door. "Right?"

"Wherever you're going, I'm going," he said lightly.

An odd gleam entered her eyes. "I wish that were true."

He wished it was, too, but he couldn't guarantee anything past the next five minutes.

Twenty-Five

Three hours later, after multiple discussions with the FBI, Homeland Security, and the NYPD, Parisa followed Jared into his apartment, and said with relief, "We're home."

"It's starting to feel like home. I just don't know how safe it is for you," he said.

She flopped down on the couch. "We were never attacked here. And I think the reason for shutting me up no longer exists."

"Only if that was the reason."

"Good point."

Jared grabbed two bottles of water out of the fridge and brought her one, sitting next to her.

She took a long swig of water, loving the cool slide of liquid against her parched throat.

"How are you feeling about everything?" he asked, downing his bottle of water in three big gulps.

"I'm relieved but also sad and angry."

"Sounds about right." He put his hand on her leg and gave it a squeeze.

"I'm happy that Jasmine is all right and that the Kumars are the wonderful people I always thought they were, including Anika. She was not having an affair with Westley. They were just plotting out the ransom drop when we saw them. I don't know if I told you that. But the Langdons..." She let out a sigh. "They're another matter."

"Neil said it started as a study group, huh?"

"Yes, but as the students got older, as more people came into the group with radical ideas, like Isaac, everything changed. The extremists took over. They became terrorists. I can understand how that happened. But the fact that Neil knew what was occurring, and he did nothing to stop it, is another matter. There had to have been moments early on, where if he had made a different choice, he could have prevented what was about to come."

"He was scared. They threatened his family."

"Still... There's a point where you have to step up, where you have to do what's right. Even a few days ago, he had a chance to get Ben to cooperate with the bureau, and he didn't take it. In fact, he did everything he could to block Ben from talking. He knew about the café in Queens. He even went there looking for Isaac. That silence could have cost Jasmine her life."

"If it wasn't for our brilliant skills of detection."

She smiled at his light words. "There's that confidence again."

"Hey, I was including you in that. You were amazing today. You shot Isaac, which prevented him from killing Anika and Jasmine. And you found Neil and alerted the FBI to get the campus evacuated before anyone could get caught in what was about to happen."

"I might have shot Isaac, but you got to Jasmine and Anika before I did. You put your body in front of theirs. Don't think I didn't see that."

He shrugged. "Instinct. You would have done the same. We make a good team."

"We do. We don't even have to talk; we're completely in sync." She paused. "I don't know if you heard, but the café has been a meeting place for Brothers of the Earth whenever they're in New York. They're rounding up a lot more people who could have been potential recruits."

"That's good to hear."

"So, you didn't know?" She gave him a speculative look. "Did the CIA come and shut you up?" She and Jared had been interviewed both together and separately, but there had been a good hour or two when she hadn't seen him.

"They did, actually. I didn't see who came to the bureau, but after making my initial statements, I was left alone in a conference room for about two hours. Then I was told you were done and ready to go. I'm sure you have more information than I do."

"Well, I think you know most of it."

"Tell me about the Raven," he said curiously. "When Isaac said the Raven was going to fly, how did you know it was Neil and it would happen at the college?"

"I knew it was Neil because he made up the story about the raven when I was in school in Bezikstan. It was one of his favorite tales. It's a fable, a metaphor for the struggle of good against evil. A huge hawk comes down and disturbs a nest of ravens and the mother is either killed or disappears. The baby ravens live on the ledge outside of a school classroom. For days on end, the kids give the ravens enough food for them to live, but it's up to them to decide when to fly away. During that time, it's storming, it's dark; the world is a sad place. One day, the bell in the courtyard peals out twelve rings, and on the twelfth note, one of the ravens decides to risk it all and fly. He finally finds his courage. The storms end. The sky opens up to sunshine, and his fellow ravens follow him into flight."

"So, it's basically a story about finding courage."

"And being who you are. A bird is supposed to fly. It has to find its wings." She paused. "It's also about fighting evil.

The ravens couldn't cower on the ledge forever. They had to be brave enough to take on whatever big birds might be in their way."

Jared gave her a thoughtful look. "In this instance, the big bird stands for the government of Bezikstan, and the raven stands for the oppressed rebels."

"Yes. It's funny how a childish tale could take on such a different meaning."

"People read into stories what they want, what they need to hear. They put their own personal experience on it, and then it becomes theirs."

"That's true. I can't imagine what Neil must have been thinking when he was forced to put on that vest, when he was told that like the raven he created, he had to fly. He knew he was going to die. But he did it to protect Elizabeth."

"Maybe it was also to protect himself," Jared suggested with a cynical note in his voice. "Who knows how involved Neil was in anything? We'll find out in the days to come, because people will talk. Sara is already talking. Perhaps he would have rather died in a somewhat heroic fashion than go to jail, be painted a terrorist, have to live with that on his name, on his family."

"That's a good point. But I'd rather think it was about protecting his family. That probably makes me a fool."

"It makes you a person who wants to see good in someone who saved her life."

"He did do that. No matter what else he did. And I'm glad that Elizabeth is physically all right, although I'm sure Neil's death and Ben's imprisonment will be very hard on her. But moving on...I wanted to talk to you about Isaac. We haven't discussed what happened in the apartment yet."

"We caught a terrorist; that's what happened."

"Were you thinking about killing him?"

Jared's green eyes darkened as his gaze met hers. "Yes, I was."

She appreciated his honesty. "Do you wish I hadn't

shown up when I did? Would it have made it easier to kill him if I hadn't been there? No one would have known. You could have claimed he went for his gun."

"I'd already decided to let him live. I couldn't kill someone who has the kind of information he has."

"Even when it would have meant justice for April?"

"That's not what she would have wanted—as you mentioned back in the apartment," he said, a smile curving his lips.

"I feel like I could have been friends with April."

"You would have had a lot in common," he agreed.

"What do you think is going to happen to you, Jared? I'm surprised no one from your agency spoke to you if they were at the FBI office while you were there."

"I'm not surprised by anything that happens."

"They can't fire you for saving people's lives."

"They can do what they want. It still infuriates me that we didn't bring Isaac in after Paris, after what he did."

"They thought he'd be more valuable spying on the group."

"But he wasn't spying for us. He was playing both sides. April figured that out. That's what she wanted to tell me and why she was killed."

She nodded. "Well, he's not going to hurt anyone else ever again. I know it won't bring April back, but you did get her killer. That's something."

"And you got Jasmine back to her family. So, you can stop feeling guilty about not saving her the night they took her."

"Let's both stop feeling guilty."

"Deal."

"Now we just have to figure out how to get you back in the good graces of the CIA."

"That one is on me, Parisa."

"What would you do if you couldn't return to the agency?"

"I have no idea. Maybe spend a lot of time riding Barnabas."

"I'm sure he'd like that, but I suspect you'd be bored in under a week."

"Maybe," he conceded. "What about you? Will you return to San Francisco now?"

"My last assignment is done. I was undercover at a tech company, using my language skills to ferret out conspirators in an industrial espionage case. I was able to assist in acquiring enough evidence to bring charges, so that case will move on to the courts. I've been offered a permanent position there, if I want to continue doing what I was doing, which was interesting, but I was getting a little burned out on trying to fake more technical skills than I actually possess."

"What else would you do?"

"There's a job in Los Angeles—also corporate crime— but my friend Bree is there, which would be fun."

"She's one of the Quantico group?"

"Yes. But I'm not sure if that's where I want to be. I also have an offer for an assignment in London. I was supposed to decide on one of those offers by Friday. I was going to spend the week here—shopping, seeing some musicals, hanging out with Damon and Sophie, and figuring out what I wanted to do next—but I got a little distracted."

"That's an understatement. It sounds like you have a lot to think about."

She didn't like the suddenly distant note in his voice. "You're on the list, Jared." She put her hand over his, as she gazed into his mesmerizing eyes. "Last night seems like a long time ago, but I haven't forgotten a single minute of it." She licked her lips. "To be honest, I'm a little overwhelmed by how strongly I feel about you. I could almost call it…love."

"I could, too," he said with a serious smile. "In fact, I *would* call it love. It's fast, it's reckless, it's fun—it's everything. I've fallen for you, Parisa."

Her heart swelled with his words. "I feel the same way, Jared. We haven't even known each other a week, but I know you almost as well as I know myself. We're connected in so many ways, at so many levels." She paused, wanting to find the right words. "I don't know how to let you go. And I don't *want* to let you go. But I also can't imagine how we can make this work."

He framed her face with his hands. "All that matters right now is that you want to make it work."

"I do. I really do."

"Good. I feel the same way, so let's start there. And we'll see where we end up." He brushed some dirt from her face with a gentle hand. "When that bomb went off, I was terrified, Parisa. I thought I was going to lose you."

"I'm sorry I put you through that. You lost your mom to a terrorist attack, and April the same way. You must have felt like it was happening again."

"Those other sad situations were on my mind. Thankfully, today was different."

She leaned forward and kissed him, wanting to not just tell him how she felt but also show him. And just like the night before, the sparks went off with one taste, one touch, creating a fever of desire, lit even hotter by the knowledge that they'd almost lost each other.

"Let's take this into the bedroom," Jared said, dragging his mouth away from hers.

"It's so far," she protested, grabbing his shoulders so she could kiss him again.

"We'll make it," he told her, pulling her to her feet.

They hadn't taken one step when a buzzer went off.

She jerked. "What was that?"

"That's the doorbell," he said blankly. "I think—I've never actually heard it."

He picked his gun up from the table where he'd set it and moved over to the intercom. She grabbed her gun, too, acting on instinct, even though it seemed unlikely someone would ring the bell before coming to attack them.

"Yes," Jared said shortly.

"This is Hank at the front desk. You have a visitor. She says her name is Daphne Hill."

Jared sucked in a quick breath. "All right. Send her up."

"Who is Daphne Hill?" she asked, as Jared put his gun back on the counter. "And what does she want?"

"She's my boss. And I have a feeling she wants to fire me."

"Oh." She saw the tension run through his eyes. "I should leave."

"No, I don't want you to go. I'll just worry about you. And I'm sure she knows you're here."

"How did she know *you* were here? I thought this place was secret."

"I told Gary where I was. He wanted to come over and talk to me later tonight. He must have told Daphne. I'm sure it was under great duress."

A sharp knock came at the door. As Jared went to answer it, she set her gun down, then moved over to stand by the kitchen table.

She didn't know what she'd been expecting, but Daphne Hill was a stunning, tall blonde, who appeared to be in her early forties. She had on a wine-colored knit dress under her black coat, which matched her black, high-heeled boots.

"Jared, you've been a busy boy," Daphne said, as she swept into the room, her assessing gaze immediately falling on Parisa. "Introduce me."

"Parisa Maxwell—Daphne Hill."

"It's nice to meet you, Agent Maxwell," Daphne said.

Parisa shook her hand, not surprised that Daphne's skin was as cool as she was. "You, too," she murmured. "I guess you know who I am."

"Yes, I've spent the last hour with Special Agent Damon Wolfe. I'm up to speed," she said crisply, removing her coat and taking a seat at the table.

"I'll leave you two alone," Parisa offered.

"It's fine," Daphne said with a wave of her hand. "From what I hear you and Jared are thick as thieves. Please sit down."

She took a seat at the far end of the table, leaving Jared to sit next to Daphne.

"You were supposed to report to Langley this morning," Daphne said to Jared.

"If you're up to speed, you know why I didn't make it."

"Yes. You carried on a mission that you were specifically ordered to stay out of. You made numerous bad decisions—breaking into a consulate, following an FBI agent to a safe house, interfering in a hostage negotiation, and the list goes on."

"You left out the part where he located Isaac Naru," Parisa interjected. She knew it wasn't her business, but she didn't care. "He also saved my life more than once. That might not matter to you, but I personally think he's a hero."

Daphne gave her a cool smile. "I wish I could say you were alone, but you're not."

"What does that mean?" Jared asked. "Why don't you cut to the chase? Am I fired?"

"No. You're probably going to get an award. Quite a few people think you're a hero despite the fact that you disobeyed my orders. However, you'll be reassigned to another division."

"What division is that?"

"I don't know where they'll put you. But you won't be in my chain of command, thank God. You need to report to Langley next Monday at nine a.m. The agency is giving you a few days off to tie up loose ends here."

"What about Naru?" Jared asked.

"He made it through surgery. We haven't had a chance to talk to him yet."

"Will the agency continue to protect him?"

"No. He will pay for everything he's done—including

what he did to April."

For the first time, Parisa saw a hint of emotion in Daphne's eyes.

"It wasn't up to me, you know," Daphne said. "The order to leave Naru alone came from above my pay grade."

"I understand."

"And you weren't the only one who mourned April's passing, Jared. I cared about her, too." Daphne cleared her throat. "At any rate, thanks to your work, there are raids going on all over the world tonight: Paris, London, and Bezikstan. We're working with the FBI and Homeland Security and our allies in Europe and the Middle East to take down the Brothers of the Earth. Sara Pillai has been extremely helpful. She has given names and locations."

"What's going to happen to her?" Parisa enquired.

"I have no idea. I'm sure your bureau will have a say in that." Daphne pushed back her chair and stood up. "That's all I have."

"You could have said that on the phone," Jared pointed out, as he rose.

"Well, I was already in the city," she said, as she put on her coat. "And I wanted to give you a chance to thank me in person."

"For saving my job?" he queried.

"And for training you to be the incredible agent that you are. You're one of the best, Jared, and I don't say that lightly. But if I can give you some advice…"

"I'm sure I can't stop you."

"You need to decide if you can continue to put the mission before everyone else, including the people you care about. You need to figure out if the life of a spy is the life you want to lead. I know you disagreed with the agency's decision to protect their asset, but there was a bigger picture, even if you couldn't see it. There's a point where every agent has to choose between staying in the field and being whoever they're needed to be and coming home and finding themselves again.

You operate on emotion, Jared. It makes you good, but it also can tear you apart. You're lucky you found someone to pay for April's death. That doesn't always happen. Sometimes you're going to lose. If you make your whole life this job, then what will you have when you lose?" Daphne let that sink in and then turned to Parisa. "It was nice meeting you, Agent Maxwell. Perhaps our paths will cross again one day."

She nodded, letting Jared usher Daphne to the door.

After Daphne left, he turned the dead bolt and walked back to her.

"So that was your boss," she said.

"Yes, for the past seven years."

"She likes you, even though she doesn't really want to."

"She has taught me a lot over the years, but we've also clashed, especially in recent months. Daphne is a rule follower, and I like to improvise. We've been on different sides on more than one occasion. She respects me, but I make her job harder. I'm sure that's why she decided to hand me off."

"Where do you think they'll assign you?"

"I don't know."

"What she said—about agents deciding when it's time to hang it up in the field and come home and be themselves—I've thought about that in regard to myself."

"What conclusion did you come to?"

"I never came up with one. I guess I'll know when it's time. What about you?"

"I have to admit her words resonated with me. The last several years have been one assignment after another. I was always on a chase, living under a different identity, using all my spy craft to get the job done, and I felt good about it. I was on a roller coaster, and while sometimes my head spun a little, I didn't see a reason to get off—until now."

"Because of April?"

"No. Because of you. When we went riding yesterday, I could suddenly see another life for myself, one that you were in."

His words made her chest tighten. "Since we met, I've had a few thoughts about that kind of life myself."

"In between stuffing our faces with tacos, making mountainous ice cream sundaes, and telling our truths over poker, I discovered a woman who makes my toes curl."

She laughed. "Good. Because I was afraid you were leaving out last night's sexy fun."

"Oh, no, that could never be left out." He put his arms around her. "I don't know where we're going, Parisa, I just know I want us to find a way to be together." His gaze grew more serious. "You told me you don't have a home anywhere in the world, no place where you feel safe, where you feel like yourself. How about right here? And I'm not talking about this apartment—I'm talking about my arms around you. I'd like to be your home, Parisa."

She drew in a shaky breath, her heart turning over with his tender, loving words. "Being with you does feel like home, Jared. I've never been able to speak to anyone the way you and I talk. Even with all our secrets, there is more truth between us than I've ever felt in my life. I want to be your home, too. But I'm a little afraid. We both live dangerous lives. We could say good-bye and never come back. You've lost two people you cared about to violence. Are you sure you don't want to find a nice preschool teacher, or a veterinarian, someone who doesn't do what I do?"

"My mom was an ordinary woman doing an ordinary job when she died. No one knows how long they have. You just have to live the day you're in. And frankly, having a minute with you is worth more to me than a lifetime with someone else."

"That's an amazing thing to say." Her eyes filled with moisture. "I feel the same way. This day is turning out to be really good."

"I know how to make it even better."

"Show me."

He lowered his head and gave her a hungry, needy, passionate kiss, and she kissed him back in exactly the same way. They really were the perfect match.

After making love, sharing a midnight Chinese food feast, making love again, and then falling asleep in each other's arms, Parisa woke up in Jared's bed Tuesday morning, feeling like she was exactly where she wanted to be. Especially when she saw Jared lying next to her.

She turned on to her side, and just let herself look at him. His features were more relaxed in sleep. In fact, there was a hint of a smile on his lips. Maybe he was thinking about her—about the night they'd shared.

It was strange how comfortable she felt with him. She'd always been fine on her own—independent, strong, happy in her own company—but this felt so much better. She and Jared were connected. They were in love. They were each other's safe harbor—each other's home.

And she'd needed home more than she'd realized. She'd always felt loved by her mother and her stepfather, but she'd also been on the outside of their intense love affair. Now, she understood their closeness, their desire to be with each other, because she was caught up in her own passionate love.

Jared was good for her and she was good for him. They brought out the best in each other, and they seemed to have a way of communicating that didn't require words.

Jared shifted and blinked open one eye, then the other. "Morning."

"Good morning," she said happily.

"You're watching me sleep?"

"Yes. I can't seem to get enough of you."

He gave her a lazy, sexy smile. "Right back at you." He rolled over on to his side and gave her a longer look. "What are you thinking about?"

"Taking a shower together."

"Good answer. But your expression is a bit more serious than that."

"Honestly?"

"Yes. No secrets between us."

"It's a little terrifying to think about how much I love you already. Facing bullets and bombs is difficult, but I'm trained in how to handle those situations. Love is a new one for me."

"For me, too."

"It will make us both vulnerable. It will influence our decisions. It could weaken us."

"Or make us stronger."

"You are definitely the more optimistic one in this relationship."

He brushed her hair away from her face. "I just know we're going to be good together."

"And you're the most confident."

"But you are the sexiest, the most beautiful, the most intelligent..." he said with a teasing smile. "Now, let's talk about that shower."

"I'm done talking. And the shower can wait."

Twenty-Six

Parisa finally got out of the shower around noon and had just finished blow-drying her hair when her phone rang. It was Damon. She took the phone into the bedroom and placed it on the nightstand, turning on the speaker, so Jared could hear the conversation while he finished getting dressed.

"How's it going, Damon?" she asked. "Is Isaac talking?"

"Not yet, but Sara has told us a lot. She was apparently compiling a lot of information in the hopes of one day being able to cut herself a deal."

"That's good news. And Ben?"

"He was shaken up by his father's death, by Neil's participation in the group. His mother is also distraught. We haven't gotten much out of her, but Ben has told us everything he knows, which isn't a lot. His only real involvement was getting Jasmine to give the kidnappers entrance to the consulate."

"What about Jasmine?"

"She was released from the hospital. She's staying with Westley in his penthouse, with an enormous amount of security. Anika and her mother are also there. Raj is working with the state department in regard to the civil war breaking out in Bezikstan."

"I'm glad the Kumars are here and not there, and that everyone is safe. I can't imagine what they think about Neil. He was such a good friend to them over the years."

"Everyone is shocked, that's for sure. How are you feeling?"

"I'm good. I would still like to know who sold out my location at the safe house and the shelter, though. Is Vincent still hanging around?"

"Yes. He and Deputy Director Hunt have been huddled together all morning. Peter just called me and asked me to bring you into the office. He wants to give you a personal report on what he's discovered."

"Which is what?"

"I don't know. He said I would find out when you found out, but that I could assure your safety with 100 percent certainty. How soon can you get here?"

She glanced at Jared, who was shaking his head, and giving her a warning look. "I don't know how comfortable I feel coming into the office when Vincent is clearly working with Peter. How do I know they're not both involved?"

"You don't, but I think you need to hear what the director has to say."

"All right. I'll be there in thirty minutes."

As she clicked off the phone, Jared immediately shook his head. "You can't go down there, Parisa. You could be walking into a trap."

"I don't think someone will try to kill me at the office."

"I'm coming with you."

"You can't, Jared." She saw the continued worry in his eyes. "I have to do this by myself. I need to hear what they've learned. I still have a job as an FBI agent, and I can't be scared of the people I work with. It sounds like they've figured out who was involved."

"Or they've found a scapegoat. You can't trust Vincent Rowland."

"No, I can't. But I need to play this out."

"Well, I'm coming with you—at least as far as the lobby." He put his hands on her hips. "I know you're a strong, independent, tough woman, but you're going to have to get used to the idea that I'm not going to be too far away."

"Until you have to be…when you eventually go back to work. We still have a lot to figure out, including whether we can find a place where we can both do our jobs."

He frowned. "I have some thoughts about that."

"What kind of thoughts?"

"Ones that are too long to get into now. You have a meeting to make."

Damon was waiting for her in a conference room with Deputy Director Peter Hunt and Vincent Rowland. Peter Hunt was in his early fifties with short, pepper-gray hair and brown eyes. She knew him only by reputation.

She drew in a hard breath as she shook their hands. She wasn't sure what was coming, but she was very interested to hear what they had to say.

"Agent Maxwell," Peter said, as they sat down at the table. "As you know, we've been trying to find the leak in the bureau since you were attacked early Saturday morning at our safe house."

"Have you done that?"

"We have," he indicated with a nod of his head. "It was an analyst by the name of Fatima Doyen. She grew up in Mumbai. She went to school with Isaac Naru."

"Really?" she asked, surprised by the revelation, and the very strong connection between Fatima and Isaac. "How did you find that out?"

Peter looked at Vincent. "Do you want to explain?"

"Yes," Vincent said. "First of all, I'd like to say that I'm very sorry you've been dealing with all this, Parisa, especially in the middle of everything going on with Jasmine. I'm very impressed with how you've handled yourself."

"Thank you. But I'm more interested in this analyst."

"I worked with Fatima's father many years ago. He was an FBI asset, who operated mostly out of Mumbai. But we also worked together in DC, when I was stationed there. I actually helped Fatima get her job when she joined the bureau three years ago."

"How do you know she's the one who was leaking information to Isaac?"

"I thought she was acting oddly, so I asked Peter to assign someone to tail her and get her phone and bank records. We found several large cash deposits in her account over the last two weeks, and she called Mr. Naru's cell phone two times in the past three days."

"That's damning. What does she have to say? Where is she? I want to talk to her."

"Unfortunately, that's not possible," Vincent said.

She frowned at his words. "Why not?"

"Because she killed herself early this morning. We went to her apartment to bring her in, and she was deceased, overdosed on pain pills. She left a note."

Peter pushed a file folder across the table to her. She opened it up and pulled out what appeared to be a photocopy.

The note was short and to the point: *I can no longer live with myself after what I've done. I've betrayed the bureau and my country. Please know that I did what I did under duress and to protect friends that I have in Bezikstan. The only way I can bring honor back to my family is to no longer be alive to shame them. Fatima.*

"May I see it?" Damon asked.

She pushed the note over to him, as she gazed back at Peter and Vincent. "Has the handwriting been analyzed?"

"It matches," Peter said. "We're still tracing the

financials, but we're confident that Fatima was the leak. She was, in fact, the person who gave Damon that particular safe house."

"Is that true?" she asked Damon.

"Yes," he said, through tense lips. "I brought her into the investigation because of her ties to India and that part of the world."

"You couldn't have known she would turn, Damon," Peter said.

"It's still a mistake," he said, as usual being very hard on himself.

"At any rate," Peter continued. "We don't believe you're in any further danger, Agent Maxwell."

"That's good to hear." She looked at Vincent, wishing she could be sure he was really on her side. "I appreciate your help on this."

"I've always felt very connected to you and Damon and the others who were Jamie's good friends. When I knew you were in trouble, I couldn't stand on the sidelines. Everyone was busy looking for Jasmine. I thought I could be more help figuring out who was after you."

"I appreciate that. Do you know how Westley and Jasmine are doing?"

"They're very happy to be together again," Vincent replied. "Jasmine feels terrible about losing the family diamond, but the Larimers are happy to see the end of that cursed stone—at least Phillip's wife is. I'm sure Phillip would have appreciated access to fifty million dollars even more. But it's done."

"I hope Jasmine doesn't hang on to that guilt; she wasn't responsible for the loss of the diamond. She didn't even want it."

"Jasmine is a kind, caring girl, and she takes things to heart. She'll be good for Westley. He can sometimes be a little hard, but when he's with her, he gets much softer."

"I'm glad they can stay together after this." She let out a

breath. "So, I guess we're done."

Peter nodded. "Four members of the radical group have been arrested in London and three more in Paris. We've also rounded up two members here in New York City. They both worked at the Indian café where you found Naru. The Bezikstan government is mobilizing troops to fight the rebels and receiving financial help from their allies, including the United States."

"What's going to happen to Ben Langdon?"

"He'll be charged with aiding and abetting the kidnapping. His case will move on to the attorneys."

"And his mother?"

Peter looked at Damon to answer.

"We don't have any evidence tying Elizabeth to the group's activities," Damon said. "She claims ignorance. Ben backs up her story. Sara said she never saw Elizabeth get involved. Right now, it looks like Mrs. Langdon is in the clear, but she's going to be interrogated for some days to come."

"That will make it easier for Kenisha Kumar to know that her best friend didn't betray her," she put in. "Is there more?"

"If you'd like a job here in New York," Peter said, "we'd be happy to have you."

"That's very nice of you. I'm weighing a couple of options at the moment."

"Put us on the list."

"Thank you."

"I'll walk you out," Damon told her, as she got to her feet.

They didn't speak until they were in the elevator. Then she gave him a questioning look. "What do you think, Damon? Fatima Doyen? Do you feel confident she was the leak?"

"Vincent made a good case against her."

"Airtight. Almost too good." She paused. "Remember Bree's situation—when her FBI file showed up at an abandoned house, and a Chicago police detective committed suicide, and they thought he was the one who had somehow gotten his hands on her file, but no one could question him? It feels a little familiar."

Damon gave her a grim look. "I'll do some more digging, but while the suicide could be homicide, how would Vincent manufacture calls between Fatima and Naru?"

"Good point. Maybe I just need to let go of the idea that Vincent is trying to mess with us."

"I wouldn't let it go, but I plan to keep an eye on him, especially if he's in New York."

"He's not always here. He was in LA before Christmas when Wyatt got into trouble." She paused. "Have you heard from Diego lately?"

"Not in months."

"He's the only one of us who hasn't had a run-in with Vincent."

"I know, but he has been warned."

"It's hard to get ready when it doesn't feel like you're the one being attacked. I only became in danger after Jasmine's kidnapping, and Vincent didn't have anything to do with that."

"At least, not that we know," Damon said. "We just need to keep our eyes open."

"We always do that."

The elevator doors opened, and they stepped into the lobby. She could see Jared pacing in front of the glass windows on the other side of the security check.

Damon followed her gaze, as they paused in the hallway. "So, what's the deal with you and the spook?"

She smiled. "I think I'm in love."

He shook his head. "That was fast."

"It's crazy, right?"

"Not really. Sophie and I made a pretty quick trip to love."

"But that was the second time around."

"Yeah, I was stupid enough to leave the first time. I wasn't going to make that mistake again. But our situation was a little easier to work out. What are you going to do? How are you going to date a spy?"

"Honestly, I don't know. What I do know is that he's important to me, and I want to make it work."

"That's all you need to know for now."

"Please, don't say *need to know*. I've already heard that a few times from Jared. It's a favorite line at the CIA."

"You want to love a spook, you better get used to secrets."

"We've managed to figure out a good way to be honest with each other, even amidst the secrets."

"Good. If you're going to be in the city a few days, Sophie and I would love to have you both over."

"I would love to see Sophie and for you to get to know Jared."

"Then we'll set it up."

She nodded. "Thanks for everything."

"You're welcome." He gave her a hug. "We'll talk soon."

She smiled and walked out to meet Jared. He grabbed her hand, impatience written all over his face, but he didn't ask her any questions until they had left the building. When they got to a park a block away, he pulled her under the shade of a tree and into his arms.

She leaned against him for a long moment, inhaling the musky scent of his cologne, and savoring the feel of his arms around hers. They finished the embrace with a kiss, and then he said, "Well?"

"Vincent Rowland has been looking into who might be leaking information about my whereabouts. He discovered that it was an analyst by the name of Fatima Doyen, who went to school with Isaac Naru in Mumbai."

"Seriously?" A look of surprise entered his eyes.

"Yes, and there were phone calls between Isaac and Fatima, as well as cash deposits made in her bank account."

"I sense there's a *but* coming."

"But she's dead. She overdosed last night. She left a suicide note apologizing for betraying her country and the bureau. She said her friends in Bezikstan were being threatened."

"So, it's all tied up with a neat bow."

She nodded, seeing the skepticism in Jared's gaze. "It seems so."

"Well, I guess that's good."

"I feel confident that I'm not in danger—at least, not at the moment. Vincent told me he had gotten involved in trying to figure out who was after me because he cares about me and Jamie's other friends. He wants us to be safe. He was very convincing. Maybe he's innocent."

"Or maybe you should keep an open mind."

"Damon and I just agreed that we should continue to do that. By the way, Damon wants us to come over for dinner one night, so you can meet Sophie, and he can get better acquainted with you."

"I'm fine with that. I like the guy."

"Me, too." She drew in a breath of chilly air and looked around at the bustling streets, teeming with people going about their days. "It's just a normal day today."

"Which is the best kind of day." Jared put his arm around her shoulders as they started to walk through the park.

"No. The best kind of day is one where you and I are together."

He smiled down at her. "Then we're going to have a lot of good days."

"I'm counting on that," she said, giving him a quick kiss, and then they headed down the street.

Epilogue

*F*_{our weeks later...}

The party reminded Jared of when he'd first met Parisa. In fact, there were many of the same people present at the wedding of Jasmine Kumar and Westley Larimer. This event was much smaller than the engagement party—only family and a few friends, less than fifty people. But there was still a large buffet, plenty of champagne, and a classical pianist adding a beautiful score to the reception at the Larimer estate in South Hampton.

Jasmine and Westley had said their *I do's* in the backyard, and now the guests were being treated to a magnificent dinner on the covered patio. It was a cold February evening, so heat lamps and candles bathed the area in a warm glow.

As he glanced around the patio, his gaze caught on Parisa. She wore a stunning dark-red silk dress with a few beads that caught the light, her legs bare, her black heels high, her hair falling down around her shoulders in luxurious, silky waves. His pulse jumped, and he felt a rush of awareness, connection, and love for the beautiful woman who had stolen his heart at first glance.

Over the past month, they'd gotten even closer, sharing all the details of their lives, learning each other's bad habits, laughing together while watching sitcoms from the seventies, competing with each other at cards and other games, spending long nights just talking about anything and everything.

Parisa wasn't just his lover; she was his best friend. *How on earth had he gotten so lucky?* He probably didn't deserve her, but he was going to spend the rest of his life trying to make her as happy as she made him.

He smiled to himself as he watched her talking to Jasmine and Anika—the friends of her youth, but also two women she'd become even closer to in the last few months. He was glad to see them smiling, laughing. It could have all ended so differently.

Parisa turned her head and caught him staring—just like she had the night of Jasmine's engagement party. She raised her champagne glass and gave him a nod, an intimate look burning up the space between them.

A moment later, she broke away from the women and walked over to join him.

"I've been neglecting you," she said, taking his hand in hers.

"Not at all. I want you to have fun."

"I have fun when I'm with you."

"You can have fun when you're not with me, too. As long as it's not *our* kind of fun," he teased.

She smiled. "You don't have to worry."

"You don't have to worry, either."

"I know." She squeezed his fingers. "It was a beautiful wedding—quiet, intimate, understated, exactly what Jasmine wanted. She found her voice with Westley."

"And he realized that getting married was about more than a big show when he almost lost her." He paused, curious about something. "What kind of wedding would you want?"

"Is that a proposal?"

He laughed. "Hell, no. When I propose to you, you will know it. And it will happen. I just want us to get everything figured out first."

"We're almost there. We both have jobs in DC now. I'm going to work on a new task force, and you're going to head the Domestic Protection Division of the CIA. You thought you were getting fired, and instead you got a big promotion."

"I'll be riding a desk, but I'll be making more money."

Her brow lifted in concern. "It is what you want, right?"

"It is. Really," he reassured her. "I'm happy to still be working toward keeping this nation safe, but I don't need to be in the field to do that. I'd rather be with you."

"In our new home in Georgetown, and our weekend getaway house in Upstate New York."

"It's all coming together. And I'm looking forward to getting to know your mother and stepfather better." They'd already spent one long evening with them, and he'd been happy with the warm welcome they'd given him.

"I haven't lived in the same city with my mother and stepfather in about eight years. It will be weird but also good to have family dinners again. I'm excited to meet your family, too," she said.

"They can't wait. We'll be in Hawaii tomorrow."

They were going to spend the week there before settling into their jobs in DC. And he had a very special evening planned—on a beach, at sunset, with the woman of his dreams—the woman he would ask to be his wife. He almost wanted to do it now, just because he couldn't wait. But this was Jasmine's night, and he wanted the proposal to be only about him and Parisa.

"Shall we dance?" Parisa asked, as the music began, and couples drifted on to the dance floor.

He set his champagne glass down on a nearby tray. As he did so, he saw a familiar face and one he didn't quite trust.

"Parisa," Vincent Rowland said.

"Vincent," she said with surprise. "Have you been here all evening?"

"No. I just arrived. My plane was late, unfortunately, and I missed the ceremony, but I heard it was lovely."

"It was," she agreed.

"It's good to see my godson so happy," Vincent added, tipping his head toward the bride and groom, who were smiling deep into each other's eyes as they danced together. "To think what they went through to get here."

"They were definitely tested, but they're going to have a long life together."

"Yes." Vincent glanced in Jared's direction. "I don't think we've officially met."

"Jared MacIntyre." His real last name was Beckham, but aside from Parisa and his family members, no one else knew that. His mother had kept her name of Montgomery when she married, so he hadn't lied when he'd told Parisa that. He'd become Jared MacIntyre when he entered the CIA, and he would remain that until he quit.

"Vincent Rowland."

"I've heard a lot about you," he drawled.

A gleam entered Vincent's eyes. "All good, I hope."

"I know your son was very important to Parisa. I'm sorry for your loss."

"Yes, thank you. Jamie was very important to me, too." Vincent cleared his throat. "I'm going to offer my congratulations to the families. Parisa—I'm sure we'll see each other again soon."

"I look forward to it," she said.

As Vincent walked away, Jared put his arm around her shoulders and gave her a tight squeeze. "I don't trust him."

"I don't, either, but it's been very quiet the last month—for both me and my fellow agents."

"You know what they say about the quiet before the storm..." He saw the frown cross her lips and regretted his comment. "Sorry."

"No, you're right. There was something creepy about the way he said he'd see me soon. But I don't want to think about Vincent tonight. I just want to be with you. Whatever comes next, we'll deal with it."

"Together," he said. "I love you, Parisa."

Her gaze warmed with pleasure. "I love you, too, Jared. Shall we dance?"

"Putting my arms around you seems like the perfect idea. And I'm a really good dancer." He swung her out onto the dance floor with a flourish.

"I would have expected nothing less."

He could have shown her some impressive moves, but once he put his arms around her, all he wanted to do was hold her. He'd show her his moves later, when they were alone, when they were in bed.

She gave him a happy smile. "I'm right where I want to be."

"Me, too. Let's stay this way forever."

"That sounds almost long enough."

THE END

Want more
OFF THE GRID: FBI Series?

Available in 2019
Dangerous Choice (#5)

About The Author

Barbara Freethy is a #1 New York Times Bestselling Author of 65 novels ranging from contemporary romance to romantic suspense and women's fiction. Traditionally published for many years, Barbara opened her own publishing company in 2011 and has since sold over 7 million books! Twenty of her titles have appeared on the New York Times and USA Today Bestseller Lists.

Known for her emotional and compelling stories of love, family, mystery and romance, Barbara enjoys writing about ordinary people caught up in extraordinary adventures. Barbara's books have won numerous awards. She is a six-time finalist for the RITA for best contemporary romance from Romance Writers of America and a two-time winner for DANIEL'S GIFT and THE WAY BACK HOME.

Barbara has lived all over the state of California and currently resides in Northern California where she draws much of her inspiration from the beautiful bay area.

For a complete listing of books, as well as excerpts and contests, and to connect with Barbara:

Visit Barbara's Website:
www.barbarafreethy.com

Join Barbara on Facebook:
www.facebook.com/barbarafreethybooks

Follow Barbara on Twitter:
www.twitter.com/barbarafreethy